JUAN FOOT IN
THE GRAVE

JUAN FOOT IN THE GRAVE

Roger Keevil

Matador
9 Priory Business Park,
Wistow Road, Kibworth Beauchamp,
Leicestershire. LE8 0RX
Tel: (+44) 116 279 2299
Fax: (+44) 116 279 2277
Email: books@troubador.co.uk
Web: www.troubador.co.uk/matador

ISBN 978 1780884 080

British Library Cataloguing in Publication Data.
A catalogue record for this book is available from the British Library.

Typeset in 11pt Adobe Garamond Pro by Troubador Publishing Ltd, Leicester, UK
Printed and bound by TJ International, Padstow, Cornwall

Matador is an imprint of Troubador Publishing Ltd

MIX
Paper from
responsible sources
FSC® C013056

*To my Ma, who took me to see
my first Agatha Christie film,
and so gave me a taste for
murder!*

Prologue

The Case of the British Connection

"Guv… "

Detective Inspector Andy Constable opened one eye. The bright colours of the floral beach shorts standing next to his sun lounger made him shut it again in a hurry.

"How many times do I have to tell you, Copper, don't call me that here. Why I ever let you talk me into coming on this holiday is beyond me."

"Well, somebody had to use the other ticket, sir." Detective Sergeant Dave Copper sounded hurt. " 'A holiday for two on the Costa Blanca', that was the prize in the station Christmas draw. And it was either you or my brother. And he's away in the Isle of Wight."

"Parkhurst, I shouldn't wonder," muttered Constable. "Anyway, what is it?"

"Well, guv… "

Constable glared. "I've told you – call me 'A.C.'"

"Sorry… A.C. It's that local police guy we were talking to in the bar yesterday – you know, Alfredo. Some bloke's been found dead, and Alfredo reckons there's a link with the British community out here, and we might be able to help him sort it out."

"Copper, if this is one of your more elaborate jokes… "

"Honestly, sir, no." The injured innocence was plain in Dave Copper's voice. "It's genuine. I mean, there's a body and everything. Alfredo's just sent his son over with the message."

"If this turns out to be a wind-up, they'll have a body soon enough. They'll be able to read the story in the local English-language papers – 'Easily Explained Death Of Holidaying British Detective'."

"It's not a joke, sir," insisted Copper.

Constable sighed. "For crying out loud. We've only been here five minutes. Talk about 'never off duty'." He pushed himself upright. "All right then, Copper – where is Alfredo?"

"Over in the bar, sir… A.C. Er, guv… couldn't you call me D.C., just while we're on holiday, like?"

Along the road in the local bar, Captain Alfredo was waiting. Finishing his brandy, he turned and took off his mirrored sunglasses as his two British colleagues entered.

"Hola, que tal?" Constable greeted him cheerily but then, wishing he'd actually completed that CD course in Spanish he'd bought three years before, lapsed into the comfort of English. "What's your problem?"

Alfredo's English was, fortunately, excellent. "It is the owner of one of the local English television companies," he explained. "A man named Rookham – his company is called CostaLot TV. His assistant found him dead on the floor when she arrived at his office this morning. We think perhaps maybe he is murdered because he is so unpopular. Maybe it is revenge."

"How's that then?" asked Copper.

"It is many different things," replied Alfredo. "It is all the time in the papers. All the English people complain of being over-charged, or the service engineers do not keep appointments, or the television goes off for no reason in the middle of the football, as it did last night, which here in Spain is a clear motive for murder! I do not know how it is in your country."

Constable found himself intrigued by the problem. "Right, then – where's your dead man? Let's see what we can do."

The offices of CostaLot TV were only a few minutes away

in Alfredo's police car. As they passed the young officer on the door – Constable couldn't help feeling a growing irritation that policemen were getting younger and better-looking these days – the two Britons noticed a faint smell of burning in the premises. On the desk, the red eye of a piece of electrical equipment was winking at them remorselessly – the only movement in the room, where the body of a middle-aged man was sprawled on the floor with an expression of horror on his face.

"I see what you mean," remarked Constable. "He's not looking too well, is he? Let's have a look – and Copper, turn off that blasted red light, whatever it is. It's driving me mad."

"Righty-ho, guv… er, I mean A.C. Ow!" Copper jumped back with a yelp of pain as sparks flew from his fingertips.

"What the hell are you playing at, man?"

"It's this thing, guv," expostulated Copper. "It's a telephone answering machine. That red light's the 'Machine Full' indicator, but the On-Off button is live. That's what gave me a shock when I touched it."

"Blasted foreign electrical equipment," snapped Constable. "Sorry, Alfredo, no offence."

"Actually," replied Alfredo, unplugging the device from the wall, "I think you will see that this is a British machine. It says "British Telefon" on the backside."

"He's right, guv. The bloke must have brought it over from England." Copper looked again closely. "But look, that's not a British plug, is it? It's a two-pin. He must have changed it so's he could use it here."

"There you are, then," retorted Constable triumphantly. "I know the identity of your murderer, and how it was done."

"So please, explain for me."

"Mr. Rookham had obviously messed about with the wiring when he changed the plug, and not earthed the machine properly. You told us that everybody was up in arms and complaining about this guy's TV service. It looks as if loads of people rang up to complain last night, more than usual because of the football, so that the answering machine exceeded its capacity and the red light started to flash. When Mr. Rookham came in first thing this morning, he must have pressed the button to turn off the light. You can check with the post-mortem, but I'm guessing that he must have had a weak heart, unlike Copper here who is as strong as a horse, and the electric shock killed him."

"So who is the murderer?" asked a slightly bewildered Alfredo.

"Obviously," replied Constable, "the entire British community. But I think," he continued, smiling, "that if you decide to charge the whole lot of them, they have a very clear case of self-defence. After all, the British are quite fond of football too."

"Perhaps you are right," agreed Alfredo. "And so I can tell my Commander that the case is solved. And perhaps you will join me for a large brandy in my bar."

"I thought you'd never ask," grinned Constable. "Another triumph for the team of A.C. and D.C. Come on, Copper – I think it's about time we started enjoying our holiday."

Chapter 1

Detective Inspector Andy Constable disliked November. It was wet, it was cold, the nights were drawing in with a vengeance, and the approach of Christmas meant that the incidence of shoplifting rocketed. Which might not be thought the worst of the world's problems, but it meant an annoying increase in the crime statistics, which led to the local papers ramping up their criticism of local policing methods, which led to the upper echelons of the County Constabulary breathing down his neck in an effort to find some success stories to offset the bad press. All of which tended to increase his load of paperwork, which was one of his un-favourite parts of the job.

Andy ran his hands through his hair, dark brown but with a bit more grey in it than he would have liked, and down across his face. His friendly brown eyes – friendly unless you found yourself on the opposite side of a table in the interview room with some explaining to do, that is – caught sight of his reflection in the glass partition facing his desk. Not too bad for forty-something, he thought. No jowls, not too many lines around the eyes, and if he took care not to let his head drop, there was absolutely no sign of even the start of a double chin. "Oh for goodness sake, get a grip and stop being miserable," he thought. And then, "Note to self. Do not bunk off more gym sessions than you absolutely have to. Do not let the waistline escape."

"Morning, guv!" Detective Sergeant Dave Copper positively bounced into the room. "How are we this bright and sunny?"

Andy Constable bit back the retort that almost sprang to his lips, and took a deep breath. "Copper, you never cease to amaze me."

"How so, sir?"

The inspector laughed. "Although your fine detective's brain will have clearly brought you to the conclusion that today is neither sunny nor particularly bright, you come bounding in here like a two-year-old with a song on your lips and a smile on your face, as if the world is a toy which you just got for Christmas. How in the name of all that's holy do you do it?"

"Power of positive thinking, sir," smiled Copper in reply. "Gets me through the day."

In his late twenties, with a shock of light brown hair which insisted on sticking up in every direction despite all attempts to tame it, Dave Copper looked as if nothing would ever be allowed to get the better of his natural good humour. His face always looked as if it was ready to burst into a grin, and in fact on more than one occasion his easy ability to see the funny side of a situation had caused many of his superiors to wonder whether he was in the right job. Andy Constable had never had quite the same doubts – in the three years or so that he had been working with his junior colleague, he had quietly enjoyed the younger man's sometimes irreverent take on the business of detection and his often surprising insights into complicated cases. And if Copper sometimes overstepped the mark, and Constable felt compelled to slap him down, no matter. Each man liked and respected the other. They made a good team.

"By the way, sir," continued Copper, "on the subject of Christmas, have you got your ticket yet for the Christmas draw?"

Constable shook his head. "No, I have not," he replied shortly.

"Oh sir, why not?" asked Copper, plonking himself into a chair across the desk from the inspector.

"Because in all likelihood, it would be singularly pointless. I've never won a thing in that raffle in all the years I've been doing it – unless you count that bottle of Blue Tower two years ago, which I could not give away quickly enough."

"Negative thinking again, sir. You really ought to give it a go. And there's a decent prize this year, for a change."

"Oh?"

"Holiday, sir. You remember that business with the guy who attempted to rob the building society, and then ran into the travel agency and tried to hold the owner hostage after our mob turned up before he could get away?"

"I do, sergeant," answered Constable. "I seem to remember you covered yourself in glory with that one, even though you weren't actually on duty at the time."

Dave Copper blushed. "It wasn't really anything, sir, and you know that. I just happened to be on the spot at the time. I was just getting some cash out of the hole in the wall, and I heard all this yelling and the alarm went off, and then somebody scooted past me and into the travel agent when one of our cars pulled up. Perfect timing by uniform, for once. Actually, the guy was a total idiot. He had one of those joke shop nose-and-glasses sets on, and a toy gun which wouldn't have fooled a seven-year-old."

"Well, it was good enough to put the wind up the building society cashier and the travel agent," remarked Constable. "Although obviously not a highly-trained detective such as yourself."

"As you say, sir," grinned Copper. "So while uniform were far... fiddling about on the pavement, I just followed him into the travel shop, where there was a lot of screaming and cowering going on, so I thought, 'I can't be doing with all this' and grabbed the guy. He wriggled and managed to get out the back door, and tried to do a runner down the back alley."

"Where, if my memory serves me correctly, you managed to

catch him and bring him down with a textbook flying tackle with his face nestling in the fragrant overspill from the fishmonger's bins."

"School rugby first fifteen, sir," said Copper. "You never lose the knack. Anyway, the whole point is, the travel agent was so grateful that he's donated a holiday to the station raffle as a prize. Which I am going to try to win."

"I can't help thinking that it would have been suitably generous if Mr. Patel had just given you a free holiday as a token of his gratitude and cut out the middle man."

"What, and run the risk of accusations of police corruption, sir?" retorted Copper in mock horror. "No, I'm going to rely on positive thinking again. If it's meant to be, it'll happen. Tell you what, guv – if I do win the holiday, I'll take you with me. Can't say fairer than that."

"Yeah, right," grunted Constable. "Good luck with that, sergeant. Anyway, if you haven't anything better to do, shall we try doing some work? Pass me that blue file off that cabinet... "

"You doing anything special over Christmas, Andy?" The custody sergeant had been in the force long enough, and had known his theoretically superior colleague long enough, to get away with both the informal address and the pair of reindeer antlers on the headband he was wearing. Together with the small twinkling fibre-optic tree on his desk, they added an incongruous festivity to the rather bleak area which led to the police station's cells.

"Not really," answered Constable. "After that business at the College Ball, I'm knackered. I thought I'd just slump in front of the television and eat myself silly for the actual three days that I've got off. Anything except chocolate, of course." He laughed.

"Too right," agreed his colleague with a grimace. "I don't reckon I'll be eating much chocolate for a while – well, not after you found what they put in the stuff! And I suppose you can't really spend Christmas with the family, can you? Where is it your sister lives?"

Constable smiled. "Vancouver. Which I think you'll agree is a bit too far to go, even for the promise of a white Christmas and a plate of roast moose, or whatever the tradition is in Canada."

"So do you ever see them?"

"She and Tom and the boys came over to the U.K. a couple of years ago on holiday, but other than that, no. We phone and email. And I dare say that tomorrow morning, or whatever time the crack of dawn is in British Columbia, I shall have the boys yelling at me on skype to say thank you for their presents."

"You ought to take a holiday and go and see them. You haven't had a holiday in ages, have you?"

"Far too busy tracking down evil-doers for you to tuck up nice and cosy in your cells," responded Constable with a laugh. "Anyway, I don't do holidays."

The custody sergeant nodded in agreement. "I suppose you're right. It's not that much fun going off on your todd. Oh well – that's what you get for being married to the job. Still, I reckon you ought to think about it. You could go on one of these singles holidays they advertise – you know, walking in the Lake District or learning how to paint watercolours in Suffolk. It'd take you out of yourself. We all have to re-charge our batteries sometime, you know. Give yourself a fresh perspective."

Andy Constable gave him a look. "Don't you start feeling sorry for me. I'm perfectly fine as I am."

"Guv!" Dave Copper's voice echoed down the corridor, and he burst through the door with a huge grin on his face. "They told me you were down here, sir. You'll never guess what! They've just done the Christmas draw, and I've only gone and won, haven't I?"

"Easy does it, sergeant," said Constable, amused at the

younger man's exuberance. "You'll go pop if you go on like this. Well done. I suppose this is all down to your famous power of positive thinking. So, what is it that you've won?"

"That's just it, sir." Copper was triumphant. "First prize, sir! I've won the holiday!"

"Good Christmas, sir?"

Andy Constable looked up from his paper-strewn desk. "Fabulous, thank you, sergeant. I did absolutely nothing."

Dave Copper perched himself on the front of his own desk, balanced the holdall he was carrying precariously on top of a stack of filing trays, and frowned. "What, nothing at all, sir? Didn't you even go out or go round to see people or anything?"

"I did not." It seemed that Constable was absolutely determined not to sound wistful. "My next-door neighbours are away on holiday in Mauritius, the pub is closed for refurbishment because they're in the middle of turning it into some sort of family carvery..." The lack of enthusiasm in the inspector's tone was evident. "... and in case you hadn't noticed, it rained most of the time on Christmas Day. So I had a very pleasant time roasting a pheasant, washing it down with one of my nicer Burgundies, and watching old films and the dancing on television. Thus fortifying myself for the exciting task of ploughing through this pile of reports on my return to work this morning. Which, if you will excuse me, I intend to get on with."

Copper was not to be put off. "Sorry, guv, but isn't that all a bit dull?" he asked. "No disrespect, sir," he added hastily. "I mean, I reckon Christmas is probably one of the only chances we get to escape from the job and enjoy ourselves. Well, apart from the poor guys on duty, scooping up drunks in the precinct, but we got away with that one, didn't we? I had a great time."

Constable pushed away the papers in front of him, leaned back, and smiled, amused almost against his will by his colleague's earnest enthusiasm. "Which you have decided to tell me about in great detail, by the sound of it. Well, go on then. Give me the blow by blow. What have you been up to?"

"Well, I went out on Christmas Eve with Lorraine… "

"Just a second. Who's Lorraine?"

"My girlfriend, sir."

"Another one? It's only five minutes ago you were going out with that other one… what was her name? Jackie?"

"No, sir, that was the one before." Dave Copper had the grace to look faintly embarrassed. "I think you're thinking of Caroline."

"And what happened to her?"

"Dumped me, sir." Copper sounded remarkably cheerful as he imparted the information.

"Sergeant, what on earth are you doing to these girls?" asked Constable in exasperation. "On second thoughts, do not on any account answer that. I do not wish to know."

"Oh, just the usual problem, guv. She couldn't be doing with the hours. Got stood up once too often, so it was the job or her." Copper chanced a grin at his superior. "Of course, sir, I blamed you."

"I don't doubt it for a moment, Copper. That is the cross I bear as your mentor and master. So where have you got this new one from?"

"She's not really that new, sir."

Constable was intrigued. "So, you're branching into the cougar market now, are you?"

Copper hastened to explain. "Do me a favour, sir! No, it's nothing like that. She's a friend of mine from when I was away at college." And in response to Constable's raised eyebrow, "Not that sort of friend. I mean we never actually… well, you know… not then. But we found each other on Facebook the other week, and it turns out she's moved back here to work for an estate agent… "

"Good steady reliable job, then," remarked Constable wryly.

"And she's only living on the other side of town, so we just met up for a drink and it sort of developed from there."

"Which was how you came to spend Christmas together."

"Exactly. We went out to a club on Christmas Eve, and then on Christmas morning… "

"Breakfast in bed?"

"I went round to her place," continued Copper with heavy emphasis and a stern look at the senior man, "and we opened our presents…" He broke off, turned away, and started to rummage in his holdall. "Hang on a sec, sir. You're going to love this. Look what she got me!" He turned back to face the inspector, proudly wearing a fur hat with ear-flaps, whose front bore the face of a grinning chimp. Copper's own grin was no less delighted. "Isn't that brilliant, sir?"

Andy Constable, against all the odds, just managed to keep a straight face. "Well, sergeant, it seems the young lady has you weighed up perfectly. She obviously knows you far better than you're admitting." And, unable to sustain the pretence any longer, he burst into peals of laughter. "Thank you, Copper," he said, wiping his eyes. "That has made my Christmas. You have just rescued me from being a grumpy old sod. I needed that."

"Anything to oblige, guv," smiled Copper. "So do you think I ought to wear this when we're next out on a case, just to liven things up?"

"Best not," replied Constable. "There are probably limits to what the brass will put up with, even from you. So…" He resumed a more business-like manner. "On the subject of cases, I suppose we ought to be earning our living. I've been looking for the forensics report on that business at the chocolate factory, and I can't find the file. Have you got it?"

"I'm sure it's here somewhere, sir," answered Copper, not sounding completely confident. "I'll have a look." He gazed helplessly at the heap of files on his desk, and started to burrow through them.

"Andy, you're tired, and you need a break."

"I really don't, sir." Andy Constable looked across the Assistant Chief Constable's desk at his boss. "I am absolutely fine. And it's not as if we aren't short of manpower already, so if I take time off it only makes things harder for the other guys."

The Assistant Chief snorted. "Come on, Andy – granted you're a brilliant officer, and yes, I know, flattery will get me nowhere, but you're not going to try the old 'crime never sleeps' line on me, are you?"

"It did cross my mind, sir," said Constable, smiling ruefully.

"For goodness' sake, man, you're a one-man detection machine," replied the other. "Give the rest a chance once in a while." He smiled, and his voice softened. "Look, I'm not blind and deaf, despite what most of the other ranks might think about me. I do have a vague idea of what goes on in this force from time to time. And I happen to know that you haven't had a proper holiday in years. And I also know that you haven't had more than a couple of days off since the Dammett Hall Fete court case. So do us all a favour, take some time off, and don't burn yourself out."

"But really, sir… "

"I'll make it an order if I have to, Andy. Take a holiday. Hard as it may be to believe, we'll cope."

When Andy Constable returned to his office, it was to find Dave Copper with his feet up on his desk. The young sergeant swiftly swung into a sitting position and hastily picked up a recently-issued memo on the subject of local crime statistics. The fact that he was holding it upside-down did not help the pretence.

"What was all that about, then, sir?" he enquired. "You don't very often get a summons from the A.C.C. He hasn't been tearing you off a strip about something, has he? Although I can't think why he would."

"No, Copper, he hasn't," replied Constable. "Far from it. In fact, it appears that I am a brilliant officer, but I am in danger of burning myself out, and I am in need of some time off."

Dave Copper leaned forward earnestly. "Well, of course, he's right, isn't he, guv? I mean about the 'brilliant officer' bit."

"Copper, if I for one moment suspected that your famous sense of humour was getting the better of your good judgement in sending up your superior… "

"Honestly not, sir." Copper was insistent. "I'm dead serious. I know I muck about a bit sometimes, but I really have learnt a hell of a lot from working with you. It's the best time I've had since I joined the force, even if you do give me a hard time every so often. But you have to take a break sometimes – even you, sir."

Constable smiled. "Thank you for the vote of confidence, sergeant. But you'd better pack it in before you end up embarrassing both of us. And as for taking a break, it doesn't seem as if I have a lot of choice. The A.C.C.'s practically ordered me to have a holiday. Although lord knows where and when."

Copper jumped to his feet in excitement. "That's brilliant, sir. You could… "

"Could what?"

"No… maybe it wouldn't be such a brilliant idea after all."

"What wouldn't? Stop talking in riddles, man, and tell me what you're on about."

Dave Copper took a deep breath. "Well, sir – you know that holiday I won in the draw at Christmas. Why don't you come with me on that?"

Constable laughed in incredulity. "You are kidding, I assume! Don't you think we get to see enough of each other at work, without having holidays together like some sort of Odd Couple? Anyway, what about that girlfriend of yours… what's her name again? Aren't you taking her?"

"Oh, Lorraine?" Copper's voice was elaborately casual. "Actually, sir, we're not seeing each other any more."

"Don't tell me – dumped you?" Copper nodded. "Couldn't stand the hours?" Another nod. "And now you know why I never got married myself, sergeant. They never stick around long enough for you to ask them the question."

"So why not, sir?" persisted Copper. "If we're both at a loose end and there's a holiday going begging. And if I promise faithfully not to talk shop…?"

Constable sighed. "Okay, tell me all about it. But I'm promising nothing."

"All passengers for DerryAir flight KY69 to Alicante, please proceed immediately to gate 17 where the flight is now boarding."

Dave Copper looked up at the Arrivals and Departures board. He grinned. "Hey, that makes a nice change, guv. Our flight's actually on time."

"I'm very pleased to hear it. Just one thing though. Do you suppose you could break the habit of calling me 'guv' while we're on holiday? For one thing, it makes you sound as if you've been watching too many 1970s television kitchen-sink cop-shows, and for another, I don't particularly want everyone to know that I'm a policeman."

"Why not, sir?"

"It alters people's attitudes. They either want to moan at you about how long it took the local station to send someone round after they'd had a garden gnome nicked, or else they feel obliged to tell you about that dodgy bloke round the corner that they're sure is dealing drugs because he's got a pit bull and they can see suspicious-looking characters calling at his house every time they twitch their net curtains. So if you don't mind, less of the 'guv'."

"Righty-ho, sir."

"Copper!"

"Sorry, si..., I mean, sorry. So what do I call you? I can't really call you Andy, sir, can I? It wouldn't feel right. I can't call you 'Mr. Constable'. And Andrew still sounds a bit formal. It is Andrew, isn't it, gu... isn't it?"

"Never you mind what it is. Let's not go there." With a sudden brisk move, and an evident firm intention of changing the subject, Andy Constable stood, picked up his flight bag, and looked up at the bright yellow signs to check the direction to the departure gate. "Speaking of which, if we don't get a move on, neither of us will be going anywhere. I think there's a pair of aircraft seats waiting for us." He set a smart pace towards the exits, with Dave Copper trotting along half a pace behind.

"Yes, but really, sir," persisted Copper. "I can't keep saying 'Oi, you', can I?"

"Look, why don't you call me 'A.C.'? It's what one of the instructors at the police college used to call me. Evidently it was his idea of a joke."

"How so, sir?"

"The name, sergeant! Call yourself a detective? Apparently he found it enormously amusing that there should be a police recruit called Constable, so what with the first initial, he thought it would be fun to upgrade me to Assistant Commissioner. Oh, how we laughed!"

"Got you! Mind you, sir," gurgled Copper, "it could turn a bit embarrassing if we run into the actual A.C."

Constable raised an eyebrow. "I seriously doubt, Copper, that the Assistant Commissioner of the Met takes his holidays in Benidorm, or wherever it is that we're going."

"It's not actually Benidorm, guv... "

"A.C.!"

"Sorry, A.C. It's just along the coast, and according to the guide book, it's quite easy to get to, once we pick up the hire car at the airport. So all we have to do is…"

"First things first, Copper. Stop burbling and get your boarding card out and show it to this nice lady."

"Righty-ho… A.C… " Copper fumbled in his bag for his passport and boarding card. "This is going to be great. I'm really looking forward to this – you know, unwinding and getting a bit of sunshine. How about you, guv?"

"Oh yes," replied Constable. His tone held reservations. "Enormously."

Chapter 2

The gigantic gleaming glass and steel cavern that was the new terminal at Alicante's El Altet airport effortlessly swallowed the hundred-or-so passengers arriving on the same flight as the two detectives. The mixture of families, returning English-language students, business travellers, and a group of giggling supermarket checkout girls whose matching pink T-shirts declared them to be 'Courtenee's Pussy Posse', formed a straggling line of marching ants as they followed the arrows towards Baggage Reclaim.

"Hen party, do you reckon... er... A.C.?" asked Dave Copper in an undertone, obviously still uncomfortable in his role of friend rather than subordinate.

"Not exactly the most difficult piece of deduction you've ever had to do in your career," responded Andy Constable in similar fashion. "Let's just hope to goodness that they're not going to the same place as us." As the luggage carousel clunked into life and suitcases began to appear, it became clear that his fears were not to be realised, as the brightly-coloured labels of a well-known tour operator were visible on each suitcase that was claimed with squeals of delight, and the group's intended destination was plainly the notorious party resort some twenty miles and an entire cultural world away. Constable breathed a sigh of relief.

Cases safely collected, Copper led the way through the Blue Channel, where the two women apparently on duty seemed to be more concerned with comparing the merits of each other's nails than identifying customs defaulters, and towards the line of booths where the names of every car hire company he had ever heard of, and not a few he hadn't, competed for the early-season market. "I've only booked the small basic car," he explained to his colleague as they stood in the queue at the only company which was doing any business. "I didn't really see the point of getting anything too big, and I got a great deal online." He gazed at the people ahead of him. "So did everyone else, by the look of it. This is going to take forever."

It didn't. The clerks behind the windows were brisk and efficient, and the line of customers was swiftly disposed of as, switching effortlessly from Spanish to English to German to Norwegian, the car hire personnel sent each client more or less happily on their way. The only hold-up seemed to be the repeated invitation to take out extra accident insurance at a substantial, and evidently unexpected, cost, but when Dave Copper's turn came, a brief and almost accidental flash of his police identification led to not only an instant waving aside of the need for any unnecessary expense, but a surprise complimentary upgrading to an open-top car, complete with electric roof, air conditioning, and an i-pod dock.

"That was a bit of luck, wasn't it, sir?" grinned Copper, as the two men headed for the multi-storey car park in search of their vehicle. "Fancy them running out of Group A's just before we got to the desk."

"Ah, the innocence of youth," smiled Constable. "You never cease to amaze me, sergeant."

"How do you mean, guv?"

"This may come as a surprise to you, but not every police force in the world suffers from the same lack of respect which we sometimes get at home. I think you'll find that, in this neck of the woods, people still tend to jump about a bit when they are dealing with the police. It's probably a left-over from the past. So that very nice young lady thought it would do no harm at all if she did you a little favour. Plus the fact that they've got three different sorts of policeman… "

"Three??"

"Yes, three. Try not to sound so envious. There's the Guardia Civil, which is national, the Local Police, which you will be astonished to hear is local, and the Traffic Police, which is a bit of both."

"So how do we know which is which? And which ones get the guns?"

"All of them, I think. Let's hope we don't need to find out."

"How come you know all this, guv?"

"Because I read the Police Gazette, which believe it or not actually contains some very useful and interesting articles from time to time, the occasional perusal of which would do your career no harm at all." And as an afterthought, "And don't call me 'guv'."

"Sorry, si… sorry, A.C. But look, it's not easy, what with you calling me 'Copper' and 'sergeant' and so on. Why couldn't you just call me 'Dave' like everybody else?"

"Exactly how chummy am I required to be on this holiday?"

"How about 'David'?" Copper's face was that of a puppy hoping to be thrown a ball.

"We'll see."

The car was a boy-racer's dream – a low-slung two-seater, bright scarlet in colour, with a long bonnet and just enough space to squeeze the bags into the boot and behind the seats. Dave Copper's attempts to conceal his glee as he slid behind the wheel were not entirely successful.

"Are you sure you don't mind if I drive?" he enquired carefully, desperately trying to keep the grin off his face. "After all, it is hired in my name, and you're only down on the paperwork as the second driver. I mean, if you'd rather drive, I suppose I could do the navigating… "

"Oh, stop burbling, man." Andy Constable's smile was good-humoured. "You would never forgive me if I took your toy away from you. Get on with it, and let's get out of here. According to the instructions, you turn right out of the car park, up to the roundabout, join the dual carriageway, and then bear right on to the main road and go through the tunnel… "

"Hang on a second, sir. I just want to… " Copper started the engine, pressed a button, and with a click and a smooth hum the roof disjointed itself, folded itself up neatly, and stowed itself away under a panel at the rear. The grin on his face grew even broader as he twisted round to reach into the bag behind his companion's seat and produced a pair of bronze-tinted aviator glasses. "Right then… shall we?"

"Nice roads," commented Copper as they headed south along the surprisingly empty highway. "I've never driven in Spain before – I expected it to all be a bit rougher round the edges."

"E.U. money," replied Constable. "So don't be too surprised, because that's some of your tax money you're driving on. And apparently the trains are brilliant. The Spanish have done very well out of all the support funds over the years."

"What, even now with all the financial stuff going on?"

"Oh, I don't say things haven't changed a bit lately – bound to have done. But if you're going to be full of money worries, I can think of worse places to do it than here."

It was true. The sun was shining, the temperature was beautifully warm but not oppressive, and the sky was the clear rich blue of a late spring Mediterranean morning. As the car topped a rise, the view opened to reveal the sea to the left, glinting in the sunlight, while closer at hand, scrambling up a hillside scored with rocky ravines and dotted with clumps of pine trees, spread the cluster of villas and low blocks in a mixture of whites, ochres and pastel blues that was their destination.

"There you go, si… A.C." said Copper happily. "San Pablo. Didn't take long, did it?"

Following the travel agent's printed instruction sheet, the detectives pulled off the main road at a sign marked '*San Pablo – urbanizacion*', past a parade of shops, bars and restaurants that was obviously one of the social centres of the village, and up a long curving hill to find themselves in another commercial area housing banks, cafes, estate agents, convenience shops, and a large building sporting a coat of arms and flying the Spanish flag from its roof.

"Stick the car in the car park on the left," instructed Constable. "Look, that's the property agency over there."

Dave Copper pulled in and parked next to two police patrol vehicles in the parking lot. As the two men got out of the car, two uniformed police officers emerged from the building and, with a great deal of smiling, laughing and back-slapping, climbed into the patrol cars and drove off.

"Isn't that great, guv?" laughed Copper. "We've only gone and parked outside the local cop shop. It's just like home from home, isn't it?"

"Highly amusing," agreed Constable drily. "And that's the last I want to have to do with the local force, if that's all right by you… David." And in response to his colleague's look of surprise, "Don't be too amazed, man. I said I would make an effort. Come on, let's go and find out where this apartment of yours is. I'm not used to this sunshine – I'm starting to get hot and sticky. I want a shower." He headed across the road towards the estate agency bearing the legend 'Lott's Property', and looked back over his shoulder. "And don't call me 'guv'."

As Constable led the way into the blessedly cool interior of the agency, passing the display boards with their array of villas and apartments for sale and to rent, a smartly-dressed woman in her thirties rose from behind a desk at the rear of the office and came forward to greet them. Her glossy dark hair, cut in a long bob and held back with a pair of white sunglasses pushed up on to the top of her head, framed a face tanned to a golden bronze, with deep red lips, large dark eyes, and immaculately sculpted eyebrows. Chunky gold gleamed at her wrist and throat. She shimmered towards them on impossibly high heels.

"Good morning, gentlemen. Is there something I can help you with?"

Andy Constable stepped aside in favour of his colleague. "You'd better do this. You've got all the guff."

Dave Copper fumbled in his shoulder bag for the paperwork. "We've got a reservation for an apartment for a week – hang on, it's here somewhere – at a place called '*La Caca del Toro*', I think." He held out the sheet of paper he had been hunting for.

The woman laughed as she took the printout. "I think you mean '*La Casa del Torero*', don't you?" she said. "You wouldn't want to get that wrong." Copper frowned in bafflement as she glanced over the form quickly. "Don't worry about it. Just a little Spanish joke. Oh yes… Mr. Copper. David, is it? Do you mind if I call you David? We're very informal round here. I'm Liza – you know, like 'Liza With A Zee'. I own the agency."

"Er yes… David's fine… er, Dave is better, actually."

Liza proffered a red-taloned hand. "Well, I'm very pleased to meet you, Dave." She arched an eyebrow towards Andy Constable. "And your… friend?"

Copper failed to stop himself blushing. "No, this is my… I mean, this is the… "

Constable stepped forward to rescue his floundering colleague. "Andy." He held out his hand. "We work together."

"Oh I see," said Liza. "So, it's a boys' out-of-the-office jolly, is it?"

"Something like that," agreed Constable. "Just a break out of the routine for a week."

"Well, you've come to the right place if you want a bit of peace and quiet," remarked Liza. "The season hasn't really got going here yet, so we haven't got that many tourists around here at the moment. Just the residents."

"Is it all English round here, then?" asked Copper.

"Oh no, Dave, not at all," said Liza. "Far from it. The owners round this bit are mostly foreigners – you know, British, German, a few French, a fair number of Norwegians, actually – but you do get quite a lot of Spanish people as well because they like to have a second home at the seaside for holidays. That's up here in the urbanisation. But once you get over the other side of the hill it's a proper Spanish town, with the fishing harbour and the marina and the shops and a few hotels. It's a nice mix."

"Have you lived here long?"

"Oh lord, yes. I've been here for years. I first came out here when the boom started. Mind you, that was then, and this is now, and it's all a bit different these days." Liza seemed to pull herself up short. "Anyway, listen to me going on, and we haven't got you sorted out." She started to leaf through a box of folders on her desk. "Here we are – '*La Casa del Torero*'." She surveyed the papers swiftly. "Yes, that's all sorted out. And you've got it all to yourselves – that'll be nice. Everything's prepaid in England, so no need for a deposit. The cleaning's all been settled in advance, and the cleaner's opened it up for you. D'you know, I can't think of a single extra to charge you for." She laughed. "There's a first! Right, here's the key, here's a little map of how to get there – it's only a couple of minutes down the road – here's my card with my mobile number on it in case you have any problems – have a lovely time." Beaming, she ushered them out on to the pavement.

'*La Casa del Torero*' came as a pleasant surprise. Utterly different from the groups of pleasant but repetitive small blocks and villas which lined the road which swept down the hill in a gentle curve, it peered over its surrounding wall like a rather grand but slightly disapproving dowager. As Dave Copper pressed the button on the key-fob which opened the electric gates and drove into the forecourt, it became clear that the building was something out of the ordinary. Dazzling white walls were dotted with intricately-carved stone balconies, draped with skeins of multi-coloured bougainvillea, and topped with toy crenellations which would not have looked out of place in a child's story-book castle. Painted shutters in varying shades of pastel blue, some partly open to reveal muslin drapes wafting gently in the soft breeze, flanked the windows. At the head of a flight of steps, an impressive front door in beautifully-grained wood was adorned with monumental cast-iron hinges and handle. Towering palm trees surrounded the building, and through a stone arch could be glimpsed a courtyard garden with the turquoise glint of a swimming pool.

"Bloody hell, sir," said Copper. "That's not bad, is it?"

"As you say, bloody hell," replied Constable. "I'm assuming you've brought us to the right place? I know Mr. Patel was grateful to you, but he's not a registered charity, is he?"

"Well, he did do me a bit of an upgrade when he knew it was me that had won the prize," grinned Copper, "but I didn't think he'd manage to get us the King of Spain's summer palace. Hang on a sec… " He leafed through the sheaf of papers on his lap. "Fret not, guv – it's not all ours." He browsed the sheet in his hand. "Apparently the guy who built it was going to use it as a holiday home, but then he changed his mind and had it converted into four separate apartments. Except Liza said there was nobody else here, so we've got it all to ourselves after all. We're in… yes, Number 3. Shall we have a look?" Eager and smiling, he hopped out of the car, popped the boot, seized his case, and led the way to the front door, as Constable followed him with an amused gleam in his eye.

The apartment was on the first floor at the rear of the

building. What had not been clear from the forecourt was that the building was perched on the rim of one of the shallow ravines which the officers had seen as they approached the town, so each of the two bedrooms offered a different view across the lower streets which faded away to open countryside with a distant vista of hazy mountains.

"Nice and quiet," remarked Constable.

The sitting room, large and leather-furnished with a tiled floor, an impressive brick fireplace containing a huge wood-burning stove, and highly-polished dark wood cabinets in traditional Spanish designs, led on to a spacious balcony overlooking the pool, with teak table and chairs and a wrought-iron spiral stair leading to the lower terrace level, where loungers and umbrellas waited expectantly.

"Any preference for which room you want, guv?" asked Dave Copper. "I mean, I don't really mind, so whichever you'd rather… " He tailed off.

"Don't pussy-foot around, man," replied Constable. "Look, sit down a minute." He took a breath. "I have been a grumpy old sod at work lately, and you have refused to be beaten down, and you have probably been the only person who could have kept me sane, and this is your treat. So you will have whichever room you want, and we will both relax and have a good time and drink sangria and sunbathe, and forget work for the week."

"Righty-ho, guv. Sounds good to me."

"And you will stop calling me 'guv', and I will make a strenuous effort to call you something other than 'sergeant'. Deal?"

"Deal, sir. Sorry… force of habit."

Constable laughed. "We'll work on it. Come on – I'm going to chuck my stuff in my room, grab a quick shower and change, and then we are going to go out and find somewhere to have lunch. And since I must admit that you have done rather well for us in sorting out this place – David – this is my treat."

Just along from the apartment stood a small row of commercial premises which housed an incongruous mixture of an opticians, a bank, a pet shop combined with a vet's surgery, a knick-knack shop which also advertised a selection of British groceries, and a large double unit which was divided into a bar and cafe to one side, and a restaurant on the other. The place seemed to have an oddly split personality – while the restaurant proudly bore the title '*El Rincon de San Pablo*' in florid Hispanic lettering, a sign over the bar door displayed the slightly more confusing legend 'The Runcorn' in good plain stolid English. The tables outside on the pavement indicated a similar mix of clientele – at one table a pair of obviously Spanish electricians, their white vans canted on the pavement at careless angles of abandonment, gesticulated in animated discussion over coffees and brandies among the debris of an extensive meal, while at another an elderly couple sipped a modest glass of beer and a rather anaemic cup of tea as they unspeakingly browsed their copies of the Daily Mail and 'Pick Me Up' magazine.

"What do you reckon to this place, then?" asked Dave Copper. "Looks as if they do food. Shall we give it a go?" And in an undertone, "And they seem to cater for the British."

"I think we should do exactly that," replied Andy Constable. "But here's a little tip I've picked up along the way. Beware of the places which do the British food – all that 'All Day Breakfast' and 'Mum's Sunday Roast' stuff. The food will always be worse and the prices will always be higher, from what I've been told. So what you have to look for is the places where the locals eat. Which they clearly do here," he added in response to a crescendo of laughter from the two Spanish customers. "Look at this." He pointed to a chalked blackboard displayed at the bar entrance.

"'*Menu del Dia*' – that's meal of the day. Three courses, choices along the way, salad and drink included – 10 Euros. That'll do me."

"Bargain, sir," agreed Copper. "Provided you know what you're ordering, that is. I haven't a clue. I can just about say '*paella*'. How's your Spanish?"

"I dare say I can get by," responded Constable airily. "I did a C.D. course a while back, so I expect we shall be fine. Well, let's give it a go."

As the detectives made to enter the bar, they almost collided with a blonde young woman who was emerging carrying a tray bearing two enormous brandies.

"*Cuidado!*" she chirped as she swerved expertly, and raised her eyebrows in interrogation.

"*Buenos dias, senorita*," began Constable hesitantly.

"With you in a second, darling," she interrupted. "Just let me get Diego and Carlos sorted out and I'll be with you. Oh, by the way," she tossed over her shoulder as she headed for the two drivers, "it's after two, so it's '*tardes*'. Go on in." And without a pause, she launched into a flurry of rapid Spanish as she delivered the drinks to the two at the table.

Constable and Copper perched on stools at the opposite end of the bar from an elderly gentleman who gave them a nod and then returned to his Telegraph crossword.

"Right, boys, what's it to be?" The young woman was back behind the bar almost before the detectives heard her approach.

"We're not too late for lunch, are we?" asked Constable. "We've only just arrived this morning, so we're running a bit late."

The barmaid laughed. Her blonde hair, piled into a confection of curls and tendrils, may well have been natural, but the huge sooty eyelashes adorning her large hazel eyes definitely were not. Fuchsia eye-shadow merging to soft brown toned with the pearlescent pale pink of her lipstick, while her animal-print top with its deeply-scooped neckline and extremely short black skirt were a perfect tribute to the 1970s. "Too late? I shouldn't think so! This is Spain, darling – everything's a bit late round here! Most of the Spanish don't even start having lunch till after two, so you're fine. Having the Menu, are you?"

"If we can."

"No problem, love. Right, let's sort you out with a drink first, and then you can grab a table outside and I'll come and get your order. So, you look like beer boys to me. Couple of pints, is it?" As she busied herself pouring the beers, the barmaid seemed disposed to chat, although her style of conversation left little room for anyone else. "Just got here this morning, then? Holiday, is it? That's nice. Bet the weather here's a bit better than at home, eh? By the way, I'm Eve. And you are...?"

"David... Dave."

"Lovely to meet you, Dave. There's your pint, darling. And...?"

"Call me Andy."

"Andy – not Andrew, then? Bet your mother used to call you 'Andrew' when you were a bad boy."

"Just 'Andy' is fine."

"Right you are, then, just Andy – and there's yours. So where are you staying?"

"Just along at the... '*Casa del Torero*'," said Dave Copper carefully, not wishing to cause any further inexplicable mirth.

"Oh, that's lovely," replied Eve with enthusiasm. "That place is really beautiful." She looked the two men up and down. "I can see I shall have to look after you two boys. You must be worth a few bob to be able to afford a place like that."

"Sorry, afraid not," responded Copper regretfully. "I won a holiday in the raffle at work. But you can still look after me if you like." He stopped short as if suddenly realising the implications of his remark.

"Well, well done you," said Eve with only a shade of disappointment. "I hope you have a good time. So, you work together, do you? What sort of job's that, then."

"Oh, just in an office," said Constable hastily. "Nothing very interesting."

"Did you hear that, Percy?" said Eve, addressing the elderly man along the bar. "Dave and Andy are staying at the '*Casa del Torero*'. That's just across the way from Percy's new place," she explained to the detectives. "He's just had this lovely new villa built, haven't you, Percy?"

"Eh? What d'you say?" The man tore himself away from his crossword.

"I said Dave and Andy here are staying at the '*Casa del Torero*' just by you," repeated Eve. "They're on holiday. Boys, this is Percy – he's one of my best customers, aren't you, darling?"

"If you say so, Eve," chuckled the man, turning to Constable and Copper. "Pay no attention – she says that about everybody." He laid aside his newspaper, rose, and extended a hand. "Percy Vere. Pleased to meet you, gentlemen."

Percy might well have come straight from a casting session for the archetypal elderly Englishman abroad. A tanned face with rosy cheeks and deeply incised laughter lines, with bright blue eyes twinkling with good humour, gazing out from beneath bushy white eyebrows which perfectly matched his luxuriant white moustache and thick head of hair, swept back in a careful wave. A bright paisley-patterned cravat added a splash of colour at the neck of his crisp white shirt, topped with a cream linen jacket, while faultlessly-polished brown brogues gleamed below immaculately-creased cavalry twill trousers. A Panama hat sat on the bar between his newspaper and what looked like a very large gin and tonic.

"So," said Andy Constable, taking the proffered hand, "are you on holiday here too?"

"Lord, no," replied Percy, laughing. "I live here, for my sins. Have done for years. I used to live further up the hill, but as Eve says, I've just had a new place built across the road from where you're staying. Just moving in this week, as it happens."

"Friday, your party, isn't it, Percy?" asked Eve. "He's having a house-warming," she explained. "Here, Percy, why don't you invite the boys along? I bet you like a party, don't you, Dave?" she said, shooting a glance at Dave Copper which might easily be read as some sort of invitation.

"Er, well… I don't know if we… " He looked desperately to his colleague for help.

"Oh, go on. Percy wouldn't mind – he'd love to have you, wouldn't you, Percy darling?"

"Of course," responded Percy expansively. "You'd be very welcome, gentlemen. We're all very sociable around here – sometimes you can't walk round the block without getting invited in for a glass of wine at least four times!" And in response to Andy Constable's evident hesitation, "Look, no pressure. You've probably got plans, and you don't want to spend your holiday being monopolised by some old fogey and a bunch of exiles. But if you'd like to pop in for a drink, please do. Friday, eight-ish. Now, not meaning to listen to other people's conversations, but weren't you wanting to order some lunch from this young lady?"

Eve's hand went to her mouth. "Sorry, loves, you were, weren't you? But that's me all over, isn't it, Percy? Once I get nattering, I just forget my own head, don't I?" Percy's smile and chuckle left no need for a reply. "Look, get yourselves a table outside and I'll be out with a menu in two seconds."

As the detectives took their seats at a table in the shade of a large umbrella, a police patrol car drew up at the kerb and the driver, a tall muscular officer in his early forties sporting designer sunglasses, an impressive holstered side-arm, and what looked like the insignia of a senior rank, seated himself at the next table. He nodded to the other two.

Eve emerged from the bar. "*Hola, Alfredo! Momentito!*" she cried to the newcomer. "Right, darlings, here's the menu. You should try the *Emperador* – it's lovely."

As the two Britons completed their order, Andy Constable murmured in a low aside to Eve, "Looks as if this place is respectable enough. You've even got the local law eating here."

Eve laughed. "I should hope so, love. He owns the place!" She turned to the Spanish officer. "Alfredo, we've got two new customers – this is Andy and Dave. They've just arrived on holiday. Boys, this is my boss Alfredo Garcia – he's the town Police Captain."

The men shook hands amidst a round of smiling "Pleased to meet you" and "*Mucho gusto*".

"*Carajillo*, Alfredo? Thought so. On my way." Eve disappeared.

"On holiday?" enquired Alfredo in a voice which carried a tone which Constable could not quite identify. "Well, I hope you gentlemen have a quiet time."

Constable smiled uncertainly. "I hope so too. Why, is there any reason why we shouldn't?"

"Not at all," replied Alfredo. "I just hope you are not here on the… what is it the English say when you are on holiday to work?"

"Busman's holiday?" suggested Copper.

"Exactly this!" agreed Alfredo. "And when you have been a policeman as long as I have, you learn to recognise certain things. Like other policemen. So, captain and sergeant, is it?"

Constable sighed ruefully. "Inspector, actually. But I promise you, this is genuinely a holiday. Work is the furthest thing from our minds. We've even got a deal not to talk shop, haven't we, sergeant… David?"

Copper nodded in confirmation.

"So if we could keep it between ourselves… "

Alfredo nodded. "I understand. I will keep your secret. So, enjoy your holiday." And as Eve arrived bearing the first of the plates, "*Buen provecho!*"

Chapter 3

"Thank you again for your help with Mr. Rookham, Andy and Dave." Alfredo raised his glass, which contained a startlingly large measure of brandy, in toast. "*Salud!*"

"It really wasn't anything," protested Constable. "Just glad to help." He sipped his drink. "Hell's teeth… this is strong!"

Alfredo laughed. "It is my best brandy. You have deserved a reward for all your hard work. And for the fact that I have – what is it you say in England – 'blown your cover'."

"Yes," agreed Constable ruefully. "So much for keeping a low profile and not talking shop on holiday."

"Actually, I do not think you will have to worry a lot about that. My officer does not speak much English, so he will not say anything to anybody. And of course," smiled Alfredo, "I will be taking all the credit for solving Mr. Rookham's death when I report it to my Commander."

"What about Eve?" put in Dave Copper. "Won't she tell people? If I know anything about barmaids… "

"No," replied Alfredo. "She was not here this morning when the body was discovered, and that is why I sent my son over to bring you. So I think your secret is safe."

At that moment, Eve emerged from the bar. "Everything all right, darlings?" she enquired as she rapidly fielded the debris from three other tables where there was clear evidence that the locals had been taking the traditional Spanish late second breakfast of coffees and croissants. "Anything else I can get you?"

Alfredo rose to his feet. "Yes… two more brandies for my friends." And as Constable started to protest, "No, you are here on holiday. You must enjoy yourselves. But I must work. So you stay here, and I will do my job to keep the streets safe for you." He smiled. "And I know how you English like to eat early, so you can stay and have lunch. On the house. So, welcome to Spain." Donning his sunglasses, he climbed into his squad car and was gone.

"Well," said Eve, "you boys have certainly made a hit there. I think my boss has taken a liking to you – he's not normally so fond of giving away the profits to every tourist that comes in here. Don't tell me you're long-lost relatives or something."

"No, no, not at all. We just got chatting," explained Constable airily. "Turned out we had some interests in common. We were talking about football mostly."

"And gadgets," added Copper.

"Well, he's the boss," shrugged Eve. "I just do what I'm told. Actually, he's very good, so I'm not complaining. So, a couple more brandies, then?"

"Any chance of a coffee to go with it?" said Copper. "Too many more like that and I shall be flat out."

"That's what the Spanish siesta was invented for," laughed Eve, "so don't you worry about that. Just let me clear those empties." She leaned forward over the table, causing Dave Copper to avert his eyes hastily from the impressive amount of cleavage revealed by her open-necked blouse.

"Here guv," hissed Copper in an undertone as Eve disappeared into the interior of the bar. "Do you reckon those are real?"

"How on earth am I supposed to know, Copper? You're meant to be a detective – if you're that bothered, you work it out."

"Hmmm," murmured Copper. "The Mystery of the Spanish Chest."

Constable sighed.

Dave Copper pored over the map spread out on the kitchen table. "Anywhere you fancy going in particular, guv?"

"A.C."

"Sorry… A.C."

"Not really, as long as it's somewhere. Look, it's Thursday already. We've been here two days, and all we've done is look at a dead body, eat, drink brandy, and sleep it off round the pool. Nice as this place is, I could easily get cabin fever. And I'm sure you are itching to go driving in that shiny new car of yours, so let's make a day of it. Any suggestions?"

"Well… as far as I can see, there's a road up through the mountains which is marked '*Ruta Turistica*', which I'm guessing means 'touristic route'… "

"Such a relief to know that all those years of training as a detective didn't go to waste!"

"… and it goes to a village which has got symbols which stand for castle and church and viewpoint, and there's a lake, so I'm guessing that might be worth the drive."

"So, you're the driver. Let's give it a go."

The drive up through the hills was spectacular, beginning with a gently meandering road through fields of olives, palms and trees laden with the white blossom of almonds, dotted with tiny hamlets where the only signs of life seemed to be a dozing dog and a black-clad old lady crocheting on a doorstep, before looping ever more tightly and steeply through groves of oranges and lemons, and passing over narrow stony bridges across deeply-cleft ravines as the rocky peaks drew nearer.

Rounding a turn in the road, the veil of pine trees drew aside to reveal a tumble of whitewashed buildings clustered around a crag topped by the stony battlements of a miniature castle. A solitary eagle circled high above the village, while at a lower level, wheeling crows cawed in accompaniment to the chimes from a church whose tiny blue dome gleamed a striking spot of vivid colour in a monochrome landscape.

"This," remarked Constable, "looks a bit more like the real Spain. None of your tourist traps here."

"I wouldn't actually bank on that," countered Dave Copper as he drove into the small and dusty square at the foot of the village. Although not crowded, the car park was populated by a significant number of hire cars bearing the stickers of a variety of rental firms, while at one end, a coach bearing a placard from a British tour company was in the process of disgorging a miscellaneous group of mature ladies in print frocks and sensible shoes, sunburnt fathers in long shorts with their skimpy-topped and high-heeled partners, and a gaggle of children who immediately marauded noisily away in several different directions.

"Elevenses, I think, don't you?" suggested Constable. "With a bit of luck, that mob is on a tour. I'm betting they'll be in and out in five minutes, once they've done their photos of the kids grinning inanely in front of whatever-it-is you grin in front of round here. Let's hope so, anyway. Right, let's apply the 'go where the locals go' rule." He pointed to a pair of elderly Spanish men engrossed in a lively game of backgammon at a table under the shade of a fig tree in the forecourt of a small cafe tucked to one side of the square.

Constable won his bet. By the time the two officers had finished their coffees, the coach party were already beginning to straggle back to their vehicle, and within a few minutes a calmer air had descended on the village.

"Shall we?"

"Why not?"

The cobbled village street wound its way steeply upwards between a mixture of houses with tightly-closed shutters but occasionally-open doors, through which shady interiors with massive wooden furniture could be glimpsed, and small shops with an astonishing profusion of surprisingly tasteful souvenirs. Passing through a tunnel cut into the rock of the crag, where a massive and ancient wooden door stood still ready to withstand an attack, the Britons emerged into an even tinier square, where the door of the church stood open to reveal the flicker of candle-light within. To one side, a steep path led through a stone arch towards the castle perched on its crest. Ahead, beyond the one-room village school with its class of attentive pupils, lay a walled terrace with a spectacular view over a deep turquoise lake several hundred feet below, and the mountains beyond it.

"Is this where I do the grinning inanely bit, guv?"

Constable smiled. "I'm never going to break you of that, am I?"

Copper laughed. "The inane grinning, or calling you 'guv', guv?"

"Both, probably. Or neither. Whatever." Constable seated himself on a stone bench and stretched contentedly. "I shall just have to put up with the 'guv', shan't I? And as for the inane grinning, I doubt if there is anything to be done about that, and unfortunately, I do not appear to have brought a camera with me, so that will have to remain unrecorded for posterity. Hard luck, David."

"You think?" Dave Copper triumphantly produced a mobile from his pocket. "Photo or HD video, do you reckon? Sorry, but the guys at the station would never forgive me if I don't." He handed the phone over to his superior. "Sorry, guv."

Constable glared severely at his colleague, took a deep breath, and the two men collapsed in helpless laughter.

The drive down from the village offered a choice of routes at a fork in the road. In one direction, the reflection of the sun on the distant sea revealed the shape of the harbour wall of a fishing port, and thoughts of lunch made the decision an easy one. After a swift descent along virtually-deserted country roads – "I could get used to driving round here," remarked Copper – the pair joined the coastal highway on the outskirts of a town which revealed itself to be a mixture of holiday resort, with a large sandy beach lined with blocks of apartments, and a working fishing village with trawler-lined quays and a commercial warehouse.

"Swim or lunch first?" enquired Copper as the two climbed out of the car on the beach-front promenade surprisingly free of any attempt to charge for parking. "I mean, it does seem a shame to waste a great beach… " he added meaningfully.

"Have you learnt nothing, man?" retorted his colleague with a smile. "Spanish hours! It's nowhere near two o'clock yet, so if we have lunch this early we shall be pointed at and mocked as tourists! Which I am not ready for."

"Swim it is, then," grinned a happy Dave Copper as he retrieved a backpack of towels and shorts from the boot of the car. "Good job I put this lot in. Forward planning and positive thinking again, you see. And it looks as if we've pretty much got the sea to ourselves. I can't believe it – can you imagine how a beach like this would be at home on a day like today? You'd be falling over people."

"It's probably still too early in the season for the locals," responded Constable. "They probably think it's still the middle of winter, and only the mad Brits go swimming at this time of year."

"In which case, guv, we're going to get pointed at and mocked as tourists whatever you say, so what the hell? Just let me get in that water."

After a brisk swim – the sea temperature was still too fresh to tempt the majority of sunbathers into the sea – and a few minutes drying-off time in the sun, the two looked about for the best choice of restaurant.

"Any preference, guv?"

"My instinct, David," replied Constable, "is to head for the harbour. I fancy fish, and I reckon we'll probably get better choice from the place they actually catch the stuff."

"Wow, guv, this is pretty impressive deductive work, if you don't mind me saying so. Do you reckon if I work very hard and pass all my exams, I could be a detective just like you?"

"Tread carefully, Sergeant Copper," growled Constable in feigned reproof. "You should beware of mocking your superior officers, for fear that they should visit the most terrible punishment upon you."

"Oh no, sir," quavered Copper. "You don't mean…?"

"Oh yes I do," laughed Constable. "You will be paying for lunch. Let that be a lesson to you."

"Deal!" smiled Copper happily.

As anticipated, the curve of the harbour was lined with over half-a-dozen restaurants, all spilling on to the pavement under extensive awnings, and each with a display of the seafood on offer in a large chilled cabinet, which was constantly basted with shovelfuls of crushed ice from a large freezer by whichever of the establishment's waiters happened to be passing. The range was huge – everything from lobsters large enough for two to share, through mackerel, mullets red and grey, and a selection of spiny goggle-eyed fish which Dave Copper had never seen before, to more familiar sardines and whitebait. Competition between the restaurants was fierce – outside each, cajoling passers-by to choose his establishment, stood a member of staff who, no matter what language any attempted brush-off was couched in, immediately responded in the same language with a fulsome description of his venue's advantages. Most offered free drinks. Some proffered trays of samples of the food on offer.

"It's a bit different from the High Street on a Friday night, isn't it," commented Dave Copper. "There we get chuckers-out

– here they have chuckers-in." He took a free glass of sangria with one hand while the other hovered over a tray of small fried seafood. "Here, what do reckon these are?"

"Well, whatever they are," answered Constable, helping himself to a portion, "they have tentacles, if you don't mind that kind of thing. Me, I'm not fussed." He took a bite. "Actually, they're rather good."

"They are *chopitos*, my friend," said the waiter holding the tray. "You're English? Baby squids. Very good. Speciality of the house. I think you like, yes?" as Constable took a second handful. "If you want, I give you portion for starter free – on the house. Yes? Table for two? Okay? Here in the shade is good. And you like Mama's famous special sangria? You want a jug for drink with your meal?" And as Dave Copper began to protest about needing to drive afterwards, "Is okay – is not too strong. Your friend can drink it all! *Mama! Una jarra de sangria!* I come back with menu in one minute." In seconds the two detectives found themselves seated with drinks in their hands and a basket of bread and garlic mayonnaise in front of them.

"I assume we're having lunch here, then, David," remarked Constable with raised eyebrows, as his colleague continued to goggle slightly at the sheer speed of events. "Good choice."

The lunch was delicious – Dave Copper's order for garlic prawns was met with an enormous platter of the largest langoustines he had ever seen, while Andy Constable's sole actually overhung the dish it was served on at both ends. A resourceful chef had even managed to squeeze a portion of chips and a serving of salad on to each plate.

"They don't want you to starve, do they, guv?" commented Copper as, after a lengthy period when conversation took a definite second place to the serious business of making inroads into the meal, the dessert of a blessedly modest portion of ice cream arrived at the table.

"They don't," agreed Constable, downing a further glass of sangria. "And I'm not that certain that they want you to remain altogether sober, despite what our waiter said, so in sheer self-defence, and in the interests of Anglo-Spanish relations, I propose to see the rest of this jug off. You, on the other hand, are the driver."

"That's fine. I'll have a coffee."

"And you think I won't? No, on the whole, I think the Spanish lifestyle most certainly suits me. All I shall require after this is a substantial siesta."

"No problem, guv. It should only take us about an hour to get back. Just strap yourself in firmly, and please try not to snore while I'm driving."

"Do they have such a thing as the Trade Description Act in Spain?"

"No idea, guv," replied Dave Copper, gingerly placing a mug of tea beside his superior as he lay stretched out on a sun lounger in the shade of the pergola at the side of the pool. "Why?"

"Because if they have, I am going back to that restaurant to have a word with our waiter and his famous mama about that sangria. 'Not strong', indeed! The only good thing about it is that I drank a great deal more of it than you did, otherwise I'm convinced you would have had us in a ditch on the way back." Andy Constable reached for his tea and groaned with the effort.

"I call that noble self-sacrifice, guv," said Copper cheerfully. "Think of it as taking one for the team. I feel absolutely fine."

"You would," grunted Constable in an undertone.

"Anyway," continued Copper, "I reckon it's all a question of culture. Don't they say that kids in the Mediterranean countries are brought up to drink wine and stuff with meals from a very early age, so they get used to it and don't go mad, unlike the mobs we get at home on a weekend who just get as much lager and whatnot down their necks as quickly as they can and then get rampant all up and down the High Street. Maybe there's something to be said for that famous 'Mediterranean diet' and 'continental cafe culture'."

"I certainly hope so," retorted Constable, who under the influence of the tea was beginning to feel fractionally more human. "Remember those two electricians who were putting away the brandy over at the bar the day we arrived? And that was lunchtime! What's the betting they were off to wire somebody's house with that lot under their belts?"

"In which case, guv, if I ever win the lottery and decide to buy my villa in the sun, remind me to check what time of day the workmen did the plumbing and the electrics," laughed Copper. "Anyway, talking of the bar, time's getting on a bit and I'm starting to rumble. Do you fancy popping over for a bite and a jar?"

"Are you completely insane? After you have eaten a lunch which consisted of half the annual prawn catch for the whole of Spain? I may never eat again. Anyway, the first time we set foot in there, it led to us getting dragged into having to think and sorting out dead bodies and other thoroughly non-holiday activities. The last thing I'm looking for is any more excitement, thank you very much. I am not up to it."

"What you need is a hair of the dog, guv. That'll see you right." Dave Copper was not to be put off. "And I just fancy some *tapas*. I don't actually know exactly what they are, but everybody goes on about them, so you have to try, don't you?" The young detective had the look of an expectant puppy.

Constable sighed and swung his feet on to the floor. "All right. Against my considerably better judgement… "

"Hello, lads! Back again? Nice to see you. With you in half a tick." In a flurry of clinking glasses, accompanied by the spluttering of the coffee machine, Eve swiftly loaded a tray with a selection of drinks and cups and disappeared towards the bar's front terrace where a group of thirty-something Spaniards were evidently unwinding at the end of the working day. "Right, now I'm all yours. You're getting to be part of my Runcorn Regulars, aren't you? Having a good time? What are you having?"

"Hi, Eve. Just a couple of pints… "

"Red wine."

"Righty-ho. Pint for me, and a glass of red for the governor here."

"Governor?" said Eve quizzically as she deftly poured the two drinks simultaneously. "That sounds awfully grand."

"Office joke," explained Constable swiftly. "He just means I'm his boss, so he has to do what I tell him. Like buying the drinks."

"So what is it you actually do?" persisted Eve. "You never did tell me."

"No, we didn't, did we?" Constable refused to be drawn. "Sorry, Eve, but we made a deal. No shop on holiday. Anyway, cheers. Now, David is looking for some advice, and I reckon you're the expert, so I think you should sort him out with what he fancies."

"Dave! Now I'm intrigued!" Eve smiled and leaned forward expectantly across the bar. "What are you after?"

"Just… just some *tapas*," spluttered Copper, with a glare at his superior who was having trouble concealing a grin of amusement. "If you do them, that is."

"Oh. Right. Course we do, love. Everybody does. Can't be a bar in Spain and not do *tapas*. They'd throw me out of the country. They're over here in the cabinet. Come along, Dave." Eve came round the bar and took Copper by the hand. "Let me show you what I've got."

As a variety of dishes was being selected, a thought struck Andy Constable.

"Eve, I'm curious."

"What about, darling?"

"The bar. It's called 'The Runcorn'. That doesn't sound very Spanish to me, so how's that come about?"

"Oh, that's quite funny," gurgled Eve as she returned behind the bar. "It's all a bit of a joke. You see, when this bit of San Pablo was first built, the restaurant was bought by this English couple from… I think it was somewhere in the Midlands. Monty and Mary, they were. Lovely couple – just retired, and they thought it would be a good idea to move to the sun and run a bar. Mind you, I'm talking about a few years ago now, back in the glory days when everybody wanted to come to Spain and the property was cheap. Of course, it's all changed a bit now. So anyway, Monty and Mary had this idea that they were going to buy a bar and cater for all the other Brits and what have you, and he was going to be the genial mine host, and she was going to perch on a bar stool all day sipping G & T. Not that they were alone! Half the Costas were full of people who had the same idea. Completely loopy!" Eve laughed. "So anyway, they bought this place, and the traditional Spanish name for a little local bar is '*Rincon*' – that's the Spanish word for a sort of cosy nook. So they called it '*El Rincon de Monty y Mary*', which was fine, except that Monty didn't have two words of Spanish to rub together, bless him, and he could never get his tongue round '*rincon*', so he was always calling it 'The Runcorn', and it sort of stuck."

"So what happened to the English owners?" Dave Copper wanted to know.

"Spain happened, that's what," said Eve shortly. "Oh don't get me wrong," she explained hastily, "it's a lovely country, and I love it here and I wouldn't live anywhere else, but the bureaucracy drives some people mad. There's a form for this, and a permit for that, and it's not so bad for me now because I speak the language, but if you're in business it can be a nightmare, and poor Monty and Mary just couldn't hack it. And I think the Spanish dream wasn't quite what they'd expected, and I reckon they missed their family in England, so they sold up and went back. And that's when Alfredo bought the place – it doesn't do any harm to have a few contacts round here – and he just kept the name for the bar, just for fun. He's actually got a sense of humour, which can be rare for a Spaniard, let alone a policeman!"

"Hmmm, yes," commented Constable. "A policeman with a sense of humour. Imagine that, eh, David?"

Copper was saved from the need to reply by a hail from the doorway.

"Eve, my dear! Set 'em up. A large measure of your finest mother's ruin, and have one for yourself!"

"Hello, Percy darling," smiled Eve in welcome. "I was wondering where you'd got to. Usually I can set my watch by you."

"Things to do, my dear, things to do." Percy Vere seated himself on a stool at the bar. "Been getting ready for tomorrow. I hope you haven't forgotten."

Eve shook her head. "Course I haven't, Percy. As if I could. I wouldn't miss one of your parties for the world. I can just see you over there with your pinny on, dusting everywhere and baking loads of sausage rolls!" She flashed a roguish wink at Constable and Copper.

"Eve," chortled Percy, "you're a very bad girl! You shouldn't take the mickey out of your more senior customers. It's bad for the old ticker." He turned to the two detectives. "Eve knows me too well," he explained. "She knows very well I can't be fussed with all that sort of thing. If you've got the money, no sense in not spending it, that's what I say. I worked hard for what I've got, so I don't see why I shouldn't enjoy it in my retirement. So I have this lovely Spanish girl who comes in to clean for me – Isabel. She's been doing it for… well, ever since I started coming out here on holiday, which is donkey's years ago now. Come to think of it, she's not so much of a girl now, is she, Eve?"

"Hardly, darling," remarked Eve. "Considering her daughter's just had her second baby."

"Well, there you are, then," continued Percy, "so she's always come in and kept the place up to scratch for me, wherever I've been. Mind you, she's had her work cut out in my new place, because there's been ten times as much builders' dust everywhere where the lads have been finishing things off – not that they have finished everything yet, because the pool's still not completed and there are still a lot of plants to put in the garden, but at least the inside is sorted. And then Isabel's got a sister who runs a bakery down in town with her husband, so I've put in my order for the food with them, and Antonio will bring it up to the villa tomorrow. So all I have to do is pop a few corks when people arrive, and Bob's your uncle."

"Percy love, you're one of the nicest men I know," said Eve. "You just love having people in, don't you."

"Friends, my dear, friends," said Percy. "That's what it's like out here… Andy, isn't it? We're all away from the old friends and family from back home – not that I ever had any family, because I was too busy working ever to get around to getting married or anything of that sort, but you know what I mean. So out here, you tend to make new friends. You're sat on your front terrace having a glass of wine, and somebody you've never clapped eyes on before comes past, and you get chatting, and the next thing you know they're sat with you having a drink, and so it goes. You've made a new friend."

"A bit different from the U.K., then," commented Dave Copper. "Where I live, I don't even know the name of the people across the road."

"Just what I say," agreed Percy. "In fact, chaps, as the newest of my friends, why don't you take me up on that invitation to come over and join the party tomorrow. It's just a few friends. Free booze!" he coaxed.

"Well, we wouldn't want to intrude. I mean, it's not as if we know anyone… "

"Go on, Dave," urged Eve. "It'll be fun. I'll be there, so you know me. So unless you've got other plans…?"

"We would love to," affirmed Andy Constable, just managing to keep a straight face at his young colleague's discomfiture.

"Excellent!" cried Percy. "Any time after eight, then. *Villa Demasiadocara*, just over the way. The one with the high wall with all the stones set into it. You can't miss it." He downed the remainder of his drink and stood. "Well, have to get on. Things to do. I will see you gentlemen tomorrow. Don't bother to dress up – we're all very casual round here. TTFN!"

As the bar door closed behind Percy, Eve again fixed Dave Copper with a determined eye. "So, Dave, how were your *tapas*?"

"Oh… er… very nice, actually."

"So, can I tempt you to any more? The *patatas bravas* are very good. Really spicy." She smiled invitingly.

"You're absolutely determined, aren't you? So we'll go."

"Well, not really, guv, but it is Friday night. You've got to go out on Friday night, haven't you."

"Obviously so, in Copper-world," said Andy Constable. "Speaking for myself, I would be perfectly content with a stroll down to the sea, a wander along the promenade, and then the difficult decision about which restaurant to go to for a bite to eat and a couple of drinks. But I suppose you have other considerations in mind," he added mischievously. "After all, the luscious Eve will be there, and I've got an idea she has plans for you."

"Oh, come on, guv," expostulated Dave Copper. "Do me a favour. She's a bit obvious for me."

"Well then, David, you will have to play your cards very carefully, won't you?" remarked Constable. "It's all my fault, I suppose, for saying yes to Percy Vere, but with the look on your face when Eve was fluttering her eyelashes at you, I couldn't resist it. Not that my idea of a perfect holiday is to stand around in a room full of total strangers making cocktail party conversation all night."

Copper thought for a moment. "Tell you what – how about a compromise? We'll pop over for a couple of drinks, stay for as little time as we decently can, and then we'll do your plan of the stroll and a meal. That way, Percy Vere gets to do his social host bit, and I'm not in your bad books for soaking up a whole evening. How does that sound?"

"Very diplomatic and resourceful," said Constable. "Excellent thinking. Plus," he commented, "it will allow you to escape the clutches of the delightful Eve, who will doubtless be severely disappointed."

"I'll live with it," grinned Copper. "Right, then. I'm ready if you are. Shall we?"

The gates of the *Villa Demasiadocara* stood open. As Constable and Copper climbed the steps, flanked by tiered walled beds which awaited their plants, towards the heavily-carved front door, they were left in no doubt that Percy Vere had spared no expense with his new construction. Elaborate wrought-iron grilles ornamented each window, and highly-glazed tiles in a deep iridescent blue covered the roof. At one end, a circular stone-clad turret opened onto a first-floor balcony shaded with tiles of a different but toning colour, while at the other, through an arch which led to the rear, could be glimpsed the corner of a wooden pergola topped with another balcony, up which a bougainvillea in a monumental terracotta pot was already beginning to writhe its colourful tentacles. A curving ramp led down to the doors of a subterranean garage beneath the house. As Andy Constable was about to place a finger on the ornate cast-iron bell-push, Percy Vere appeared through the arch.

"Good evening, gentlemen – glad you could come. This way – we're all round here." He ushered the two detectives round the corner of the house and on to a terrace, where a group of evidently non-British guests stood in a sheepish huddle at one end with glasses in their hands. Mostly young men in their twenties, with one or two wives or girlfriends hanging on to their partner's arms, they smiled tentatively at the newcomers and some murmured a collective "*Buenas tardes*", before reforming what looked rather like a defensive circle. Nobody else was to be seen.

Constable was concerned. "We're not too early, are we? Because you did say sometime after eight… "

"Oh, don't worry about that," boomed Percy. "Nobody gets anywhere on time around here. Spanish time, you know – it's a very flexible thing." In response to Constable's raised eyebrow and slight nod of the head towards the other group, Percy lowered his voice. "Mind you, if it's a case of a free drink, the Spaniards can be as punctual as you like. It's the builder's lads," he explained as Constable continued to look puzzled. "Spanish plus a few oddments. I couldn't really not invite them, considering the amount of work they've all put into building the place for me, and all in all I'm very pleased with what they've done so far, so I thought it would be a nice gesture. Of course," he said, indicating the still-unfinished back garden, "there's still a lot to do, but that's mostly the people from the garden centre, so I think I owe these chaps a bit of a thank-you. They've only got a few bits of finishing up to do, like the garden lighting and the pool and the barbecue area."

"I hope you haven't got them coming in to do your lighting in the morning," commented Dave Copper. "The last electricians we saw were putting away the booze like there was no tomorrow. I wouldn't have fancied letting them do my electrics."

"Don't fret about that," chuckled Percy. "For these lads, there is no tomorrow!"

"Sorry?"

"It's a fiesta day. Nobody's working at all, so they can have as much as they like. Now, listen to me – I'm standing here chatting, and you haven't got a drink. I've got plenty of fizz standing by inside – come on in and get a glass, and then I'll give you the conducted tour before anyone else arrives."

As the three passed through wide double doors into a spacious sitting room, they almost collided with a man emerging with a glass in his hand, who swerved adroitly and, with a murmured *'Perdon!'*, joined the group on the terrace. Constable had a brief impression of thick black swept-back hair, a deep tan, piercing eyes and a white smile, and a pair of shiny patent electric-blue trainers.

"That's Juan," said Percy over his shoulder.

"One what?" asked Copper, slightly puzzled.

Percy laughed. "No, that's his name. Juan Manuel," he explained as he headed for a marble table bearing glasses and several rows of bottles. "He's the foreman – keeps that little lot in order. Most of them don't speak much English, so he keeps the wheels turning. Anyway, what'll you have?"

With glasses in their hands, the visitors dutifully followed Percy as he showed them the seeming acres of marble, granite and tile which made up his new domain. Swags of carved velvet flanked the windows. Stainless steel gleamed everywhere in the kitchen. Bronze fittings and Moorish motifs adorned the several bathrooms.

"D'you reckon there's much more of this?" hissed Dave Copper in an aside to Andy Constable as yet another lavish guest bedroom was revealed. "Only I'm starting to get a bit ravenous."

"Well, what do you think of the place?" enquired a beaming Percy as the three descended the curving staircase.

"It's a beautiful house," replied Constable, draining his glass. "Unfortunately," he added ruefully, "it's a bit above my pay grade."

"Mine too," put in Copper.

"Oh, I say, look – the tide's gone out," remarked Percy, indicating the pair's empty glasses. "Come along, let me get you a top-up. I'm sure the others will be here soon."

"Look, Percy, it's very kind of you, but would you be terribly offended if we sneak off now?" asked Constable. "I'm sure everyone's very nice, but we really don't know anyone, and David here's getting rather peckish… "

"Not at all, lads, not at all!" cried Percy. "No, you go off and enjoy yourselves. After all, you're on your holidays, aren't you. You don't want to be taking up your time listening to an old buffer swanking on about his new house. I don't know what I was thinking of. Lord knows I've been bored to death by people I don't care about at enough parties in my time. Go on, off you go – if you're quick, you can probably make your escape before I have to start introducing you to everyone, and then you'd never get away! I'll see you out," he added, heading for the hall.

As if on cue, the front door bell sounded.

"Right then, Plan B," said Percy with a twinkle. "Always have a Plan B. Learnt that when I did my National Service! Nip round the side of the house while I answer the door, and then you can slope off before anyone sees you. Thanks for coming anyway – although I can think of a certain young lady who's going to be disappointed that young David here isn't present." With a cheery wave and a wink, he headed for the door as the two detectives hurried out through the patio doors towards the terrace and, under the slightly puzzled gaze of the group of workmen, sidled around the corner of the building and down the drive as the door closed to Percy's cries of welcome for the new guests.

"Lucky escape there, young David," commented Constable

with a smile. "Otherwise that certain young lady might have tried to ply you with drink, and lord knows where that would have led. You'd have needed a snatch squad to come in and rescue you."

"Can we not go into that too deeply, guv, if you don't mind," protested Copper. "You wouldn't want to spoil my appetite, would you?"

Andy Constable took pity on his colleague. "Right, then – food it is. You're the chauffeur. Get the keys, and you can have the pleasure of driving us into town in that nice shiny car of yours to find a restaurant. And as my reward for saving you from a grisly fate at the hands of the lovely Eve, I will delegate the choice to you, and as a special treat, I'll even let you pay."

"You're good to me, guv," grinned Copper. "Just a sec while I work out whether I should be grateful."

"Oh, that's ridiculous!" Constable slowly focussed his eyes on the clock display of the radio at the side of his bed. "Who the hell is ringing the door-bell at quarter past seven on a Saturday morning, for God's sake?" he muttered to himself, as he swung his feet around and stood up.

"It's okay, guv, I'm there." Dave Copper, in a pair of boxer shorts with a colourful pattern of capering teddy bears, trotted past the bedroom door.

"Nice shorts," called Constable.

"Christmas present," retorted Copper shortly, and opened the door. During the murmured conversation which followed, Constable swiftly climbed into a T-shirt and shorts, and emerged to find Captain Alfredo standing at the door, with a junior officer hovering behind him.

"Good morning, Andy. I am sorry to call on you at this hour... "

"Morning, Alfredo. What's up?"

"There is a problem. There is something across the road that I think you ought to see."

"What sort of problem?" asked Constable warily. This did not sound good.

"We have found something. And since you were so kind as to help me with Mr. Rookham… "

"Oh strewth!" groaned Constable. "Not another one!"

Chapter 4

"But I still can't see that we can be much help to you," protested Constable, slumping back on the sofa. "Surely you're much better placed to carry out an investigation than we would be?"

"But it is fiesta," replied Alfredo simply.

"So what difference does that make?"

"Ah, the *Fiesta de San Pablo* is the biggest fiesta of the whole year here in the town, and so we have big celebrations for three days, starting today. There is the landing on the beach, and the battle, and the big processions, and the special masses in the church, and the fireworks."

"So what's all that in aid of?" asked Copper, intrigued.

"It is celebrating our history," explained Alfredo. "Hundreds of years ago there was a big struggle between the Christians and the Moors about who would rule Spain, and there were many fights. And in this place there was a little castle, and a lot of boats full of Moors came to attack it, and there were few Spanish soldiers in the castle, but many Moors. But the Christians prayed to San Pablo to help them, and it is said he appeared on a white horse and helped them to win the battle. So the town was born, and every year they have the fiesta to remember the story."

"So how does that stop you investigating a case?" asked Constable.

"Ah, you do not understand," smiled Alfredo. "It is Spain. Here, fiesta is sacred, and nobody works. All my offices are closed until Tuesday – you know, the investigators of the blood and the fingerprints…?"

"Forensics?" suggested Copper.

"Yes, that is it. And also, the thing is that all the people that could have done it are English, or some piece English, and I think you understand the English mind better than I do, so you will see better if they do not tell the truth or are hiding some things."

Constable capitulated. "Okay, Alfredo. Tell us all about it. What exactly has happened?"

Alfredo stood. "You had better come to see."

The *Villa Demasiadocara* stood still and silent as Alfredo led the way round the corner of the building and down past the patio to the building works surrounding the pool. There, among a jumble of builder's rubble, odd chunks of timber, broken terracotta pipes, and discarded workmen's tools, running between the pool and what appeared to be a small pump-house lay a trench which had been partially and not particularly expertly filled in. Startling in its incongruity, there protruded from the rough soil infill a foot encased in a shiny blue trainer. Standing by, and looking very young and rather scared, was another junior police officer.

"I recognise that shoe," said Andy Constable. He turned to Dave Copper. "That's that Spanish builder guy who was here last night – the one we almost bumped into when Percy was showing us around."

"Juan something, wasn't it? Oh yes, I remember those shoes. I thought they were a bit over-the-top at the time. That's if they're the same ones, guv."

"Something of a coincidence if they aren't."

"Yes, we think it is Juan Manuel Laborero," confirmed Alfredo. "Mr. Vere has said he was here."

"I suppose you're absolutely sure he's dead?" enquired Copper, turning to Alfredo. "I mean, I don't know if you get a pulse in the ankle or anything, but I suppose you have checked."

"We have," answered Alfredo shortly. "Nothing."

"In which case, sir," commented Copper, "this has to be the nastiest case of trench foot I've ever seen."

"Copper," responded Constable, "your penchant for graveyard humour never ceases to amaze me."

"Oh, I can do much better than that, guv, given a bit of thinking time." Copper was in no way abashed by his superior's disapproval. "So, if we're on the case, shouldn't we start digging for clues?"

Constable was not to be drawn. "Alfredo," he said, "hadn't you better get the poor chap out of the ground? We might be able to tell more if we know how he died." He crouched down. "For a start, take a look at this." He gestured to what seemed to be part of a sturdy stair-post lying nearby. "If I'm not much mistaken, that looks like blood on the corner of that, so that's worth taking a closer look at."

"You are right," said Alfredo. "I had not noticed that, because I was hurrying to come to see you to ask your help. But I will have my boys wrap it and take it. And I will have them dig up the body, and then we will know for sure if it is Juan Manuel, and maybe we know how he died." He issued rapid instructions in Spanish to his two junior colleagues.

"Hold it!" ejaculated Constable, as one of the two reached for a spade which was lying alongside the trench. "Don't touch that! Look at the handle – I think there seems to be blood on that as well. That's another one for your forensics team when they finally get back to work, Alfredo."

"What if they use some gloves? Look, we have some gloves here." Alfredo gestured to a pair of dust-covered and tattered gloves lying nearby on a spoil-heap. He stooped to reach for them.

"Whoa!" cried Constable urgently. "For all we know, the

murderer might have used those as well, in which case you'll be able to get DNA off the insides. I'd send those off to forensics too if I were you. Not that I'm trying to tell you how to do your job," he added.

"We will get other spades," said Alfredo, sighing and gesturing to his juniors. "Thank you."

"Fine," replied Constable. "Right, next step. Who found him, and when?"

"We will go indoors. Mr. Vere will tell you."

Seated in the villa's living room, with a still-shaken-looking Percy Vere appearing small and shrunken in a huge leather armchair, Alfredo consulted a notebook.

"So, Mr. Vere, Andy and David have agreed to help me, so I would like you to tell them what you have said to me."

"Alfredo says you two are policemen, then," said Percy, sitting up a little straighter and seeming to make an effort to gather his wits. "You kept that a bit quiet, didn't you? What, over here on a case, are you? I must say, I take a dim view of it if you're doing some sort of investigation and making use of me and my house."

"No, I promise you it's nothing at all like that," Andy Constable reassured him. "It's absolutely one hundred percent coincidence that David and I happened to be here. We are genuinely on holiday, and I can assure you that nothing was further from my mind than getting involved in a suspicious death."

"Two, sir, actually."

"Thank you, Copper, for that very helpful addition to the conversation," said Constable drily. "Look, Mr. Vere, let me introduce myself properly. I'm Andy Constable – I'm a detective inspector in the U.K., and I'm sorry to have to tell you that this bright young spark is Detective Sergeant Dave Copper, who works with me. And if I'm being honest, I'm blaming him for the whole thing." He smiled slightly to take the seriousness out of his words.

"Fair do's, guv," responded Copper. "I just won the holiday. None of this was my idea."

"Be that as it may," continued Constable, "I'm afraid that Alfredo spotted us on our first day here. Policeman's instinct is obviously international. Anyway, he asked us to help sort out a little problem he had… "

"If you can call a dead body a little problem," commented Copper.

"Which we were happy to do," pressed on Constable, "but we asked him not to mention the fact to anyone, and not to mention that we are police officers, because we just wanted to have a normal holiday. Somebody, however," he added heavily, "seems to have other ideas."

"I see," said Percy, mollified. "So now he wants you to help with our 'little problem', does he?"

"Yes," said Alfredo, taking charge. "So, Andy – I will still call you Andy, yes? I will tell you about this morning. Mr. Vere says he woke up early, and when he looked out at his window, he saw the foot as you have seen. Is this correct, Mr. Vere?"

"That's right, Alfredo. I woke up because I wanted to – well, you know, it was the party last night, and I'd had quite a few drinks, and none of us is getting any younger, and when you get to my age… anyway, I needed to go to the bathroom, and when I came back, I opened up the shutters, looked out, and saw that… that foot sticking out of the ground. Couldn't believe it. So then I must admit, the old brain went a bit fuzzy. I thought, 'I've got to tell somebody', and I suppose I must have thought of Alfredo subconsciously because I chucked a dressing gown on and went over to the restaurant and started banging on the door. Must have looked a right fool!"

"So what happened?" asked Andy Constable.

"Well, as luck would have it, Eve heard me, and came down."

"Eve Stropper," confirmed Alfredo. "She is my waitress. You know her. She lives in the apartment above the restaurant."

"Ah yes, the lovely Eve," said Constable. "David's… admirer."

"And what did she do?" hurried on Dave Copper, anxious not to linger.

"She telephoned me," replied Alfredo, "and I came here, and then I called my two officers to come here with me, and then I came to you."

"And very generously placed the ball firmly in our court," said Constable in tones which did not exactly convey warm gratitude. "So, that's the what. Now how about the who. Who do you have in the frame for this? After all, Mr. Vere here had a houseful last night, didn't you?"

Alfredo consulted his notebook again. "Actually, it is not so bad. We only have six or seven people who were still here when Mr. Laborero was last seen, and they have all to do with the building of Mr. Vere's villa, and as I tell you, all English, so this is why I have asked you to help."

"But what about that bunch of builders who were here when we arrived?" protested Dave Copper. "How come you aren't including them?"

"Oh, they'd all gone by that time," explained Percy. "Can't say I blame them. Lot of young chaps with their wives and girlfriends, they don't want to be hanging round here all night listening to a group of foreigners trying to talk to them in bad Spanish just for the sake of politeness. They'd much rather be off down into town making a start on the fiesta weekend. So they were all gone… oh, not that long after you two went, actually. Certainly by nine o'clock, and Juan Manuel was still alive and kicking then." He pulled a face. "Sorry – unfortunate choice of words."

"So," asked Constable, "who was still here?"

"Look, Alfredo, can I leave this to you," said Percy, who seemed to be beginning to wilt. "You've got all the names, and I'm feeling a bit knocked about – I could really do with a shower and a cup of tea. Would you mind awfully?"

"That is no problem, Mr. Vere," replied Alfredo. "I will take Andy and David up to my office. I have on my computer all information about foreigners who are resident in my area, so I can give you all the names and pictures too. I think this will help perhaps. So it is okay if you go and shower and put clothes on, but please do not go away anywhere."

"Of course not," bristled Percy. "Why would I?"

"What I think Alfredo means," interjected Constable soothingly, "is that we shall probably want to have another word with you when we come back, when you're feeling a bit more up to it."

"And also," added Alfredo, as the sound of digging began to filter in through the open patio doors, "my officers are still here, remember. Come, Andy and Dave – we take my car."

The car park outside the police station was deserted, and as the three officers entered the building, their footsteps echoed down the silence of the tiled corridor which led to Alfredo's office.

"You weren't kidding about this fiesta business, Alfredo," remarked Dave Copper. "I can't believe there's not a soul about. At home, they're more likely to drag us in for extra shifts when it's a holiday weekend. No wonder your two guys were looking a bit cheesed off. Here guv, can you imagine what it would be like at home if we all took public holidays off?"

"A great deal more restful," replied Andy Constable drily. "After all, nobody wants to work on holiday, do they?"

Alfredo affected not to hear the comment as he turned into his office, seated himself behind his desk and booted his computer. A few clicks later, after consulting a file from a cabinet alongside the desk, he swivelled the monitor and gestured to the two Britons to take a seat alongside him.

"These are the people who were at the house of Mr. Vere last night." With each click, a face appeared on the screen. "This is Mr. Connor, who is the builder of the villa... this is Philippa – she is his girlfriend, and she also works for me sometimes in my bar."

"Did you say you've got pictures on file of all the foreigners who live on your patch?" asked Dave Copper, incredulous. "I bet it comes in handy sometimes, like now for instance, but don't the civil rights people go mental about something like that? I know they would at home."

"This is because you do not have identity cards in England," said Alfredo. "Here, we have them, so everybody has to carry their papers with them, and if you are a foreigner you have to apply for a card if you want to live here, and so we have all the pictures on the national computer."

"Yeah, we nearly got I.D. cards in the U.K. a while back," said Copper, "but it never came to anything."

"But it is changing here also," said Alfredo, "and they will stop the cards with pictures for the foreign people. This makes my job much more hard. But for us Spanish, we are used to it, so we do not worry, and it is necessary for getting jobs and driving licences."

"So who else have you got to show us?" interrupted Constable, anxious to return to the matter in hand. "Are there many more?"

"Not too many. Look, here is also Eve, who you know from my bar..." Another face appeared.

"Oh, we know her too, don't we?" said Copper. "That's the estate agent woman we got the keys from... Liza something... "

"Liza Lott," resumed Alfredo. "Yes, she has the office just

across the road. And then here is Mr. Berman... he is employed by Mr. Connor... and here is Mr. Torrance, who works for him as well. They are both on his... what is the word?"

"Workforce?" suggested Copper.

"Yes, that is it. I can tell you the addresses of all these people, because I think you will want to talk to them all, yes?"

"Absolutely, why not?" responded Constable with ironic cheerfulness. "As we seem to be on the case, we'd better make a proper job of it, hadn't we, David?"

"As you say, sir, absolutely," agreed Copper with a smile. "I was getting a bit bored anyway. So, is that the lot, Alfredo?"

"No, I have two more." Click. "Look, this is Mrs. Stone... she has a business which works with Mr. Connor on his buildings." Another click. "And this last one is Mr. Husami."

"Mr. Whose what?" enquired Copper. "I thought you said they were all English. That doesn't sound too English to me." He examined the image of the deeply-tanned face on the screen. "He doesn't look all that English either. Sorry, that doesn't sound very P.C., does it?"

"It is Mr. Husami," repeated Alfredo. "Hoo-sah-mee. Sorry, I know I say English, but to us in Spain you are all English. It is because you have all different names for your country – sometimes it is England, sometimes it is United Kingdom, sometimes it is Britain, so for us it is easier to say English. He sounds English to me when he talks. I think he is half British. You will meet him – he will tell you."

"And that's it?"

"Yes. Here, I give you addresses for all these people." Alfredo swiftly scribbled on a sheet of paper.

"In which case, I suppose we'd better get on with it," said Constable, getting to his feet.

"Andy, I have to tell you, I am very grateful to you for this help." Alfredo stood and proffered his hand to his two colleagues.

"But you see, with the fiesta I have no people, and maybe if we do not start quickly… "

"Yes, I know," replied Constable. "Strike while the iron's hot, that's what we say. Come on, David – duty calls. Don't bother about giving us a lift, Alfredo," he added as the Spaniard reached for his car keys. "We'll walk. I think better on my feet."

"Just a thought, guv," said Dave Copper. "If we're on duty, can I go back to calling you 'sir'?"

"Sergeant," smiled Andy Constable, "I think that would be a very good idea."

On the steps of the police station, Alfredo once again offered his hand in farewell. As the two Britons turned to leave, a car drew into the car park, and a familiar figure stepped out and crossed the road towards the row of shops opposite.

"Look, guv," said Copper. "That's the woman from the property agency, isn't it?"

"It is," agreed Constable, consulting the sheet Alfredo had given him. "Estate agent Liza Lott. Well, I did say something about striking while the iron was hot, and I don't suppose it will get much hotter than this. Why don't we go and have a word with her now?" He turned to Alfredo. "I imagine the word hasn't got around yet about your dead man, so we may achieve something with an element of surprise. I'm assuming she knew this Juan Manuel, of course?"

"You are right, Andy," replied Alfredo. "But everybody knew Juan Manuel, because he was a very popular guy, so this will not mean anything special."

"Not universally popular, it seems to me," commented Dave Copper in an undertone to his superior. "Otherwise he wouldn't be lying in a hole in Percy Vere's garden with his feet sticking up in the air."

"Perspicacious as ever, sergeant, if not particularly tasteful," said Constable with a raised eyebrow. A thought struck him. "Look, Alfredo, I'm only too happy to help you out on this one – well, maybe that's overstating it a bit, but we are where we are. But as far as these suspects – I suppose we have to call them that – as far as they're concerned, I'm just some bloke on holiday, or worse, a total stranger. I can't think that they're going to take kindly to it if I just go barging in on my own say-so and start asking questions about a murder. I think you are going to have to give us some sort of authority, otherwise nobody's going to co-operate."

"You are right, Andy. What I will do, I will call all the people and I will tell them that I have arranged the help of an English detective… "

"… because of specialist knowledge of the British community," put in Dave Copper. "That might make whoever did this a bit jumpy if they think we know more than we do."

"Good bluff. I like it." Constable nodded approvingly. "So shall we make a start with Liza Lott?" He gestured towards the other side of the road, where the estate agent had disappeared into her premises. "Alfredo, if you wouldn't mind, could you come over and do the introduction in person, as you're here. It might save a few minutes."

As the two-tone bleep sounded as the door to the agency opened to admit the three officers, Liza Lott looked up in surprise.

"Sorry, gentlemen, you're a bit early. I've only just got here myself, and we don't actually open until nine o'clock." She took in the identity of her visitors. "It's David and Andy from the '*Casa del Torero*', isn't it? Is everything all right down there? I hope you haven't come in with a complaint. That's usually the only reason anyone comes in to see me this early in the day." In response to the silence which greeted her remarks, the professional smile on her face faded. "Captain Alfredo, I don't very often see you in here." The uncertainly in her voice became more pronounced. "Is there some sort of a problem?"

"Yes, I think you can say that. And I have asked my two friends here if they will help me to solve it, and now I ask you if you will help them and answer their questions."

"What questions? What about? And why are they asking me? Look, will somebody tell me what this is all about."

Andy Constable stepped forward. "I think I'd better introduce myself properly, madam. I'm Detective Inspector Constable, and this is my colleague Detective Sergeant Copper."

"You're British police?" Liza's surprise was evident. "I thought you were here on holiday. That's what you told me. Are you telling me you're here on some sort of investigation?"

"I'm afraid that it wouldn't be prudent to comment on that, madam," responded Constable smoothly. "But in fact, the reason we're in Spain has nothing to do with the reason we're here now. Captain Alfredo has asked us to assist him as… "

"Consultants."

"Thank you, Copper. That was very well put. As consultants, as my sergeant says, into a case which has unexpectedly arisen. Unfortunately, there has been a suspicious death."

Liza's eyes opened wide. "Whose death? What do you mean, suspicious? Who's died?"

Andy Constable turned to Alfredo. "Captain…?"

Alfredo assumed a more official tone. "This morning we have discovered, at the villa of Mr. Vere, a body which we believe to be Juan Manuel Laborero."

"Juan Manuel? He's dead? Are you sure?" Liza's shock appeared genuine.

"Yes, we are sure that he is dead," replied Alfredo grimly. "And by now, I think we will also be sure that it is Mr. Laborero. And as we know you were at the party last night where he was last seen, we want you to tell us what you know."

Liza subsided on to a chair, pale beneath her tan. "Juan Manuel's dead? I can't believe it. And that's why you're here?" There was incredulity in her voice, mixed with a trace of something else which Constable could not quite put his finger on. The incongruity nagged at him. He put it aside in his mind for the time being.

"I'm happy to take it from here, Captain Alfredo, if that's all right by you." A formal note had entered Constable's voice.

"Of course, Andy – Inspector. I will go and make those telephone calls. And here is my card with my mobile number on it. If you want anything, you call me."

"Good point. Copper, let Captain Alfredo have your mobile number as well. Then if anything comes up, no doubt you will let us know."

"Of course." Alfredo shook hands again "And then I will go back to Mr. Vere's house. Perhaps I will see you there later?"

As the agency door closed behind Alfredo, Constable turned back to Liza Lott.

"If you don't mind, Miss Lott, I'll make a start on those few questions, if you're up to it?"

"Yes, inspector," said Liza, taking a deep breath and recovering a more normal colour.

"Do you mind if we sit down?" Constable seated himself on a leather sofa in the reception area. "Oh, and I don't suppose you could let my sergeant here have some paper and a pen so that he can make a few notes if he has to. We haven't really come equipped this morning." He smiled blandly.

"Help yourself, sergeant," said Liza, gesturing to the front desk. "There should be some shorthand notepads in the top drawer, if that is any good to you."

"Perfect, madam. You're very kind." Copper seated himself alongside the inspector.

Andy Constable marshalled his thoughts. "It's obviously come as a shock, and I apologise that it's probably something of an imposition, having to answer questions from a British policeman, but the Captain was very anxious not to lose any time over the investigation, bearing in mind that, as he told us, his facilities are somewhat limited over the fiesta weekend. So if you're all right…"

"Please."

"Right then, Miss Lott. It is Miss, is it?"

"Yes, inspector. Elizabeth Angela Marguerite Lott, if you want the full name, which is why everyone shortens it to Liza."

"With a Zee," confirmed Copper.

"Yes," replied Liza. "So, inspector, what do you want to know?" Her voice had regained its former calm assurance, but Constable couldn't help noticing the tremor in the scarlet-taloned hands which twisted in her lap.

"I think some background would help us find our feet, Miss Lott," smiled Constable affably. "How you knew the dead man, how come you were at the party last night, that sort of thing."

Liza took a deep breath. "Well, inspector, you'd better have the full life story then, hadn't you?"

"Just as much as you think relevant, Miss Lott. I don't want my sergeant here getting writer's cramp too early in the day. Can I assume that you know Mr. Vere through his new villa?"

"That's right. The estate agency business here isn't all I do – we've also got a side of the business which caters for people coming out from the U.K. who want to come and live on the Costa."

"Do they still do that?" Constable was surprised. "From what I'd read in the papers, the whole Spanish property bubble had burst, and a lot of people had lost a lot of money. So you're telling me that's wrong?"

"Not exactly," explained Liza. "It used to be like that – there were loads of companies setting up in competition to sell holiday flats and villas, and a lot of Spanish building firms who were building whole hillsides of apartments. It was all speculation, mostly on borrowed money. That's what I was doing in the early days, to be honest – that's how this side of San Pablo started to develop. But since the crash, that's all fallen apart. A lot of people have gone bust."

"But not you."

"No. Not me. Because whatever you might have heard, there are still people with money, so they're quite happy to come in and snap up the bargains."

"Spanish people?"

"More than you'd think."

"I've heard," interrupted Dave Copper, "that they say there are more 500 Euro notes under Spanish mattresses than there are in circulation in the rest of Europe. Do you reckon that's right?"

"Black money, sergeant," answered Liza. "That's what they call it. Not that I have anything to do with that kind of thing. But to answer your question," she went on, "not just Spanish people. Scandinavians – East Europeans – Russians… "

"Russians?"

"Oh yes. Not your ordinary Russian-in-the-street, of course. Businessmen, shall we say – a certain type of businessmen, I imagine, but I don't see any point in asking too many questions. Their money's as good as anyone's. But anyway, all of this means that I'm quite busy on the agency side handling the normal run of property re-sales."

"But you mentioned the other side of your business. British people who want to move out here?"

"That's right. In fact, that is how I first met Percy – Mr. Vere. We do a service for people like him – they're mostly retired, and they've got a bit of a nest-egg and they have a house in the U.K. which is worth a lot more now than when they bought it years ago… "

"Even today?"

"Of course. I mean, if you bought a house, say, thirty years ago, the value of it has gone up a huge amount, and most of these people have paid off their mortgages by now. Even if they haven't, the amount left to clear is probably only back-pocket money, so a lot of people have got a lot of cash, and they'd rather spend their retirement in the sun instead of slipping about on icy pavements during a British winter."

"It sounds as if there's a fair amount of cash floating about. And that's where you come in?"

"That's where we come in. What we do is… "

"Sorry, that's the second time you've said 'we'," broke in Andy Constable. "And by 'we' you mean…?"

"I've got an arrangement with the construction firm who build the villas."

Copper fished in a pocket for the list of names he had noted down at Alfredo's office. "Would that be Mr. Connor, madam?"

"Yes. We work together. In fact, what we can offer is the complete package." Liza launched into what was obviously a well-rehearsed sales pitch. "We run small ads in the property papers in the U.K. which direct people to our website, and then what we do is arrange inspection tours so that people can fly out here. We book the flights, put them up in hotels, and then we take them round and show them all the sites which I identify through my local contacts. Then once they decide to go ahead, we arrange all the permissions, deal with the architects, and then the property is built by Mr. Connor's company. And so you end up with a happy customer like Percy Vere."

"Which must be very gratifying for you," remarked Constable. "Well, no doubt we'll be having a chat with Mr. Connor a bit later, so he can tell us more about where Mr. Laborero fitted in to all this."

"Oh, he was in with us all along," said Liza. "As he was the foreman on the works, it was the most obvious thing to do, because he spoke really good English. Most of our British customers don't speak a word of Spanish, and my Spanish isn't up to dealing with technical and legal terminology, so we always had Juan Manuel along to interpret for all the official matters – he was very good at taking care of things like that." She paused and the animation drained from her face. "Yes, we make a really good team, the three of us. Sorry – made. We could never have done it without Juan Manuel's help. I can't really think how we'll go on now."

Dave Copper leant forward. "Can you just tell me about what happened at the party last night, madam?"

Liza sighed and looked up in thought. "I can't really tell you all that much, David – sergeant. I got there about nine-ish, and I just spent the evening chatting to various people as you do. Juan was there, and I talked to him at some point, but I was in and out, and he was in and out with other people – to be honest, I didn't really pay much attention."

"So you couldn't say when you saw him last?"

"Not really. I'm sure he hadn't left by the time I came away, because I didn't want to stay too late because I had to come in here to open up this morning."

"He never left at all, by the look of it," replied Dave Copper bluntly, "seeing as he's still there now, lying under half a ton of dirt, so that's not much help to me, is it, madam?"

"Thank you, sergeant," said Andy Constable swiftly. "If Miss Lott doesn't know, she can't very well tell us, can she?" He turned to Liza. "My sergeant gets frustrated sometimes when the information doesn't fall into his lap as easily as he'd wish. So I think we'll have to settle for what you've told us." He got to his feet. "For now."

"Of course, sir," said Copper, standing. "We shall just have to see what else we can unearth from other people." And in response to a glare from his superior, "Sorry. Just slipped out."

As the two British officers headed for the door, Constable turned back as a thought seemed to occur to him. "Actually, Miss Lott, I'm quite surprised to see you here today at all, bearing in mind what the Captain told us about this weekend being a fiesta. I'd have thought that all the businesses would be shut down."

"Oh, all the Spanish ones are," replied Liza, as she stood and smoothed her skirt. "Except for the bars and the restaurants, which will all be doing a roaring trade. There's nothing the locals enjoy more than a fiesta. But most of the British-owned businesses carry on as normal. After all, somebody has to sell the milk and the bread, and you never know when someone is going to get it into their head that today's the day they start looking for a new house. I can't afford to let a chance slip by, can I?" She smiled, her calm professional glamour restored.

"And we mustn't take up any more of your time. We have other people we need to talk to – perhaps we'll start with your Mr. Connor. We may want to have another chat later, but for now, we'll get out of your way and do our job and let you get on with yours." Constable shook her hand in farewell. "No rest for the wicked, eh?"

As Constable and Copper made their way across the street, Liza Lott stood for a moment in thought. Then she turned, made her way to her desk, and picked up the phone.

Chapter 5

"So who next, sir?"

"We might as well start at the top of the list and work down. Who have you got?"

"The first one is the builder Liza Lott was talking about – Mr. X.P. Connor, according to Alfredo's computer."

"X? Who the hell has a name starting with X?"

"Don't know, sir," replied Copper. "I just got the initials. Maybe it's a clue," he added facetiously. "Mr. X, the man of mystery, criminal mastermind! X marks the spot – dig here!"

"Hmmm. Enough digging references, I think, sergeant."

"Sorry, guv. It just happens, I'm afraid. I just open my mouth and put my foot in it."

"Copper!"

"I'll just shut up, then, shall I, sir?"

"No. Make yourself useful and tell me where we find this Mr. Connor."

"I've got the address here, sir, And," triumphantly producing a map from the pocket of his shorts, "I picked another one of these up from Liza's office, so we can see how to get there. In fact," Copper juggled with the several pieces of paper in his hands, "as far as I can see, it's only a couple of hundred yards down this road here on the left – number 42. And, even better, the address for the next person is the same – Philippa – that's the one Alfredo said was his girlfriend."

"Girlfriend, eh? Good thinking, sergeant. Well done."

"Well, at least I've done one thing right," smiled Copper ruefully. "With a bit of luck they'll both be home. Then we can kill two birds with one stone."

"Copper," sighed Constable, "I don't know how you do it."

On the drive of the villa in question, a large and ferocious-looking Italian sports car was being polished by a burly man in his forties, with crinkled greying hair and surprisingly bright blue eyes. He straightened as the two detectives entered the property.

"Looks as if the building lark pays well, guv," murmured Copper in an aside to his superior. "We're obviously in the wrong business."

"Good morning, gentlemen," said the man, stepping forward to meet the visitors. "I'm assuming you're the two policemen I've been warned to expect."

"We are, sir," confirmed Constable. "I'm Detective Inspector Constable, this is my sergeant D.S. Copper. And I assume you're Mr. Connor?"

"X-Pat. Call me X-Pat. Everyone does."

"That's a bit unusual, isn't it, sir?" said Dave Copper, producing his notebook. "Is that actually your name?"

"If you want the whole thing, it's Xavier Patrick Connor."

"Thank you, sir. I was wondering what the X stood for."

X-Pat smiled. "That's what you get for being born into a religious family in Armagh, son."

"Hence the Irish accent, sir. Sorry, forgive the surprise, but Captain Alfredo told us that all the people who were involved were English."

"Ah, well that's the Spanish for you. Some of them couldn't tell English from a hole in the ground."

"Sorry to sound nosey, sir, but how come the name?"

"Put that down to the school. Half the boys in my class were called either Michael or Patrick, so you can imagine the chaos if the teacher called on Pat or Mike. So it was Mike G or Pat F, just to avoid the confusion."

"So why not just Xavier?"

"Come off it. I was a seven-year-old boy. What boy wants to be called Xavier in school? I wasn't having that!"

"Pat C? No, on second thoughts, I see your problem with that."

"So then, X-Pat. Easy. Now, any other family history you'd like? Grandmother's maiden name? Shoe size?"

Inspector Constable swiftly took control as Sergeant Copper looked faintly abashed. "Forgive my sergeant, Mr. Connor. He does get side-tracked sometimes, and I'm sure you'd much rather get on with the matter in hand. I gather you know why we're here."

"Yes," replied X-Pat easily. "I had a call from Liza Lott a little while ago. She told me about Juan – that's a shock, I must say. And she said there'd be two British policemen coming to see me, although I have to say I'm still not sure why. You said 'involved' just now – I can't say I like the sound of that."

"That's all down to Captain Alfredo, sir – I imagine you know him?" X-Pat nodded assent. "Of course, I don't have any official jurisdiction, which is why my colleague and I haven't been showing you our warrant cards, but as we were on his patch for… well, shall we say, unconnected reasons… the Captain asked for our help in looking into the case. I'm sure if you wish to contact him, he'll be pleased to confirm that we're acting on his behalf. Of course, you're under no compulsion to answer any questions, but I'm sure the local authorities would be very appreciative of any co-operation you could give us." The implication as to how any lack of co-operation might be viewed was skilfully left unvoiced.

"Ask away, then, gentlemen," beamed X-Pat. "I'm always only too happy to assist the law in any way I can. Poor old Juan didn't deserve to be killed, whatever he'd done. You'd better come and sit down." He led the way to a shaded front terrace where a group of wicker chairs waited, and waved a hand the size of a shovel towards a sofa. "So, what can I tell you?"

"Well, Miss Lott has given us a certain amount of background," said Constable, sitting with a thump on the deceptively under-stuffed cushions. "I understand that you and she work very closely together?"

"Oh, yes, Liza and I go back a long way," smiled X-Pat. "We've been together for years – there's not a thing we don't know about each other."

"Excuse me, sir," put in Dave Copper, preparing to make notes. "When you say together…?"

"Ah, no, not that kind of together," said X-Pat. "I mean in business. She rustles up the punters – I get to do the donkey work. Well, I say donkey-work, because that's how it was in the early days when we were just starting, and I was just an ambitious brickie."

"I couldn't help noticing the car, sir," said Copper. "It looks as if you've moved on a bit from just brickieing these days."

"You're right at that," responded X-Pat with a smile of satisfaction. "Well, it's my own firm, so I think I deserve some of the rewards."

"And the work involves…?" Andy Constable resumed control of the conversation.

"It's pretty much all one-off builds all up and down the Costa," answered X-Pat. "I suppose you've seen Percy Vere's place? Well, villas like that. There's quite a number of people like Mr. Vere who've got a bit of money to spend, and they'd rather have something individual rather than one of these places you see so many of, like in the song – you know, 'little boxes on the hillside'. No, they want something architect-designed, so that's where Liza and I come in."

"You manage to cope with the bureaucracy, then?" asked Constable. "I remember somebody told us that the officialdom here is a nightmare, what with forms and permits and so on."

"Easy as you like," said X-Pat. "I don't say you don't have to be careful, what with all the zoning laws and the different building regulations depending on which local authority you're dealing with, but we've never had any trouble in that line. It's all a question of knowing the right people to contact. You know what it's like in some offices – some people are right jobsworths, and others are only too pleased to help you out along the way. Juan was a genius at sorting stuff like that out."

"So had he been working for you for long?"

"Pretty much since I started up. He kicked off just as a foreman, recruiting the lads for me, but over time he turned into my main interpreter and Mr. Fixit. So I've got a bit of a problem now that he's got himself killed." X-Pat stopped short. "I suppose you're sure that he has been murdered? I mean, there's no possibility of an accident? There's a lot of people who die on Spanish building sites without anybody crying foul play. Not with us, of course," he explained hastily. "Our record's fine. But I don't think they pay too much attention to health and safety at work in this country."

"I think you can take it as read that Mr. Laborero didn't die as the result of an accident," replied Constable heavily. "If he did, it's not like any accident I've ever seen."

"So how did he die?"

"Collision with a rather large piece of wood, sir, we think," said Copper before Constable could stop him.

"But I'd be grateful if you could keep that just between ourselves," said the inspector hastily, with a sideways glare at his colleague that promised trouble later.

X-Pat shook his head. "Poor devil."

"So I'm assuming you must have known him pretty well. Any

ideas as to who might have wanted to do him any harm?"

"Sorry, inspector, but I can't think of a soul." X-Pat's expression was as open and guileless as anyone could wish. "Juan was just everyone's friend. And it's going to be a real pain getting by without him, but I guess we'll have to manage somehow. I wish I could help you more."

"Perhaps you can, Mr. Connor. It might be a help to know something about Mr. Laborero's movements at the party last night. That's mainly why we're here – everything else is just background really. Now I understand that you were at the party, so if you can tell us anything about who you saw with the dead man, and when you saw him last, it should enable us to put the jigsaw together."

"Right." X-Pat thought for a moment. "D'you know, inspector, I think I'm going to be no use to you at all. I reckon Phil and I got there somewhere between eight and nine… that's Philippa, the girlfriend," he added in clarification. "We walked down – it's not so far, and I wanted to have a few drinks to start off the weekend, so I didn't want to drive in case any of Alfredo's boys took it into their heads to start clamping down on drink-driving. He's a good lad, but some of his new guys don't know yet who's a friend of the boss and who isn't, and you can imagine I'd not be best pleased if they took away my licence to drive that little baby." He gestured to his car. "Anyway, we got there while it was still light, so that must have been before nine. And Juan Manuel and a bunch of the lads from the firm were still there at that time." He laughed in recollection. "Actually, it was quite funny. When Phil and I strolled in, the boys all looked like startled rabbits, and before you knew it, they were off like a shot from a gun, so it was a case of 'Hola and adios'. Juan stayed, of course. I had a little chat with him, but as to what happened after that and when, I couldn't honestly say. I didn't see him around when Phil and I left, but I have no idea where he went or when."

"That would be because he didn't leave, sir," said Dave Copper. "He is very much still there."

"Ah now, but are you sure of that?" said X-Pat. "How do you know he didn't leave and then come back later? Maybe that's something you ought to check with Percy Vere."

"We will, sir, don't worry," said Copper, slightly thrown by the unexpected suggestion. "We'll be doing quite a bit of checking with everyone. Which reminds me, you mentioned your lady friend. I understand she lives here too – would it be possible to have a word with her as well? As we're here." He turned to the inspector. "If that's all right with you, guv?"

"Carry on, sergeant, if Mr. Connor doesn't mind."

"She's round the back by the pool, I think," said X-Pat, rising to his feet. "Do you want me to get her?"

The two policemen stood. "That's fine," said Constable. "We'll go to her, if you can show us the way. I wouldn't want to disturb her more than we have to on a Saturday morning. And I dare say you'll be wanting to get back to finishing off that very nice car of yours before the sun gets too hot. I'm sure you wouldn't want it ending up covered in streaks." The intention of conducting the interview without Mr. Connor's presence was plain if unspoken.

"No problem." X-Pat's smile was broad and untroubled. "Through the front door there, left at the end, and that'll bring you out to the back terrace."

"Thank you, sir." Constable smiled no less genially. "We'll find our way. We'll let you get on with it." He turned and led the way into the house.

The rear terrace extended across the full width of the property, wrapped around a large swimming pool whose sinuous curves terminated at one end in a flight of steps which led down into the gently rippling water. To one side, shaded by a group of palm trees, stood a pool house which incorporated a well-stocked bar, an outdoor kitchen which gleamed with stainless steel, and louvred saloon doors which Constable surmised led to changing rooms within. At the other, next to an enormous jacuzzi beneath a rustic canopy, in the only patch of sun which, at that early hour, fell upon the patio, a young woman in a bikini was stretched out on a sun lounger. In response to Constable's discreet clearing of the throat, she looked up in surprise, sat up, and hastily pulled around her the loose silk wrap which she wore.

"What are you doing here? Who let you in?"

Inspector Constable was at his most emollient. "I do apologise if we startled you, Miss, but Mr. Connor said it would be all right."

"Oh. You've seen X-Pat, have you? Well, what is it you want?" The tension in her voice was obvious.

"I'm so sorry, Miss, if we're disturbing you, but I'm afraid we're here on a police matter." The young woman looked the two officers up and down, her disbelief plain. "Yes, I know we may not look the part at the moment, but I'm Detective Inspector Constable, this is my colleague Sergeant Copper, and we've been asked to assist the local force in an investigation. And I understand that you are Miss Philippa…?" The query hung in the air.

"Philippa Glass."

"And you are Mr. Connor's… friend?"

"Yes."

"And you also live here, miss?"

"That's right."

Copper slid his notebook out of his pocket and made an unobtrusive note. "Thank you, miss."

"This is about Juan, isn't it?" said Philippa. And in response to Constable's nod of affirmation, "But I don't understand. You're English. Why are you coming asking questions about something that's happened here in Spain? What's it got to do with you?"

By now, Andy Constable was becoming well-rehearsed in his explanation. "The Captain of the local force has asked for our help because of… another matter we had been involved in, so we are working in conjunction with him. Why, would that be a problem for you?"

"No, not at all. I suppose if Alfredo has sent you… " The unease in her tone belied her words. "So what do you want to ask me?"

Constable chose his words with care. "I take it you know that Mr. Laborero has been found dead this morning at Mr. Vere's villa, in circumstances which mean that the local authorities have started a murder investigation."

"Yes. X-Pat told me. Liza phoned him earlier. But that's got nothing to do with me."

"Of course not, Miss Glass. Nobody has suggested that it has." Copper could clearly hear the unvoiced 'yet' in the seemingly soothing words of the inspector's response. "But the thing is, the last time Mr. Laborero was seen with any certainty was last night at Mr. Vere's party, so we are having to ask everyone who was there at the same time what they can tell us, in the hope that we can garner some helpful information."

"I see." Philippa appeared to grow more relaxed. She sat up, tied back her long dark-blonde hair in a bandeau, wrapped her robe more closely around herself, and gestured to the two detectives to seat themselves at a table alongside her. "So, what is it you want to know?"

"Background, miss, as much as anything," replied Copper. "We've met one or two of the people concerned, but I have to say that Inspector Constable and I are still struggling slightly to work out who is who and who fits in where. Yourself, for example."

"All right. So, I'm X-Pat's girlfriend, but you say you know that."

"And you've known him for…?"

"It must be nearly five years now." She smiled tentatively. "Lord, is it really that long? Anyway, I first met him when I was working as a temp when I originally came over here to live, and he wanted someone to do some secretarial work. And then we just went on from there. I still do some of his paperwork for him sometimes, because he doesn't always get the chance to clear everything out of the way at the office, what with being out and about and on site so much of the time. Not that I need to work now, of course, because there's some really good money in this building business, but you can't lie around all day topping up the tan, can you?"

"I suppose you can't, miss."

"Well, not every day, anyway." All Philippa's reserved manner seemed to have fallen away from her. "That's why I do a couple of nights a week down at the bar."

"Bar, miss?"

"Yes. The Runcorn. Alfredo's place. I work with Eve."

"Of course, Miss Glass. Yes, we've met Miss Stropper." Andy Constable took over with a sideways glance and a slight smile in the direction of his junior colleague. "So, you two work together, then? So, how do you find that? A bit different from secretarial work, I should imagine."

"It's fine." There was an echo of defensiveness in the way Philippa spoke. "It's a good way of meeting new people. It's not always easy here, you know, if you're not working. You might have a lovely house, and the weather's beautiful, but for a lot of the time, you're living behind walls, so you don't get much of a social life unless you go out and mix. So that's what's so good about the bar. Eve's a laugh, and there's different people coming in all the time, so it makes a nice change. Oh, I'm not complaining," she added hastily. "Don't think that. It's just that…" She tailed off.

"Yes, of course. I think I understand." Exactly what the inspector understood was not specified. "So that's how you met Mr. Laborero, was it?"

"Oh no," replied Philippa. "He was working for X-Pat long before I started to. But it was probably in the bar that I got to know him a bit better. He used to come in for a drink most nights after he finished work – several of the boys did, but Juan Manuel was always the one with all the bunny." A smile of reminiscence passed over her face and was gone almost at once.

"So you got on well with him?"

"Yes, of course. I liked him, but then, I think most of the girls did. It was quite funny – sometimes the boys off the site would come in with their wives or girlfriends, and Juan would always flirt with them. He had that sort of smile, you see… " Philippa stopped short and her hand went to her mouth. "Oh my god! Listen to me. He's not been dead five minutes, and here I am talking about him in the past as if it's the easiest thing… oh, that's horrible." She seemed suddenly shaken. "And to think I was only talking to him a few hours ago."

"So you were…," the inspector trod delicately, "quite close to him, then?"

Philippa's denial came swiftly and emphatically. "Not at all! We were just friends, that's all. There was nothing going on, if that's what you're implying. No… it's just a bit of a shock, that's all."

"I'm afraid sudden death does have that effect, miss," said Constable. "And I'm sorry if it can be upsetting, but that's why we need to speak to everyone concerned as soon as possible so that the facts of the case are still clear in their minds."

"How did he die?" asked Philippa. "You never said."

"I don't think we're quite ready to discuss that at the moment, Miss Glass," responded the inspector. "I believe the Captain is still establishing the details of that, and I wouldn't want to release any information prematurely. All I'm seeking to do at the moment is to establish some sort of sequence of events from Mr. Vere's party last night so that we can find out who saw Mr. Laborero last, where that was, who spoke to him – that sort of thing." He waited, eyebrows raised in expectation.

Philippa shifted uneasily. "Well, I chatted to him last night, of course, but then I think everyone did. Why, hasn't X-Pat told you what happened?"

"He has indeed, miss, but you'd be surprised how often people forget little details, and how sometimes one person remembers something which has completely escaped the notice of someone else."

The shutters appeared to come down. "Sorry, but I can't really tell you any more than that. I'm afraid I didn't spend my evening looking at my watch, so I don't know anything about times. I just wanted to enjoy myself… " He hand went to her mouth again, and she blinked several times. "Sorry."

Inspector Constable bowed to the inevitable. It was clear that there was no more to be learnt at this stage. He stood. "Then we'll leave you alone, Miss Glass. But if, while you're thinking things over, you happen to remember anything that might be of help to us, I hope you'll let us know. You can always get in touch with us via Captain Alfredo. I imagine you can do that fairly easily." In response to Philippa's nod, the two detectives turned and made their way back through the house to the front drive, where X-Pat was just giving a final polish to the car's windows.

"Waste of time, really," he greeted them.

"Sir?"

"Cleaning this." He looked up into the sky where the flawless blue was beginning to be marred by an encroaching bank of cloud from the south-west. "It just takes a little shower, and this'll be covered over with little spots of red dust, and I'll have to start all over again. It all comes over from the Sahara, you see," he explained, "but, ah, what can you do? What's a Saturday morning without the ritual of cleaning the car?"

"I never seem to have the time to do mine, sir," responded Dave Copper. "Sometimes I don't know whether I should clean it or plant it."

"All done?" enquired X-Pat.

"Certainly for the moment, sir," said Andy Constable. "We've had a word with Miss Glass, but I'm not sure she was able to add much to what you'd already told us. But we might want a further chat later, if that's all right with you."

"Just as you like. If I'm not here, I'll probably be at the office."

"Which is where, sir?"

"First floor, just above 'Lott's Property' opposite the cop-shop. You know where that is, I'm sure."

"Oh yes, sir. No problem there. So, thank you again for your help, and we'll get out of your way."

As the two detectives left the property, X-Pat stood and watched them, then turned to re-enter the house.

"What do you make of that then, sir?" asked Copper.

"I think that our Mr. Connor seems very charming, very amiable, and very helpful," said Constable. "I also think that I wouldn't be inclined to trust him as far as I could throw him. There's a sort of smile which goes all over the face but never seems to get to the eyes, and that's what I detect in Mr. Connor. There's a story there. But I'd be happier if you hadn't mentioned how we think Juan died. Let's keep all the advantages we have, if you don't mind."

"Sorry, guv – didn't think," said Copper humbly. "And what about Philippa Glass? She's jumpy about something. And I reckon he keeps her on a tight rein."

"Hmmm. I think you're right. Well, if we're any good at our job, I dare say we shall winkle it out. Let's just let it stew for a bit." He turned his mind to other matters. "I'm more concerned at the moment in getting back to Percy Vere's villa and finding out if Alfredo has any more news about how Juan died. Ready for a walk?"

Chapter 6

At the *Villa Demasiadocara,* two police cars were parked in the road outside alongside a blue sports car, while a plain black van with tinted windows stood on the drive.

"I recognise that," commented Dave Copper. "They've sent the meat wagon, so Alfredo's probably got matey out of the ground by now."

"Come on, Copper," frowned his superior in response. "Let's have a bit of respect for the poor guy. Nobody deserves to get whacked on the head and then end up six feet under on somebody's building site."

"If that's what happened, sir."

"Well, I suggest we go and talk to Alfredo and find out."

Standing guard at the villa's front door stood the junior officer who had accompanied Alfredo that morning. In reply to Constable's hesitant "*El Capitan?*", the young man nodded and gestured wordlessly to the path which led around the side of the house towards the rear garden. Rounding the corner of the building, the two British officers were greeted with the sight of two white-overall-clad men lifting the body of Juan Manuel Laborero on to a stretcher, assisted by the other young officer from Alfredo's squad, while the captain himself stood and watched.

"This is mad, guv," commented Copper in an aside to his superior. "At home we'd have SOCO crawling all over the place. These guys might be missing evidence left, right and centre."

"Shhh! Don't go treading on toes," warned the inspector in lowered tones.

"Ah, Andy," Alfredo greeted Constable sombrely. "You see we have at last had success in getting the dead man from the ground. It has taken a longer time than I thought, but it is because I have told my two boys to be careful and be slow."

"Very wise," agreed Constable. "The last thing you want is to be mucking up the body."

"Sorry? Mucking up…?"

"I mean causing any other injuries, apart from those that were there already," explained Constable.

"Good thought, sir," added Copper. "I remember one case we had where the victim had been battered about with a shovel. Poor bloke looked like he'd been through the mincer. You don't want your guys complicating things with a bit of over-enthusiastic spadework, do you, Alfredo?"

"Thank you, sergeant. I don't think we need to tell the captain how to do his job," said Constable in reproof. "So, Alfredo, are you any clearer as to how Juan died?"

"I will know for sure when the doctor at the mortuary has examined him, but I think you were right in what you thought. Come and see." Alfredo knelt down alongside the stretcher and gestured to the two Britons to approach. He spoke briefly to the two mortuary assistants, who stepped aside several paces. "Look, here is a big wound to the head – just one. I believe it is as you said – that piece of wood with the blood, it has been used to hit him, and I think that the one blow has killed him."

"From in front or from behind, do you reckon, sir?" Copper craned over the body.

"Couldn't begin to guess, sergeant. That's one for Alfredo's forensics people – they can sort out direction and speed of the blow fairly easily when they start work on Tuesday, I expect."

"Yes, on Tuesday," confirmed Alfredo heavily. "I am sorry

that it will not be sooner. I think this does not help you."

"Don't fret, Alfredo," smiled Constable as he straightened. "We'll do our best with what we've got. Oh, just a thought. Anything useful on the body? You know, stuff in his pockets."

"We have his wallet with some money and his papers – his identity card and his driving licence."

"Any car keys?"

"Yes, we have those too. And I believe that his car is parked out in the road."

"I bet that's that blue one, guv," said Copper. "Matches the shoes."

"I think so," said Alfredo, "so I will look in that now."

"You're ahead of me. Look, I want to have another word with Mr. Vere, so if you want to get things sorted out with the body, Copper and I can come and find you afterwards, if that's okay by you."

"It is good, Andy. Mr. Vere is I know in the house. I will have Juan Manuel taken away now, and we will speak soon." Alfredo turned back to his Spanish colleagues and began to issue instructions as the two British officers climbed the steps towards the villa.

Percy Vere was seated as before in the large leather armchair facing the patio doors, but in contrast to his earlier dishevelled state, he had resumed his customary dapper appearance, dressed in a white shirt with a cravat and dark-blue cardigan. As Constable and Copper entered, he rose to his feet.

"Come in, gentlemen. I've been waiting for you." He raised the cut-glass tumbler in his hand. "Thought I'd have a spot of G & T to go on with. I don't normally start this early in the day but… well, special circumstances and all that. I suppose you wouldn't care to join me? No? I thought probably not. Well, do sit down. You'll want to get on with it, I dare say."

"Thank you, Mr. Vere," said Constable. "We'll try not to take up too much of your time. I can see that this must all be a severe shock."

"I'm fine, inspector," responded Percy. He sounded robust. "I'm pretty tough. You don't get to my age without encountering a few surprises along the way. Not usually this kind of surprise, though, I have to say. This is all a bit of a turn-up for the books. I've never been mixed up with the law before."

"Well, Mr. Vere, I wouldn't go so far as to say that you're actually mixed up with the law on this occasion. For instance, we don't know that you had any sort of motive to do the dead man harm. But obviously, when it's a case of murder, we do have to look into everybody's relationship with the victim. So let's say that we need your help in our investigation."

"Hmm. Sounds a lot like being mixed up with the law to me," muttered Percy. "Anyway, as I say, this is all new territory to me. The closest I ever came to this sort of thing was when we had the VAT people in to do an investigation into the books when I ran my printing business back in the U.K. Not that there was anything dodgy there, of course, but you're always on tenterhooks because these blasted officials are invariably on the lookout for the tiniest thing, and you can never tell whether you might have made the most trivial mistake which they're going to pounce upon. I do hope you're not going to pounce upon me, inspector."

"We'll do our best not to, Mr. Vere," smiled Constable. "If we can just get a few facts straight – I'm sure you won't mind if my colleague here makes a few notes."

"Ask me anything you like," said Percy. "My life's always been an open book. Ha ha! Sorry – very old printer's joke. But then, I'm a very old printer. Well, I was – forty-odd years I was in the business. When I first started out as a grubby apprentice, some people were still using hot metal. D'you know, sometimes I can still smell that smell – very evocative stuff, molten lead. But I worked my way up, got to the top, and made a very good living out of it. Finally sold up about five years ago. I think I got out at the right time, too – there have been so many changes over the last few years that I don't think I'd even know my way around my old plant now. Well, that's progress, I suppose." It seemed to dawn on Percy that he was straying from the point. "Anyway, gentlemen, you don't want to hear my life story. You're wanting to get on with trying to find out who killed poor old Juan. I suppose you are certain that it's murder?"

"Oh yes, sir," replied Constable. "Having seen the body, I don't think there can be any doubt about that. So had you known the dead man long?"

"Not really, no. Only since we started on the villa. I think I first met him when I was at Liza's office one day – that must have been very early on, because at that stage I was looking for a plot of land to build on, and Juan happened to come in, and Liza introduced him to me as the man who could do anything. Seemed a straight sort of chap, and that's what you need around here, they say."

"Oh, sir? In what way?"

"Well." Percy looked around furtively and, to Constable's surprise, lowered his voice. "I was chatting to my solicitor the other day. Nice woman, Isabella – she's Spanish, but she's got an English mother, so she speaks perfect English. Well, I say perfect, because she's the only Spaniard I know who speaks with a Brummie accent! Anyway, I digress. She and I were arranging for her to go off to see the notary to sort out the final transfer of the deeds to the property. It's not like the U.K., where you get an exchange of contracts, and then a month later you get completion. No, you all go and sit round a desk, and then some chap jabbers on for an age with all the legal jargon, and then somebody hands over a cheque and you walk away with the keys.

At least, that's the way it works when you're just buying or selling an existing property. But when I sold my old place, I gave Isabella my power of attorney because I couldn't be fussed with all that malarkey. But I didn't want to take any chances with this place."

"What do you mean, chances, sir?"

"As I say, according to what Isabella was telling me, there's a big corruption scandal in the wind. She's heard that there's going to be an investigation by the regional government into all these allegations of fake building permits being sold by some of the planning officials in some of the *Ayunt…* – the *Ayuntim…* – oh, dammit, the Town Halls. Blasted language! I shall never get my tongue round it. Wouldn't it be wonderful if everybody spoke English, but there's no chance of that!"

Dave Copper looked up in interest. "So what's all this about fake building permits, then, sir?"

"Oh, of course, you wouldn't know, sergeant, not being a local. But there have been all sorts of stories in the papers about mayors in towns up along the coast taking back-handers to turn a blind eye to unofficial building developments. They have a great deal of power in Spain, local mayors. Mind you," he chortled, "not that it does some of them a lot of good. There's at least two in prison that I can think of, and in one place they had to knock half the town down because it was all illegally constructed."

"Doesn't that worry you, sir?"

"Lord, no. There's no problem with this place. I know that, because I sorted it all out myself. I had to go to the Town Hall in person with Liza – several times, in fact – and every time we took Juan along as interpreter. Well, he knew all the people there and he had all the lingo for what we needed to sort out, so it was pretty obvious really. Very useful chap – I shall miss him about the place. Always smiling, you know. And he was very good with the lads, keeping them up to the mark."

"So Juan Manuel was instrumental in arranging the whole building project, then, Mr. Vere?" resumed the inspector.

"Absolutely. He explained it all to me as we went along, because as I said, it's so very different from the English system. And it's not just the legalities, you see. There are so many things that have to be paid in cash, because apparently that's the way the system works here."

"How do you mean, sir?"

"Well, from what he and Liza told me, there are two rates of tax for things, one rate if you pay in cash and another if you pay by cheque or bank transfer. Sounds mad, I know, but that's the way the Spanish government wants it, I'm told, and if I can make a saving by paying up front in cash, that's what I'm going to do. I'm not daft, and money doesn't grow on trees, does it?"

"Well, it would certainly be foolish to spend money you don't have to," agreed Constable.

"Ah, but then you've got the other side of the coin," continued Percy. "You get prices changing all the time, so sometimes the building costs suddenly go up, and then the government can change the tax rate completely at the drop of a hat, so you never know where you are. That's why people like Liza and Juan have been such a godsend. Oh, and X-Pat too. I remember one time when we all met up at Liza's office, and when I arrived, X-Pat was there on the phone, checking our appointment I think, and he said to whoever it was on the other end, 'That's going to cost a lot more'."

"Did you have any idea who he was talking to?"

"Good grief, no! Could have been any one of a dozen people, I expect. I completely lost track of all the officials we met at one time or another – you know, one chap in glasses behind a desk looks very much like another. That's why I was so pleased that I could put myself in the hands of Liza and the others. I've spent enough years fussing about with accountants and the like – it's the last thing I want to have to do now I'm retired." He drained his glass and stood. "Well, I have to say that went down a treat. I think I shall have another." He headed for the drinks table. "Are you sure I can't tempt you chaps?"

"Positive, thank you, sir," said Copper.

"Still rather early in the day for me too, Mr. Vere," added Constable.

"Yes, of course, quite understand," said Percy, splashing a generous measure of gin into his glass and topping it up with a microscopic amount of tonic. "Got to have a clear head in your line of work. And here I am getting you off track. So what else can I tell you?"

"It seems to me, sir," said Andy Constable, "that there's something of a thread of money running through all this. Tell me if I'm wrong."

"No, no, inspector," responded Percy, resuming his seat. "I think you're absolutely right. They all get so het up about money, don't they? What, do you think somebody might have killed Juan over some sort of money problem? Debts, or something like that? Or even… " his eyes gleamed, "what about blackmail? That'd be a motive, wouldn't it?"

"Now why on earth would you suggest blackmail?" Constable wanted to know. "Do you mean that Juan was a blackmailer, or that someone else might be blackmailing him?"

"I'm sorry, inspector. I really don't know what on earth I meant. Just got carried away in the moment. But the thing is, they've all got their fingers in so many pies, I suppose you're bound to run up against a wrong 'un at some point."

"Sorry, sir, but I'm still not too clear on who you're talking about. Who do you mean by 'they'?"

"Well, you've got Ewan, for a start. He's got so many business schemes on the go that I'd be surprised if he can keep track of them all."

"That would be Mr. Husami, I assume, guv," chimed in Dave Copper. "You remember, that businessman that Alfredo told us about. He was here too last night, wasn't he, Mr. Vere?"

"That's right," affirmed Percy. "Not much goes on round here that Ewan hasn't got something to do with somewhere along the line. Have you met him?"

"Not as yet," said Constable. "He's certainly on our list to chat to. Assuming we can track him down, if he's as busy as you say."

"Ah, well, I've got an idea that even he might be over-stretching himself these days. I think he might be planning on selling some of these businesses off, because I heard Juan talking to him at the party last night, and Ewan was talking about disposing of things, and Juan said something like 'someone's going to be in trouble if I don't get my share'."

"Sounds a bit like a threat to me, guv," remarked Copper. "That's the first hint we've had of anything like that. Mind you, of course, it's the wrong way round, isn't it. That's this Mr. Husami on the receiving end of it, and not our dead man. Did you get any idea of exactly what it was they were talking about, sir?"

Percy coloured a little. "Well, a chap doesn't like to eavesdrop and all that, so I may have got it completely wrong, but it might have had something to do with Ewan's agency for casual labourers. That's all to do with X-Pat, you see."

"Yes, sir?"

"I'm assuming that, with the work on this place coming to an end soon, X-Pat is going to move his lads on to some other job. Or, in fact, thinking about it, I think some of them may be about to get the push, because Ewan said 'they'll get their cards soon enough, don't you worry about that', and then Juan said something like 'I hope so, because I've got a busy day on Tuesday and I may not be around here much'. Which actually I thought was a bit odd at the time, because of course he ought to have been on here on site."

"Did you have a chance to ask him what he was referring to?" asked Constable.

"Lord, no. In fact, I didn't really see a lot of Juan last night because I was so busy going round chatting to everyone. Oh, I do remember one thing. There was one of those lulls in the conversation that you get sometimes at a party when everyone stops talking at once, and Juan said that he was just going outside, and somebody made a joke about 'I may be some time', and there was some remark about oats, and someone laughed. I thought, what's funny about that, but then of course I realised that they were talking about Captain Oates – you know, the chap on Scott's expedition who walked off into the night and was never seen again." Percy shivered suddenly. "Actually, that's not a very pleasant thought – I never did see Juan again after that. Bit of a coincidence, that, eh, inspector?"

"As you say, sir," replied Constable. "Not that I'm a great fan of coincidences. I'd rather stick to plain mundane facts – they tend to be rather more productive. So, the last you saw of Juan was when he went out into the garden."

"Yes, I thought he might be popping out to check up on the workers, because they tend to huddle together and not mix, even though you try your best, but then of course I realised that they'd pushed off hours before."

"So this was when, sir? Any idea?" enquired Copper, poised to make a note.

Percy wrinkled his brow in thought. "Must have been about half-past nine or so. Yes, the lads were long gone by then."

"And was anyone else out there at that point?"

"Not that I know of, sergeant, but I can't be positive – sorry. Oh, I noticed Philippa went out into the garden about five minutes later – goodness knows why, because the lighting out there isn't working yet, and you can't really see a thing, but you do get a lovely view out over the bay when it's dark, what with the lamps along the coast road, and you also get the twinkling of the lights from the villages up in the mountains in the distance. Ah!" Percy snapped his fingers. "I do recall, X-Pat went out into the garden looking for Philippa about five minutes after that. Don't know if he saw Juan, but I dare say he'll tell you if you ask him. And that's about it."

"Nothing else useful that you recollect, sir?"

"Sadly not." Percy sounded apologetic. "I'm afraid it's all a bit hazy after that, because I was on the old Shampoo all night, and I probably got a tad squiffy. Well, it was my party, after all. So of course, people all eventually drifted away, and for goodness' sake don't ask me who left when because I haven't got the foggiest. And then I toddled off to bed, slept the sleep of the righteous, woke up this morning, and looked out the window. And I think you know the story after that."

"I think we do, sir." Andy Constable got to his feet. "Look, we'll leave it at that for now, Mr. Vere. We have some other people to talk to, but if you remember anything else, please let us know."

As the two detectives descended the front steps of Percy's villa, Constable shook his head in frustration. "Well, this is all very helpful. Everybody loved Juan Manuel, everybody saw him but nobody can remember when, and nobody's got any idea why anybody else would want to do him harm!"

"Par for the course, though, isn't it, guv?" replied Copper. "Aren't we used to this sort of thing?"

"You're right, of course," sighed Constable. "Doesn't make it any less frustrating, though."

Dave Copper smiled slowly. "You're actually getting caught up in this thing, aren't you, sir? Whatever happened to 'I'm on my holidays and there'll be no shop talk, thank you very much'?"

Andy Constable grinned ruefully. "Must be something in the genes, sergeant. Why, are you wishing we'd never got dragged into this business?"

"Not at all, guv. To be honest, I was getting rather bored doing nothing much, and it's actually fun to have a bit of a challenge. No disrespect to the dead guy, of course," Copper added hastily, "but there's something different about doing an investigation when it's not actually your job to do it. I mean, it's not as if there's anything on the line, is it?"

"Except our reputations as standard-bearers for the British detecting community, sergeant."

"Ah, well in that case, sir, we're stuffed."

"How so?"

"Because at the moment, I haven't got a clue."

Constable laughed. "Oh, I'm sure you've got some, Copper. You just haven't recognised them yet." A thought struck him. "What you need is some intellectual stimulation. Let's go and see your friend Eve."

"Excuse me, sir. Eve and intellectual stimulation? How do they belong in the same sentence?"

"Coffee, sergeant. Let's go and see if your brain can be jolted into activity by one of Eve's famously strong shots of caffeine." He glanced at his watch. "Perfect timing – elevenses at the Runcorn, I think."

Chapter 7

As the two detectives approached the bar, they were surprised to see that the establishment was doing a lively morning trade. Spanish family groups, seemingly including everyone from shambling toddlers to elegantly-groomed matrons, were clustered around the tables. Adolescent boys, bravely sporting the shadows of their first moustache, were assiduously helping frail grandmothers to find a comfortable seat in the shade. Thirty-something fathers, sharply suited as if modelling for a fashion shoot, glanced anxiously over the shoulders of their young teenage daughters whose thumbs moved in a continuous digital blur of messaging on their smart-phones, while their wives swept back their long dark hair as they turned from one friend to another in an animated exchange of gossip.

Eve, emerging from the door with a tray laden with coffees and toasted rolls, greeted the Britons with a sort of flustered relief. "Dave, Andy, I'm so glad you're here. I have to talk to you."

"I take it the news has got around, then," said Andy Constable, gesturing to the buzzing restaurant clientele.

"What... ? Oh no," replied Eve. "This is nothing to do with that. This is all for the fiesta. Everyone goes into town for the procession round the square on the Saturday morning before the first Mass at mid-day, so they all come in for the late breakfast first."

"So that's why they're all togged up in the Sunday best, is it?" queried Dave Copper. "I thought they were a bit over-dressed."

"Look," said Eve, "I'm rushed off my feet, so you sit down somewhere, let me get everyone sorted and I'll come over." She took a deep breath. "Alfredo's told me a bit about what's happened. Honestly, I still can't believe it. Juan of all people – he was such a nice guy. And you two being policemen and all – you never told me that, did you, Dave? Well… no, we'll have a talk in a minute." She was away to a distant table before the detectives could utter another word.

"Intriguing," remarked Constable. "I wonder what that's all about." He led the way to one of the few vacant tables.

"I'm back," said Eve, materialising unexpectedly at his shoulder. "I've just realised, there's someone else you ought to have a word with. Hold on." She scurried to the door of the bar, pushed it open, and leant in calling, "Tim! Could you come out here a minute?" She rushed back to Constable's table. "You should talk to Tim – he was there last night."

In response to Eve's call, a tall rangy man had appeared in the bar doorway. Eve beckoned, and he approached. "Tim, this is Andy and Dave. They're the ones I told you about – the ones Alfredo has asked to help him. Andy, this is Tim – he used to work with Juan."

"Good morning, gentlemen." The man proffered his hand. "Tim Berman. How can I help you?"

"Mr. Berman," replied Constable. "Well, this is a fortunate coincidence."

"Really? In what way?"

"Because your name happens to be on the list of people we need to talk to about the death of Mr. Laborero. A list given to us by Captain Alfredo. And I was saying to my colleague here only a little while ago, funny thing, coincidence, isn't it, sergeant?"

"Sergeant?"

"Indeed, sir. Sorry, didn't Eve mention the fact? I am

surprised. Well, in that case, we really ought to introduce ourselves properly. I am Detective Inspector Constable, my colleague here is Detective Sergeant Copper, and as Eve has said, we have been invited by the local police Captain to assist with the investigation into the murder of your friend Mr Laborero." Constable smiled blandly. "I am assuming he was your friend, sir?"

"If I'm to be grilled, I take it I may sit down, inspector?" Tim Berman's tone was sardonic. Without waiting for a reply, he pulled out a chair, turned it around, and hitched one long jeans-clad leg over it to sit with arms resting on the chair-back. The rolled-back sleeves of his check shirt revealed slim but well-muscled forearms, ending in large hands with unexpectedly stubby fingers, the nails short and well-kept. His light brown hair showed a sprinkle of grey and there were white creases around the laughter-lines of his deep-set brown eyes, which had deep dark circles beneath them. Late thirties, Constable estimated.

"Not grilled at all, Mr. Berman," responded the inspector easily. "Far from it. We haven't the authority to do anything of the kind, as I'm sure you probably realise. It's simply that Captain Alfredo finds himself in need of a little assistance in looking into your friend's death and gathering some of the facts from those individuals who were present last evening, and as we were on the spot, we were only too happy to help."

"As a sort of professional courtesy?"

"Something like that, sir," smiled Constable in agreement. "If you can spare us a moment…?"

There was a shade of reluctance in Tim's voice. "Very well. Although I've got a pint getting warm inside… "

"We'll try not to keep you from it too long, sir. So, then – Mr. Laborero. Your friend…?"

"Friend… colleague… whatever you like, inspector." Tim Berman did not seem disposed to offer more information than was absolutely necessary.

Andy Constable paused. "Look, Mr. Berman, can we start again? I get the impression that you think I'm trying to trap you into something, which I'm not. My colleague and I are just attempting to help a fellow policeman look into a rather unpleasant murder, and giving up our holiday into the bargain. So a few basic facts, and then we can get out of your way. How's that?"

Tim seemed to relax. "Sorry, inspector. You're right, of course. I'm afraid that after living in this country for a while, I've rather adopted the customary native truculence in response to questioning from officialdom. It's purely a defence mechanism – it doesn't necessarily mean anything. So, what would you like to know?"

"As much as you care to tell me, Mr. Berman. At the moment, all we have is your name. It might be useful if we knew how you came to know the dead man. I take it you won't object if my sergeant makes a couple of notes?"

"Building up the dossier, eh?" Tim gave a wry smile. "Sorry, there I go again. Right. Juan Manuel and I work together – worked, I suppose I have to say now. We're… damn! We were both with X-Pat's firm." He looked quizzically at the inspector. "I suppose you do know who I'm talking about – X-Pat Connor, the builder?"

"Yes, we've met Mr. Connor, sir," affirmed Constable, "so we know who he is. And you're one of his associates?"

"You could say that, inspector. I'm his chief carpenter."

"Doors and kitchens, then, sir?" interposed Dave Copper. "Is that the sort of thing?"

"Thank you, sergeant," replied Tim. "You make it sound so impressive." The irony in his voice was plain. "Yes, shutters, balconies, balustrades, built-in fitments – anything involving carpentry. All the villas which X-Pat builds are individual commissions, which means that virtually nothing is standard.

Everything has to be tailor-made to fit the particular building, plus we're very often working with unusual woods rather than the standard softwoods and oak and such. So I am in control of a group of skilled craftsmen."

"And this was what brought you into contact with Mr. Laborero?"

"Of course, sergeant. I would work very closely with Juan, because he had overall control of the schedule of the building works, and I had to make sure that my team of chippies were always standing by at just the right moment so that we didn't get any delays. It's all a jigsaw."

"You use jigsaws, sir?"

Tim laughed softly. "No, sergeant," he explained with a pitying smile. "The scheduling. I can't afford to have my lads hanging around between jobs getting paid for doing nothing. So the builds are sequenced so that the electricians, for instance, go in and work on a particular project, then they move on to the next job and the plasterers move in, then as soon as they've finished my team takes over, then the decorators, and so on. That way, each team makes the most effective use of its time."

"Like a conveyor belt, then, sir?"

"Exactly."

"And that's what cuts out the delays?"

"Yes. X-Pat has never been one to put up with delays. Not conducive to a good bottom line. It costs a great deal to build some of these villas, so you have to keep a very tight rein. As soon as you've got somebody standing about doing nothing, you might as well start setting fire to bundles of Euro notes. Mind you, having said that, it's always going to cost that bit extra to have a permanent workforce rather than just hiring casuals as and when."

"Bit of a financial juggling act then, sir, by the sound of it."

"As you say, sergeant. And don't forget the fact that you have to tie up a lot of money in stock so that you've always got stuff available."

"Sounds a nightmare."

Tim smiled. "You're not wrong, but fortunately it's X-Pat's nightmare and not mine. He obviously does well out of it, so it must be worth it in the long run. And even these days, the clients seem to have plenty of cash, so there's no problem."

Andy Constable decided to resume the questioning. "I'm sure that all this background is going to stand us in good stead, sir, and if my sergeant here ever decides to start up a construction enterprise, he'll have a head start on the competition. However, I'm rather more concerned with getting a little more detail on the events of last night at Mr. Vere's party, which I am given to understand that you, in common with the dead man, attended. Correct?"

"Correct, inspector." In response to the increase in formality in Constable's voice, Tim sat up a little straighter. "And…?"

"And therefore, sir, we'd be very glad if you can tell us anything about what happened when, anything about who Mr. Laborero talked to, what he did – I'm sure you understand what we need."

"Come off it, inspector – you really can't expect me to remember the whole evening so that I can give you a blow-by-blow of what went on! It was a party. You know what it's like." A thought seemed to hit him. "In fact, I've just realised – you know exactly what it was like. You two were there, weren't you? I remember Percy was going on about two chaps who were over here on holiday, that he'd asked along, but that they'd gone before we arrived. That was you two, wasn't it?"

"It was," affirmed Constable.

"Well then, I might just as well ask the two of you about your movements on the night in question," challenged Tim. "I think that's the jargon, isn't it?"

Constable sighed. "Mr. Berman, this isn't helping."

Tim subsided. "I'm sorry, inspector," he said. "I'm off again. I think it's the shock of Juan being killed – it's only just starting to hit me. And I wish I could tell you chapter and verse about who did what to whom last night, and if I'd known I was going to need to give an account of things, I would have paid more attention. But as it is, I'm just an ordinary bloke without a photographic memory. Yes, I saw Juan on and off last night, and I spoke to him, but then I spoke to a lot of people."

"And do you remember when you saw him last?"

"Ah. That's a thought." Tim screwed up his face in recollection. "I remember when I *didn't* see him."

"How do you mean, sir?"

"Well, I wanted a word with him about… oh, something or other, I forget what… and I went looking for him, but I couldn't find him. I think I assumed he must have gone off with the Spanish lads, because they all left early. No, hang on – he was still there after they left." Tim smiled helplessly. "I suppose that's not the slightest use to you, is it, inspector?"

Constable knew when he had reached an impasse. "Look, Mr. Berman, don't worry about it too much. I know that sometimes, the harder you look at something, the more difficult it is to see. We still have to track down a couple of the people who were at Mr. Vere's last night, so it's entirely possible that they will be able to fill in some of the blanks. And also, you never know, you may well remember something that's slipped your mind now, so we'll probably come and have another word with you at some time. So I suggest you go back to your drink inside, and we'll see you later." He smiled in a friendly fashion. Dave Copper, who knew that smile, tried not to wince too obviously, as Tim stood and, with a slightly uncertain nod, re-entered the bar.

"Can't make him out, sir," said Copper as Tim disappeared.

"Is he being unhelpful on purpose, or was he just too ratted to remember?"

"That I couldn't tell you. But he does have one thing in common with everybody else, which does strike me as a little odd."

"And what's that, sir?"

"Apart from Mr. Connor, I don't think anyone's asked us yet how Juan Manuel Laborero died. Don't you find that strange?"

"And Philippa Glass, guv, don't forget. But you're right. It does seem a bit peculiar. You'd think that'd be one of the first questions, wouldn't you?" As he mused, Dave Copper's mobile suddenly sprang into musical life.

"Good grief, Copper, what the hell is that?"

"My ringtone, guv? Don't you like it?"

"What is it?"

"Disco song, sir. 'Let's Hear It For The Boy'. One of my old girlfriends put it on there, and I never got around to changing it. Actually, I'm quite fond of it now."

"Fine. Just don't sit there boogying to it. Answer the wretched thing."

"Hello… oh, hi… yes… right… we'll be there." And in response to Andy Constable's enquiring look, "Alfredo, guv. He's got something for us. Up at the station."

"Did he say what?"

"Something about stuff in the dead man's car, sir. He didn't specify."

"Then I suppose we'd better go and see what he's found. Looks as if you're not getting that coffee I promised you. We might as well take the car – I'm getting too old to keep walking up and down hills in the sun, and it'll give you another chance to show off your toy. Come on then, sergeant – fire up the Quattro."

The front desk at the police station was manned by the young officer who had accompanied Alfredo that morning. Recognising the two Britons, he smiled shyly and pointed down the silent corridor behind him in the direction of Alfredo's office.

"Thanks, mate – we ought to know the way by now," Dave Copper greeted him cheerily, receiving a slightly baffled nod in reply.

Alfredo rose from behind his desk as his visitors entered. "Andy, David, thank you for coming. I thought you would want to know some new information. I have things to show you." He gestured to the items in front of him.

Spread out on the desktop, and encased in the clear plastic evidence bags with which the detectives were very familiar, was an incongruous array of objects. Most startling was a large padded envelope such as would normally be used to send books or documents in the post, but it was not the envelope but its contents which caused Constable's eyebrows to rise in surprise. Bundles of high-denomination Euro notes, ranging from garish orange fifties up to sophisticated purple five-hundreds, were tumbled together in random order, held together with a mixture of paper-clips and rubber bands.

"That," remarked Copper, "is a helluva lot of dosh. How much is there, for goodness sake?"

"It is twelve thousand Euros," replied Alfredo. "I have counted it." And as Constable drew breath as if to voice objection, Alfredo held up a hand to forestall him. "Do not worry, Andy. I am not so foolish as not to have worn gloves to do this. If there are any fingerprints on the money, I think they will still be there, but I do not have a big hope for this. It is money. It is all the time in people's hands."

"What, even the five hundreds?"

"No, you are right. Those you do not see every day, so we will try."

"On Tuesday, I presume?"

Alfredo grimaced. "Of course, yes, on Tuesday, when everybody else is working, and we do not have to do this all by ourselves."

"And the envelope too, I take it."

"Yes, that too, and you can see, it is not new. It has been used before, and the address label has been carefully… pulled off, is it you say?"

"Peeled off. Right. So maybe somebody was anxious not to reveal who had been the original recipient."

"This may be. But look here." Alfredo turned the envelope over. "It is clear who was the… recipient, did you say… now." In bold black letters, written in marker pen, were the words '*JML* – FOR THE NEXT 3'. "It is Juan Manuel Laborero."

"And you found this where?"

"It was in his car, under the seat – not of the driver, but the other side."

"The front passenger seat?"

"Yes, Andy. And this I think is also strange. The car was not locked."

"That's a bit dodgy, guv, isn't it," said Dave Copper. "He should have been a bit more careful than that. Anybody could have taken it."

"Or… " Andy Constable paused in reflection. "Or, anybody could have put it there. Unobtrusively. By arrangement. You don't necessarily go handing over envelopes containing stacks of cash in the middle of a crowd, do you? Depending on what you're up to, of course."

"So what's this 'NEXT 3' business?" enquired Copper. "Do we know what that's about?"

"As yet, no," replied Alfredo.

"It's got to be something pretty substantial, hasn't it? After all, twelve thousand Euros, that's about… " Copper did a quick mental calculation. "Strewth, that's about ten thousand quid! That's a nice little earner. Do you reckon it's all tied up with the building business, guv?"

"It could easily be, Copper. We keep getting told that there's a lot of dealing done in cash."

"So, supplies, permits, the sort of stuff Percy and Liza were going on about?"

"That is one explanation, sergeant. I could think of others. So, Alfredo, we have a large amount of cash and no immediate explanation as to its origin or purpose. That's fine for starters. What else have you got?"

"There is this." Alfredo held up a second plastic envelope, which contained a crumpled hand-written note. "It was in Juan Manuel's pocket."

"Let's have a look, sir," said Dave Copper. "Dreadful writing. '*Ewan*'," he read aloud, "'*If you think it's hot here, try the Atlas. I've got some friends who will pay for a free one-way ticket for you if I talk to them. Think about it!*' That doesn't sound too friendly, sir, does it?" he remarked, handing over the plastic bag to his superior for a closer examination.

"Okay. This was in Juan Manuel's possession, but it's addressed to someone else," said Constable. "So, do we think it's from Juan, but he never got to pass it on, or is it from someone else entirely, and he has somehow come into possession of it? And look at the writing compared to the envelope with all the cash. Does that look the same to you?" He held the two up together and scrutinised them.

"Difficult to say, sir. But I don't know about you, but that handwriting doesn't look English to me. And are we to assume that this Ewan is the Mr. Husami who's on my list as being at the party, sir?"

"Not a stupid assumption, sergeant. You may be right. When we track him down for a little conversation, we'll have an interesting ice-breaker, shan't we? Excellent. More questions than answers. The story of our lives. Okay, Alfredo, what else have you got to confuse us?"

"There is this. It was in another pocket." Alfredo pushed a third bag across the desk to Constable. Inside lay several hundred pounds-worth of gleaming smart-phone.

"Copper?" The inspector turned to his junior colleague. "More your field than mine. You're the technology expert."

"Nice one," commented Copper. "That's cost him a few quid. It's a damn sight better than mine. Looks as if we're ruling out robbery as a motive then, guv?" he added facetiously. "Have you had a look at it, Alfredo? Is it locked?" And in response to the Spanish officer's negative, "Do you mind if I have a butcher's?" He picked up the phone with care and gave a few exploratory dabs and swipes to its screen through the plastic bag. "This is daft. He's not even put the most elementary security on it, guv. A two-year-old could pinch it and use it. That's pretty naïve. What was he, stupid?"

Alfredo smiled grimly. "I think whatever you could say about Juan Manuel, from what I know, you would not say he was stupid."

"Hold on a sec." Copper reacted to an icon blinking on the phone's display. "There's an unread message here. Just let me… there you go. Hey, that's interesting. Have a look at this, sir." He handed the phone to the inspector.

"'*Juan,*'" read Constable aloud, "'*This business ends now – it's too dangerous. Act as usual in public, but no more private arrangements, okay? Don't even think about not doing what I say. You know I mean it.*' Unsigned. Of course. I suppose there's no way of telling where that's come from?" he asked, passing the phone back to Dave Copper.

After a few moments fiddling, the sergeant shook his head. "Sorry, guv. No can do. Looks as if it's come in as an email, but the sender's identity is concealed. We get that a lot in cyber-bullying cases, if you remember. Just another one of the little advantages that technology gives the villain. Maybe Alfredo's techno-boys can get something out of it if they get it into their lab…"

"… On Tuesday," chorused the Britons.

"But can't we get anything from the content?" continued Copper. "I mean, whoever-it-is is talking about 'business' and 'private arrangements' – that'd go with the cash and all this talk about permits and liaison with the authorities and whatnot, wouldn't it?"

"But 'dangerous'? Where does that fit in?" objected Constable. "And 'Act as usual in public'? No, my instinct is that it's something more personal than that. Don't ask me why – it's just the smell of it."

"Well, Andy," said Alfredo. "Do you think all this helps us?"

"I'm sure it does, Alfredo," responded Constable. "But at the moment, I have to admit, I have absolutely no idea how. But we've still got people to talk to, so maybe something will jump out at us. Let us have a bit of a think. And I promised young Mr. Copper here a coffee before we came up here, so he won't be firing on all cylinders either."

"You need a coffee, there is a bar over the road," pointed out Alfredo. "My officers go there all the time, in special when they want to talk about me." He smiled. "Of course, it is not so good as my own bar…"

"I reckon it'll do fine, sir," interjected Dave Copper. "And we'll stand more chance of having a chat without being overheard by… anyone," he finished lamely.

"Yes, the lovely Eve again," mused Constable. "Which reminds me, she had something she wanted to tell us, so we're going to have to go back later anyway. But for now, I shall take pity on you. Over the road will do fine."

Chapter 8

In the shade of the awning on the bar terrace, Dave Copper took a long draught of coffee and sighed. "I'll tell you one thing, guv. They do make a fine cup of coffee over here. I doubt if I shall be able to drink that swill they serve in the station canteen ever again. So, what do you reckon? Recap?"

"I'm not sure that we've got all that much to recap at present," replied Constable.

"Well, sir, let's look on the positive side. We know who's dead, and we think we know how he died. We know where he died, because I can't believe that he left the site without anybody seeing him, and then got smacked on the head and brought back at some time during the night, so we don't have to go tracing his movements from where he was last seen to where the body was found." Copper's voice grew gradually more enthusiastic as he warmed to his theme. "And also we've got a reasonable time-frame for when he died, or at least when he was last seen by various people. Not only that, but we've got a pretty restricted list of who was there and when, so we're not thrashing around in the dark trying to identify suspects. I call that a bit of a result for a morning's work." He looked hopefully at his superior.

"Okay, Copper," agreed the inspector. "That's not a bad analysis as far as it goes. The main problem is that it only goes so far and no further. For a start, we haven't got a sniff of a motive. From what everybody has been telling us so far, Juan Manuel

Laborero was the nicest guy in the world and the best thing since sliced bread when it came to organising the building business. Everybody loved him."

"Self-evidently not everybody, guv, or else we'd be lying around the pool gently sizzling with a glass of beer in our hands instead of wondering why he's lying on a slab."

"True."

"Also, sir, you say no motive, but surely we've got something. We just don't know what it is."

"By which you mean…?"

"Well, there's the note, and that message on his phone. It's obvious that somebody isn't somebody's favourite bunny. And what's he doing with that great wodge of cash? I don't go around with envelopes containing ten thousand quid lying about in my car. Somebody must have an explanation for that, and I've had enough dealings with dodgy characters since I joined the force to know that it's highly unlikely to be an innocent one."

"Yes, well, don't let the brass hear you talking about dodgy characters and large lumps of cash in the same sentence when we get back home," advised Constable with a smile. "Put that together with your obvious skill in finding your way into other people's mobiles, and I reckon the police force is in enough trouble with the press without giving them any more gratuitous ammunition to chuck at us."

"Righty-ho, guv," grinned Copper in response. "So shall we revert to normal boring old foot-slogging detective work? In which case… " He fished in the pocket of his shorts and produced his notebook, "… as the character says in 'The Mikado', 'I've got a little list'."

"I have to say, Copper, that I never had you down as a fan of Gilbert and Sullivan."

"There are many things you don't know about me, sir," said Copper. "Some of which I shall take great care that you never find out. So, my little list. We've already got quite a long way down the list of names Alfredo gave us… "

"Yes, and to singularly little effect," objected Constable. "Not only did nobody have a bad word to say about Laborero, but everybody was infuriatingly vague about when they saw him and where."

"Fret not, guv. For a start, we haven't finished speaking to everyone. I bet you that somewhere in this lot, we shall turn up a diamond. And, we've always got the chance to go back and talk to people again. You know as well as I do that that's when the cracks begin to show. That's when we get 'em. If we start to tell A what B has said, then chances are that the stories are going to start to change."

"They'd better. We've only got a couple more days. Don't forget we fly home on Tuesday."

Copper refused to be depressed. "We'll get there, sir. I've got a feeling. You'll do it."

Constable could not fail to be amused by his junior's unbounded confidence. "This is your famous power of positive thinking again, isn't it?"

"That or the caffeine, guv. You decide."

A shadow fell across their table. Constable looked up. Liza Lott stood there. Her face was drawn.

"Miss Lott?" Constable half-stood. "Were you wanting something?"

"Not really, inspector," she replied. "I've just locked up because I'm totally wasting my time working today. The place is absolutely dead… " She caught her breath. "I mean, there's no business about, so I've decided to pack it in and go home. I noticed you here and I thought I should just tell you."

"Thank you, Miss Lott. That's thoughtful of you."

"Liza, please. Otherwise it all seems so official. You make me sound as if I'm some sort of suspect."

"Very well. Liza, then." Constable declined to deny Liza's assumption. He simply sat and looked up at her without speaking.

Liza grew restive. "I suppose I shouldn't ask if you're making headway on the case, gentlemen?" she said.

"I can't really say at this stage," said Constable neutrally. "Early days."

"Well…" Liza shifted awkwardly. "I'll be off." As she turned to leave, another woman hurried on to the bar terrace. She held out her hands to Liza, and the two women embraced.

"Rox," said Liza. "You've heard."

"Yes," said the newcomer. "X-Pat phoned me. I was just coming up to pop into my office and I saw you here. What a dreadful thing."

"Rox, I think you ought to talk to these two," said Liza, gesturing to the two Britons. "Alfredo has put them on the case. They're policemen from England."

The woman frowned in disbelief. "You're what?"

"English police," repeated Liza. "They're investigating Juan's death. They're talking to everyone who was at Percy's last night. They came and saw me first thing this morning. That was the first I heard of it."

"And what have you said to them?"

"I've just told them what I know," sighed Liza wearily. "Look, I can't be doing with all this. I've got a splitting headache. I'm just going home. If that's all right with you, inspector…?"

"Of course, Miss Lott. You go. We'll find you if we need you." As Liza turned and left, Constable gestured to an empty chair. "Do sit down, Miss… ?"

"Stone. Mrs. And Liza called you 'inspector'."

"That's right, Mrs. Stone." Constable performed the introductions. "I'm rather glad you're here, because it saves us the task of tracking you down. You see, your name is on a list which the local police have given us of those people who were present last night at Mr. Vere's party when, to the best of our knowledge, Mr. Laborero was killed. Is that correct?"

"Yes, I was there," agreed the new arrival. In contrast to the immaculately-turned-out Liza, she presented an altogether less groomed appearance. Her longish mousey-coloured hair was untidily drawn back into a loose ponytail, and the faded jeans and pale-blue polo shirt which she wore concealed a figure which looked to be on the verge of turning plump. A plain gold ring and a substantial solitaire diamond gleamed on her left hand, but she was otherwise devoid of jewellery. A touch of lipstick was the sole concession to make-up. She looked at the detectives with calm hazel eyes and waited. Just turned forty at a guess, thought Constable, and could be quite good-looking with a little more effort.

"You said Mr. Connor has told you what's happened, Mrs. Stone. Did he give you any details?"

"No, just that Juan had been found dead in Percy's garden, and that the police think it's murder. He didn't say anything about when or how or who."

"And I'm afraid that we're not in any position to fill in any of those gaps for you at this stage, madam," said Constable with a disarming smile. "At the moment I'm rather more concerned with gathering information than handing it out. Now, if I can just establish a few basic facts, and I take it that you won't mind if my sergeant makes a couple of notes."

"I'd better have your full name to start with, madam, if you don't mind," interjected Copper.

"Of course. It's Roxanne Stone."

Constable picked up the questioning again. "So, Mrs. Stone, I'm under the impression that the majority of people at Mr. Vere's little get-together last night were in some way connected with the building of the villa. So do you fit into that category as well?"

"Yes. I run a building supplies company."

"Really?" Constable sounded faintly surprised.

"Yes, inspector. I know it might sound like an unusual job for a woman, but the firm was started by my late husband, Ed Stone, and I took it over when he died a while ago."

"So am I to take it that you worked with Mr. Connor on the construction project for Mr. Vere's villa?"

"Oh, not just that one. X-Pat and I have been working in conjunction for quite some while now. Our businesses dovetail quite well. We're both quite specialised, and neither of us caters for what you might call the bread-and-butter end of the market. Just as well, really," she snorted derisively, "with the bottom end of the market being what it is at the moment – not that much bread, and precious little butter. But in our line of work, we're not too affected by the crash. Never mind what the saying is about the poor – as far as we're concerned, I'm pleased to say that the rich are always with us."

"And the rich are your clients." Constable made it a statement rather than a question.

"Certainly. We do a lot of sandstone and marble and granite – premium building materials. Most of X-Pat's clients aren't the sort of people who would want a house built out of those cheap terracotta bricks. One bump with a car, and you've lost an entire wall. No, our clients are looking for the best, so of course they're more than happy to pay extra. So with me supplying the finest materials, and X-Pat's expertise in the construction business, our clients have the complete package." She stopped abruptly. "Listen to me, launching into the sales spiel. I'm sorry, but when I start talking shop, I tend to go on to auto-pilot. And none of it is what you want to hear, I expect."

"Information is never wasted, Mrs. Stone," Constable reassured her. "But you're right, it's information about last night's events that I'm more concerned about at this point. Now unfortunately, most of the people we've already spoken to have been rather vague about their contacts with Mr. Laborero last night. I don't suppose you can help us out with a bit more detail, can you?"

"Yes, of course I can, inspector."

"That'll make a nice change," muttered Dave Copper in the background.

"Now, let me think. I got there not far off nine o'clock – yes, because X-Pat and Philippa had got there just before me. And then Percy insisted that he give me a complete tour of the house, because I hadn't been there since it was pretty much an unfinished shell, and we had been around choosing the materials and finishes for his bathrooms and kitchen and so on. But then once I'd escaped from him, I went and got myself another drink, and then I was talking to Juan for quite a while. But then, you know what it's like, someone else came up and Juan got talking to them – it might have been Philippa, but I'm not sure – and then I got grabbed again by Percy because he was intent on making sure that all his guests circulated and didn't get into a huddle with anyone in particular. I did want to have another chat with Juan a bit later, and I went looking for him, but he was nowhere to be found."

"Did you want him for any particular reason?" asked Constable.

"Oh no," replied Roxanne. "It was just something I'd suddenly thought of about the business. Juan was always managing to find new suppliers for me, because he knew everyone, so I wanted a word about that. Nothing important." Her face fell. "It's all very sad. Juan was a really nice guy."

"So everyone has told us," remarked Constable. "Which makes it that much more unbelievable to think that, in the absence of any surprising new information concerning some outsiders we know nothing about, one of his friends must have killed him." He sat back to watch the reaction to his remark.

"That's a horrible thought, inspector," said Roxanne quietly. "I hope you do find it was someone from the outside. Otherwise, how can the rest of us…?" She tailed off.

After a moment's awkward silence, Dave Copper came to the rescue. "Well, Mrs. Stone," he said, closing his notebook, "I think I've got everything. Unless you need anything else, sir?" He glanced enquiringly at his superior.

"I think not."

Copper stood. "So in that case, sir, should we be getting on? You did say you wanted to… "

Constable swiftly picked up the hint and got to his feet. "Yes, you're right, sergeant. We must get on. Things to do, Mrs. Stone – people to talk to. I'm sure you understand. But perhaps we can talk again later."

As the two detectives returned to their car, Constable looked quizzically at his colleague. "What was all that about, Copper? You plainly wanted to get away, but what's the hurry?"

"The thought occurred to me, sir," answered Copper, "that the phones have been buzzing. Everybody has heard about this business from somebody else. Wouldn't it be nice if we could get to someone before they've heard the news? You never know, it might stop somebody having the chance to get their story straight before we talk to them."

"Anyone in particular in mind?"

"Not at all, sir. But I have to say, I'm looking forward to having a chat with this elusive Mr. Husami."

"Good thinking, Copper. Right, let's see if we can track him down. Any ideas?"

"Alfredo? He'll probably know if anyone does."

"Right then, sergeant – back across the road. You know, we're spending so much time in this station, I'm starting to think we might as well get a transfer."

As Constable and Copper entered Alfredo's office, he was just hanging up the phone on his form-strewn desk.

"I have just spoken to my Commander," he explained. "I succeeded in finding him at last. He was not pleased that I disturb him on fiesta day, but when I told him about Mr. Laborero's murder, he became very interested. I do not know why in special, but he has given me the permission to make a search of Juan Manuel's office. It is part of Mr. Connor's place. Who knows, I may find something with his work that is a help."

"Yes, Mr. Connor told us about his office. Do you want us to come with you? It's over the road above the estate agent's, he said."

"No," contradicted Alfredo. "This is where he meets his clients. There are many offices above those shops. Mrs. Stone has one too. No, Mr. Connor's real office where he runs his business is at his house. His company is based in his home, so his managers all have their offices there."

"Whereabouts?" enquired Copper, intrigued. "We never saw any sign of an office when we were there, did we, guv?"

"It is in his *sotano*… underground… "

"Basement?"

"Yes, that is it. Many of the big houses are built with a garage underneath the house – Mr. Connor has made his into his offices."

"You're pretty well-up on the people on your patch, aren't you, Alfredo," remarked Copper admiringly.

"It is my job," replied Alfredo simply. "And the people with much money, those I like to know a little more about."

"So," repeated Constable, "any objections if we tag along when you go visiting?"

"Not at all, but I do not think I will have time to go today. I have many things here that I must do." He gestured to the paperwork in front of him. "But I will go tomorrow."

"Thanks. Actually, that's not why we came to see you. We wondered if you might know where we can track down the last couple of people on the list you gave us. Mr. Husami, for instance."

Alfredo thought for a moment. "It may be difficult on fiesta day. I do not think he will be working, and his house is out in the country many kilometres. But he has a boat in the marina in San Pablo port, so I think at a weekend he is very often there."

"Another one of your wealthy locals you keep an eye on?" queried Copper with a grin.

"Of course."

"We'll give it a go, then, sir, shall we?" Copper swept an arm towards the door in a florid gesture. "Your carriage awaits."

The drive into San Pablo was short, but as the car approached the centre, the roads became ever more filled with crowds streaming away from the direction of the main square.

"It's busy today, sir," commented Copper as he negotiated a particularly large family group who seemed determined to cross the road as one single unit.

"Of course," said Constable. "Don't you remember those people at the Runcorn, all dressed up? Eve told us there was a procession and a church service – I bet it's just turned out, so they're all off for their lunch."

"Well, if they're all off somewhere, guv, we might stand a chance of getting somewhere to park."

Copper was in luck. As he approached the road along the harbour front, lined with restaurants whose terraces, overflowing the pavements and spilling on to the road, were becoming ever more crowded, an elegant limousine with tinted windows slid out of a space just in front of him.

"More money, guv," remarked Copper as he reversed into the gap.

"As you say. We're certainly in the right place for it."

The quays of the marina stretched away to the left behind a gleaming white and flag-decked yacht clubhouse. Vessels of every sort, from simple chubby 28-foot motor-sailers to the most gleaming confections in aluminium, glass, teak and chrome, nestled against the pontoons. One cruiser in particular caught Copper's eye.

"Will you take a look at that one, sir!" The boat was well worth admiration. The long sleek lines of the craft moored alongside the pier were a delight to the eye. From a waterline poised to cut the ocean like the sharpest of knives, the bow flared proudly up and out, and the hull in deepest graphite grey streaked back towards the stern as if poised to pounce. Above, a dazzling white superstructure, punctuated with smoky grey windows in an elongated diamond form which echoed the racing lines of the vessel, rose to a roofed cockpit where chrome shone on the impressive wheel, and coloured glints from the navigational lights provided the only relief from the beautifully stark monochrome theme. Whiplash aerials and a radar golf-ball topped the structure. Aft, beneath a striped awning in shades of grey, lay an immaculately-patterned timber open deck, bleached to the palest buff, where varnished wooden steamer chairs were placed around a table alongside an open locker containing an impressive array of spirits. Astern, in the slight chop of the marina's waters, danced a miniature acolyte which proclaimed its identity as 'Tender to Medea'. "That," breathed Copper, "is worth a pretty penny."

"I see you're admiring my boat, gentlemen." The soft Scots burr at their shoulder caused the detectives to spin round in surprise. Rather more surprising was the appearance of the owner of the voice. Of middling height, and with receding grey-brown hair with a pronounced kink in it, the man smiled at them with an array of white teeth in an olive complexioned face, whose eyes were concealed behind mirrored aviator shades. A pale turquoise open-necked shirt beneath a crisply-tailored cream linen suit shrieked 'designer'. White leather snake-skin patterned shoes matched the glimpse of belt. "Would you like to take a closer look at her?"

Copper could not restrain his enthusiasm. "Wow! Would I?"

"Ewan Husami."

"You what?"

"Ewan Husami." The man extended his hand. "The Medea is my boat. And you, if I'm not much mistaken, are the two gentlemen from the British police who are anxious to speak to me about this sad matter of Juan Manuel. Don't tell me I'm wrong."

"No, sir, you're not, but how…?"

Ewan waved his hand airily. "One hears things. San Pablo is a very small place. Now, are we going to stand here in the sun, or are you going to come aboard, sit down, have a drink, and talk about things in a civilised manner?" Without waiting for an answer, he led the way on board, seemingly confident that the two detectives would follow.

"Another of those amazing coincidences you're so un-fond of, guv?" hissed Copper out of the side of his mouth.

"Shut up and get on board!"

"Take a seat, gentlemen," said Ewan, indicating a pair of cushioned seats under the awning. "You'll have a drink, I'm sure. I can do you a beer or something a little more interesting, or I have soft drinks as well. It all depends on whether you're going to give me that old 'not while I'm on duty, sir' line."

"A beer will do very nicely, sir, thank you," replied Constable. "You're very kind. And we're not officially what you might call 'on duty'. It's just that we have become acquainted with the local police captain, and he has enlisted our help over Mr. Laborero's death. But from what you say, I'm assuming you know this already."

Ewan nodded in affirmation. "In fact, there are really only two things I don't know. One is precisely who you are… " Constable told him. "And the other is, how you think I can help you."

"Not necessarily you in particular, sir," said Constable, accepting a tall beer-glass already covered with condensation in the warmth of the afternoon. "But we're interviewing – at Captain Alfredo's request, you understand – all those who were at Mr. Vere's house-warming party in the hope of gleaning some significant piece of information which may lead us to the killer. And you, we are told, were present. Can I ask in what capacity? Are you a friend of Mr. Vere's, or is it a business connection?"

Ewan seated himself, leaned back and stretched out his legs, and tossed his sun-glasses carelessly on to the table-top. "Do you know, Mr. Constable, that is probably one of the more difficult questions to answer," he mused. "I have so many business interests, I hardly know what to call myself. I suppose, if you force me to it, I would have to say I'm an entrepreneur."

"Which, I'm afraid, sir, tells me everything and nothing. Could you be a little more explicit."

"By all means, inspector." Ewan smiled. "I'm sorry, I'm rather teasing you. Specifics, then. The reason I was there last night was because I've known Percy Vere slightly for several years – he comes into the bar here at the yacht club occasionally, so of course you get chatting – but also because I have a connection to his new villa through X-Pat Connor, who I think you have met." Constable nodded a confirmation in response to an interrogative eyebrow. "I have a lot of dealings with X-Pat and Liza Lott because I have a cousin who has an architect's practice in Alicante. I'm a partner in the practice, so we work very closely together with their clients to generate the designs for the villas they commission."

"I see, sir. So that's mainly what you do? And that's how you came into contact with Mr. Laborero?"

"Oh, not at all. No, I'm no architect myself – I just have an investment in the business. My main dealings with Juan were through another cousin of mine who runs the agency I own for freelance building labourers."

"Here in San Pablo, sir?"

"No, no, up and down the coast. And inland, up towards the mountains, for that matter. Despite what you may have read in the press, there's always a ready market for special houses – people coming in from Eastern Europe are some of our best clients, you may be surprised to hear. So wherever there's building going on, there's always going to be a demand for flexible labour. A man like Juan wouldn't necessarily know what workforce he'd need from one day to the next. Just for the routine labouring, you understand – the skilled men are a different matter altogether." He chuckled in amusement. "My cousin's certainly kept on the hop juggling everybody's needs."

"I think Mr. Vere may have mentioned something about it, sir. So, pretty big family business then," commented Dave Copper. "I see what you mean when you say you have trouble deciding what exactly you do."

Ewan laughed. "Hey, that's not all of it. There's the site security. And, we have a lot of people coming in from abroad when they first get the idea of building a holiday home out here, so we need to organise a lot of flights. Fortunately, another one of my businesses is a travel agency, so one way and another, we get to keep a pretty tight control on the whole project."

"You're not going to tell me that the agency is run by another one of your cousins, are you, sir?"

"Where on earth would you get an idea like that, sergeant?" A sigh of mock relief from Copper. "He's my second cousin."

"Forgive me for sounding nosey, sir," persisted Copper, "but if you don't mind me saying so, the Scottish accent doesn't quite seem to go with the name. I've never met anyone called Husami before."

"That, sergeant, is probably because you've never been to

Morocco." Copper looked baffled. "It's perfectly simple, sergeant. My dad was from Morocco, and when he was young he worked for a time at a hotel in London. He was a waiter. While he was there he met this wee Scottish girl who was a dancer at one of the theatres, who took a fancy to him, and they got married. Result, me! So you see before you a right mixture. I was born in England, the surname's from my dad, the first name's from my granddad in Glasgow, the accent's from my mum… " He drained his glass. "And the beer's from the fridge. Another, either of you?"

Just as Dave Copper seemed disposed to take up the offer, Andy Constable leant forward to resume charge of the conversation. "We won't, sir, thank you all the same. This isn't really a social call. We're actually more interested in what you can tell us about the events of last evening."

"What can I say, inspector? It was a very pleasant party, with Percy playing the part of the genial host as he does so well, and the rest of us simply having a good time among friends, chatting and enjoying Percy's generous liquid hospitality."

"Did you have any particular dealings with Juan Manuel?"

"Dealings? What an odd word. I had a few conversations with him, and a few drinks, if that's what you mean, but I really wasn't there to talk business. No, I came, I saw, I conversed – and at the end of it I went home."

"And was Mr. Laborero still around when you left?"

"I have no idea, inspector. I don't remember seeing him, but I wasn't checking up on everybody's movements. Forgive me for not having thought of it."

Inspector Constable rose to his feet. His tone was brusque. "Then we'll take up no more of your time, Mr. Husami. I'm sure you've helped us all you can, so we'll leave it at that for now. Thank you for the drink – we'll be on our way." He led the way ashore briskly, while Dave Copper hastily bolted down the remains of his beer and trotted in his wake.

Chapter 9

"Now there's a very smooth gentleman," remarked Copper as the Britons headed down the pier towards dry land once more. "Not the most helpful individual we've ever interviewed, eh, guv?"

"Well spotted, Copper – ten out of ten," snapped Constable, and immediately relented. "Sorry, David – I shouldn't take it out on you. No, you're quite right, of course. Blood out of a stone doesn't come into it. And I do resent characters like that seeking to amuse themselves at our expense."

"So you reckon he was being deliberately obstructive then, guv? All this 'oh dear, if only I could remember' guff is just a load of old hogwash? You think he's got something to hide?"

"I'm absolutely certain he has. Now, whether that's got anything to do with Juan's death or not, I wouldn't like to say."

"But you don't think that the old 'detective's nose' is letting you down?"

"I don't." Constable smiled. "As a mere youthful whipper-snapper, you should recognise that my many years' seniority in both age and experience gives me a considerable advantage over you. I've met more slippery customers than you've had hot dinners. So first, remember that you should never judge a book by its cover. But at the same time, just ask yourself, how come the son of a foreign waiter and a British chorus girl ends up owning a boat which probably cost more than you will earn during your entire career in the police force. Not to mention a clutch of businesses, of which we've possibly only heard about a few of the tentacles."

"Eggs with tentacles, guv? Sounds nasty!"

"You know perfectly well what I mean, sergeant, mixed metaphor or not."

"Sorry, sir. Yes, sir. I do. But as to how, could be any number of reasons, couldn't it? Brilliant entrepreneurial skills – ruthless ambition and a determination to tread on the opposition – after all, we've all seen 'The Apprentice' – just plain ordinary luck?"

"Luck!" snorted Constable in derision. "Did you not notice the boat? Who gets that lucky?"

"Can I make a suggestion, sir?"

"Go on."

"You won't like it."

"I'm listening."

"Could you sit down and take a deep breath, guv." Constable gave his junior a look, then sat on a nearby bench as it became clear that Copper was not intending to proceed unless he complied.

"Well?"

"Shall we pack it in for today, sir? I think it's getting to us."

"'It' being the case. And by 'us' you mean me. Yes?"

"Look at it like this. We've been at it since first thing this morning. We've been asking questions all day, talking to people who either can't or won't tell us anything useful. And it's not even as if it's our case – we've just been dragged into it to help somebody out. I know you've got the bit between your teeth, sir, because that's what you do, and I'll admit that I want to know what happened, probably almost as much as you do. But we are supposed to be on holiday, and it is Saturday, and for crying out loud, we're the only ones working in this whole blasted town!"

Constable sat for a few moments as he digested what for

Dave Copper was an unusually impassioned speech. Eventually the tension drained from his body, and he nodded.

"Sergeant… David… you are a great deal cleverer than I sometimes give you credit for. You are absolutely right. Even Alfredo said he can't do anything more before tomorrow. So we will bale out, and do our damnedest to find something else to occupy our thoughts. Any suggestions?"

"Well, guv, it was probably the mention of hot dinners that did it. Could we please find some food? I can't survive on the odd beer and coffee – I'll start to twitch. We haven't had a thing to eat so far today, and even the Spanish probably think this is a bit late to call lunch-time. We missed breakfast this morning when Alfredo came calling, and now I am so utterly starving that my stomach thinks my throat's been cut."

"God help us!" ejaculated Constable. "Let's not go there. One gruesome death in one day, Sergeant Copper, may be regarded as a misfortune," he intoned. "Two looks like carelessness." He got to his feet and surveyed the still-milling crowds along the promenade. "Come on – fiesta or no, there'll be a table somewhere."

The restaurant could by no means be called chic, but it was certainly popular. A dozen or so busy tables were scattered under an awning between two rather dusty-looking mimosa trees, while through the full range of glazed doors, now standing open to take advantage of the spring sunshine, an interior furnished with simple pine tables and chairs appeared packed. A chalked blackboard alongside a serving hatch listed the dishes offered on the ubiquitous '*menu del dia*' at a gratifyingly normal 10 Euros. Lettering along the front of the awning proclaimed the establishment to be '*El Rincon de Hanibal*'. As Constable and Copper approached, a couple rose from a table and, with a smile and a nod, departed as the two officers slid gratefully into their places. Miraculously, within seconds the table had been swept clear of used plates and glasses by a briskly-efficient passing waitress, and a basket of bread, a plate of salad, and a bottle of water accompanied by two glasses appeared unbidden as if by magic.

"Another '*Rincon*', guv," remarked Copper. 'No relation to the Runcorn, I hope."

"If by that you mean you're anxious to avoid the attentions of the delicious Eve, I should imagine you're relatively safe," responded Constable, his good humour thoroughly restored. He nodded in the direction of a youthful curly-headed individual who was circulating from table to table with smiles and handshakes. "That, I'm deducing, is Hanibal, and I suspect you may not be his type at all."

"Bit of an unusual name, guv, isn't it? I mean, you don't meet many Hannibals on the average day."

"Ah, but I suspect you may in this neck of the woods. Something of a local hero, is Hannibal."

"We are talking about the same Hannibal, aren't we, guv? The guy with the elephants? I thought he came from Carthage. Isn't that North Africa?"

"Yes, yes, yes, and yes, in that order. And your problem is what exactly?"

"Oh no." Dave Copper groaned and put his head in his hands. "I know that look. I'm about to get one of those history lessons from your fabulous education, aren't I, sir?"

"You will walk into these things, Copper." Constable leaned back and stretched expansively. "We shall use these few moments of precious relaxation to improve your knowledge of ancient history. Unless you have any objection, of course?"

"Just one question before you start, guv. Who's paying for lunch?"

"As I am now back in a good mood, sergeant, you will be pleased to hear that I am."

"In which case, sir, I don't mind a bit. Bash on."

"Hannibal," began Constable, "was indeed a member of a very famous Carthaginian ruling family. Have you heard of Hasdrubal?"

"Vaguely, I think, guv. Was he another general? In the Punic Wars?"

"Absolutely right. Maybe your education hasn't been as badly neglected as I suspected. So, Hasdrubal Barca was Hannibal's brother-in-law, and he was ruler of the city of Cartagena, just down the coast."

"What, here in Spain?"

"The Romans weren't the only ones with an empire, you know. In fact, that's why the Romans and the Carthaginians came into conflict. Rival imperial ambitions, and this part of Spain was the front line. At one time, this was all part of Carthage's empire, so when the Romans started spreading west, the Barca family didn't take too kindly to it."

"So Hannibal loaded up his elephants and headed over the Alps?"

"That's skipping one or two steps, but in essence, yes. Of course, it did him no good in the long run, and the Romans ended up with pretty much all of the Iberian peninsula, and Carthage ended up as a pile of rubble with salt ploughed into its fields. Ruthless people, the Romans, when it suited them. But although Hannibal was gone, he wasn't forgotten. He somehow hung on in local legend as a symbol of resistance to foreign oppression."

"What, some sort of North African Robin Hood?" laughed Copper.

"You mock, but there's a long tradition of conquest and underdogs in this part of the world. It's not like in England – we have 1066, and apart from the occasional kerfuffle involving roses or Roundheads, nobody's come tramping in from the outside to tread the people down. They have long memories around here, and there's still more than a hint of North African influence left. Not just from the Carthaginians, of course, but you remember what Alfredo told us about the origins of this weekend's fiesta – from the Moors as well."

"And still carrying on," observed Copper, "with our friend Mr. Husami." He suddenly guffawed. "Here, guv," he gurgled in delight. "Does that make him one of the Scottish Moors?"

"I shall pretend I didn't hear that," said Constable severely. "I have taken your advice and switched off. Unless you want to witness the return of the snarling old grouch who was here earlier, I suggest we stay away from that subject for the rest of the day."

Dave Copper was spared further criticism by the timely arrival of the waitress, order pad at the ready, with a cheery '*Y que toman los señores?*'. Constable took a deep breath, and wrenched his concentration to the Herculean task of plundering his meagre reserves of Spanish sufficiently to order the meal.

"Er… "

The waitress took pity. "And what do you like to eat?"

Andy Constable was awoken on Sunday morning by the almighty splash from the pool beneath his bedroom window. Throwing back the sheet, he wrapped a towel around himself and padded out on to the balcony, from where he could see Dave Copper below flailing through the water in an inelegant but speedy front crawl. The sergeant glanced up and, with a cheerful flash of teeth and a wave, disappeared beneath the surface to emerge at the end of the pool in a flurry of spray and with much noisy puffing.

"Insomnia?" enquired Constable mildly.

"Too good a morning to waste, guv," came the reply. "It's gone nine, you know."

"Couldn't be bothered to shower?"

"Sets you up, guv, a brisk swim first thing. Gets the blood circulating. You should give it a try."

"What, 'come on in, the water's lovely'? I suppose that's your next line."

"Please yourself, guv. I'm only saying."

Thirty seconds was enough for Constable to pull on a pair of beach shorts and, with a noisy impact that scattered water for several yards, join his colleague in the pool. "You know what, David?" he spluttered as he surfaced. "You're absolutely right. This was a very good idea."

"Recovered from yesterday, then, guv?"

Constable flexed experimentally. "Well, the old bones don't seem to be aching all that much, but I suspect my feet may be killing me for quite a while."

"Occupational hazard of being a flat-foot," suggested Copper with a grin.

Following their conversation at the restaurant table the previous day, the two had done well to stick to their agreement to avoid any further mention of the case in hand at all costs. Shop talk was ruthlessly prohibited. After a protracted and very pleasurable lunch – "This fish is brilliant, guv; I could live on fish if it didn't cost an arm and a leg back home" – lubricated with a bottle of the restaurant's house rosé – "I've had more than you, sir; you'd better drive. Here's the car keys; just *please* don't bend it!" – the pair had come to the mutual conclusion that the Spanish tradition of siesta had a great deal to be said for it. Constable was the first to arise from hibernation. With mug in hand, he tapped at Dave Copper's door and, in response to the muffled grunt which he took as an invitation to enter, did so and drew back the half-closed curtains to illuminate a tousled figure blinking at him.

"Medicinal tea," he explained, placing the mug at the bedside.

"Thanks, guv," croaked Copper. "You know, I think I'm going to stay away from wine in future. It sneaks up on you. I'll stick to beer – you know where you are with beer."

Constable laughed. "You've had about an eggcup-full, man. Don't whinge. Just think what all the Friday-nighters must feel like after a heavy session in the bars in town at home."

"I have no sympathy for them," retorted Copper. "They deserve everything they get. Including a night in the cells."

"No such luxury for you," breezed Constable. "Rise and shine – I have a cunning plan."

"I thought I was supposed to be the one who said that sort of thing, sir."

"Yes, well, who said an old dog can't learn new tricks? Come on, drag yourself from your pit, boy – we're going out. Alicante beckons."

A shower and a shave later, the two were on their way along the coastal highway. "I can't get over how clear the roads are around here," remarked Dave Copper. "You try driving into town on a Saturday night at home – it's a nightmare. And," he added a few minutes later as he manoeuvred the car into a parking space near to the city's marina and adjacent to a large entertainment centre with cinemas and a gaggle of restaurants, "I can't believe they actually let you park somewhere like this for free."

"Thinking of moving to Spain?" asked Andy Constable, not entirely joking.

"Maybe when I get my pension, guv," replied Copper in the same vein.

Alicante had the feel of a traditional Mediterranean city, a million miles away from the image of golden beaches backed by high-rise hotels so often seen in holiday brochures. There were high-rises, but they did not dominate the city's skyline. There was a beach, mere yards from one of the main avenues of the town, where even in the fading light of the cooling early evening, a scattering of groups of locals sprawled and chatted as children played around them. But the beach was backed by a spectacular promenade, tree-shaded and with a swirling pattern of tiles along its booth-lined length, where spot-lit stalls sold a rich variety of crafts, jewellery, leatherwares, and mystic paraphernalia, while buskers played and artists sketched caricatures of self-conscious young men as their giggling girlfriends looked on. Smartly-dressed mature ladies in fur-trimmed coats, their iron-grey hair immaculately coiffed into metallic armour, walked their tiny dogs in minute shrub-shrouded public gardens. Palm-lined pedestrianised avenues, wrought-iron lamp standards beginning to twinkle, led up to spectacular fountains on roundabouts at the centre of a burst of radiating boulevards. Balconied town-houses with sinuous art-nouveau architectural lines rubbed shoulders with glamorous marble and crystal boutiques whose windows displayed an exuberant froth of bridal silk and lace. In the heart of the old town, a massive cathedral, its gloomy interior punctuated with red and yellow spots of candle-light and the gleam of silver from ornate reliquaries, spread its protective presence over the muddle of narrow twisting lanes crouched beneath its skirts. Above, watching over all, the huge castle threw curtains of masonry around its high crag, as the banners of Spain floated proudly from its topmost tower.

The two Britons gratefully immersed themselves in the relaxing atmosphere of the city, strolling aimlessly among the crowds, commenting occasionally as a colourfully tiled shop-front or a gleaming pepper-pot dome caught their eye. They laughed as, joining the queue at a street stall for generous portions of ice-cream, they were unable to stop drips from the cones from running down their chins and over their knuckles. They ventured among the alleys in the ancient quarter where, grasping their courage firmly in their hands and entering a bar in search of a snack, they were surprised to find themselves being taken through the extensive *tapas* menu in flawless English by a Swedish student working his way through Spanish university. And finally, as the sky eventually abandoned its struggle to hold on to the dark blue of late evening and gave in to a star-scattered black, they climbed the long steep spiral up to the castle where, perched on a parapet, they sipped a final beer from the tiny one-man booth and gazed across the bay towards the distant headland of San Pablo, the coast road a glinting necklace of orange, as the lights of the occasional aircraft drifted silently downwards into the airport.

"David," sighed Andy Constable. "This trip was a very good idea of yours. I actually feel as if I'm on holiday. I have now unwound. Good man."

"Cheers, guv," responded Dave Copper in slight embarrassment. "Glad you're enjoying it. But don't relax too much just yet. Don't forget, we've still got a long walk back to the car."

"Oh rats!" retorted Constable good-humouredly.

"Not only that, guv, but in case you've forgotten, tomorrow we've got to… "

"Tomorrow is tomorrow," Constable interrupted him firmly. "I refuse to think about it." He drained the last few drops from his bottle and hoisted himself off the parapet. "Ouch! My dogs, as my old granny used to say, are barking. Tomorrow is when I shall pay for all this walking. And, while we're on the subject of wise old saws, in the words of the Chinese, the longest journey begins with a single step. Come on – let's go."

The evening had ended companionably at the '*Casa del Torero*' with a poolside glass of brandy from a bottle unexpectedly discovered at the back of a kitchen cupboard. But now, as Andy Constable towelled himself off briskly in the aftermath of the morning swim, he realised that time to conclude the investigation was slipping inexorably past. "Right," he said, "enough pleasure.

We've been enjoying ourselves far too much. Better get back to the grindstone and see if we can sort out Alfredo's little problem."

"You know what, guv?" countered Dave Copper. "I know it's against all your instincts, but I could murder a Full English. I know they do them at the Runcorn. I don't suppose you could consider compromising your instincts just this once?"

"Sergeant Copper," said Constable. "I wish you'd stop having these good ideas. You're on. Get your kit on, and we'll see what delights Eve can offer you first thing in the morning."

"Oh, spare me," muttered Copper in despair.

At the Runcorn, trade was brisk. Several Spanish families, their young daughters draped in white *mantillas* and evidently heading for mass, sipped coffees or dunked *churros* into mugs of chocolate. Two tables of obviously retired British expatriates were ploughing wordlessly through large platters of bacon, eggs, and fried bread, accompanied by incongruous pints of lager, as they surveyed the football reports in the back pages of their Sunday papers. The detectives hardly had a chance to take their seats at a table on the terrace before Eve burst forth from the interior of the bar.

"Morning, boys – how's it all going?" she enquired breathlessly. "Are you getting anywhere?"

"Hello, Eve," replied Constable, refusing to be drawn. "You seem to be here all the hours God sends. Can't they run this place without you?"

"Don't!" returned Eve with a grimace. "Sorry, darling, but I'm not my usual happy self this morning."

"Why's that then?"

"Because... " Eve sighed. "Because I was supposed to be having this morning off, and Philippa was supposed to be working, but she's phoned up at about ten minutes' notice to say she's not up to it, bless her, so can I cover for her?"

"Ill, is she?" asked Copper.

Eve threw her hands up. "Don't ask me what goes through that girl's mind sometimes, darling. I just know that she's not coming in, so I'm chief cook and bottle-washer until the chef comes in to start the lunches."

"Maybe she's upset over Juan Manuel's death?" hazarded Copper.

Eve glanced around before lowering her voice. "Yes, well, I could tell you a thing or two there."

"You did say you wanted to talk to us yesterday, and we never got the chance," Constable reminded her.

"I do, but not now. Let me get on with things here, and we'll have a chat when I've got a minute to myself. Whenever that may be… *Si, si, un momento*," she cried in response to a raised hand across the terrace, and was gone.

A chair scraped as it was drawn up to a table close behind the detectives. Turning slightly, Constable saw a man in his forties with a shock of dark red hair and a friendly creased face whose complexion was evidently not designed to cope with prolonged exposure to the sun. The slightly bulbous nose was red and peeling. The man nodded and smiled slightly, murmuring a subdued 'Morning' before raising his voice to hail Eve as she headed for the restaurant door.

"Good morning, young lady! I'll have the usual, when you're ready!"

"Oh, Wally, I didn't notice you come in." Eve bustled over. "Sorry, love, I'm running about like a mad thing. Usual full breakfast, is it?"

"Aye, and mind you don't forget the black pudding like you tried to the other day."

"Could we order the same while you're at it?" interjected Andy Constable as Eve seemed poised to depart.

Eve's hand went to her mouth. "Andy, Dave, I'm so sorry,"

she apologised. "I never did take your order. Honestly, I don't know where I am today." She took a breath and pulled herself together. "Right, three breakfasts coming up. Won't keep you." As she was about to leave, a thought appeared to strike her, and she turned back. "I've just realised. Andy, this is Wally. He was at Percy's party as well, so I bet you'll want to talk to him."

"Mr.... Torrance, would it be?" produced Constable after a moment's frenzied digging in the memory banks.

"Aye, that's right," confirmed the other.

"Well, in that case, Eve is absolutely right. We would be grateful for a word, if it's not too much trouble."

"Ah. I heard this might be in the wind. This'll be about Juan, no doubt?"

"That's right, sir. I ought to tell you, my colleague and I are police officers." Constable effected the introductions and explained Captain Alfredo's request for help. "We've already spoken to most of the people who were present at Mr. Vere's house on Friday night – we got a list from Captain Alfredo, and I think yours is the last name on it."

"I see. Well, in that case, you'll already have had your wee chat with the rich member of the family." And in response to Constable's look of uncertainty, "Ewan, I mean."

"Ewan? Family? What, you mean you and Ewan...?"

"He's my cousin, inspector. Did he not tell you? Well, I guess he did not, otherwise it wouldn't come as a surprise to you. Aye, we're cousins, because his mum and my mum were sisters, although you'd never think it to look at us, would you. Chalk and cheese, eh?" Walter chuckled. "But family nonetheless. Which is how he came to get me this job out here, working for X-Pat on his new villas."

"Well, if you wouldn't mind my sergeant here making a few notes... Copper, I don't suppose you've got that notebook handy, have you?"

"Never leaves my person, guv," responded Copper.

"Another from your department of amazing coincidences?" enquired Constable in an undertone.

"On so many levels, sir," replied his colleague. "So, sir, it's Mr. Torrance. And is Wally short for…?"

"Walter. Walter Torrance. I'm X-Pat's chief plumber."

"So, Copper, another of Mr. Husami's many cousins," commented Constable with only minimal irony. "Who'd have thought it? I think I remember you remarking that Mr. Husami's family seemed unusually large."

"Oh, I'm not the half of it," broke in Walter. "You wouldn't believe the number of Moroccan cousins he's got."

"We have heard about his other businesses."

"No, no, I mean in the building trade – the younger guys. I've got some of them working for me. Not that they arrive with all the skills they need, by any means, but given a bit of training, they soon come up to scratch. They're quick learners."

"Sorry, hold on a second. Arrive? What, you mean you bring in the workforce from outside the country? How does that go down with the locals?"

"No, they might come from North Africa originally, but they're all residents, just as much as me. It's all legal and above-board – I see all their I.D. cards when I take them on, and there's not a thing wrong with them. You can't mess about with that kind of thing – those famous Spanish bureaucrats would be down on you like a ton of bricks."

"I don't recall any of these chaps being pointed out to us at the party, guv," said Dave Copper.

"There's a good reason for that," answered Walter. "They weren't there. They wouldn't have enjoyed it, and most of them don't drink anyway, so I told them to take the night off – it was the start of the fiesta weekend, after all. I shouldn't be surprised if they did what they usually do when they've got time off – go fishing."

"Fishing?" Copper sounded surprised.

"Aye, they're off all the time. They love it, for some reason. Mind you, having said that, they're not the only ones. Tim's a bit of a fisherman himself. I could never see it myself, but there's loads of people around here who are out there at all hours. Apparently this coastline is special, for some reason. Have you not seen them all along that rocky bit of coast the other side of town down towards Torrenueva?"

"No, we've not been down that far, sir."

"Car-loads of them, sometimes. And every so often I think Ewan takes some of them out on night-fishing trips on that great big boat of his."

"The 'Medea'? Yes, we've seen Mr. Husami's boat. Not exactly your average trawler, is it?" remarked Copper wryly.

"You could say that," agreed Walter with a smile. "But he's pretty good to the lads. Off he goes in the middle of the night, and whenever I see him coming back in the morning, it turns out he's been out there with a bunch of his cousins. They must go miles, the amount he spends on fuel. Well, he can afford it, so it's no skin off my nose. And he's always saying to me, 'You should have seen the fish Ali caught – what a whopper'. He always laughs – great sense of humour, our Ewan. And to tell the truth, I wouldn't know who on earth he's talking about, because I don't know that side of the family at all well, and they all seem to be called Ali anyway. It's funny, sometimes at work I'm halfway through a job and I need a hand with something, so I yell 'Ali!', and two or three guys come running up. Half the time I can't tell one from another."

"So all these cousins are also connected with Mr. Connor's building business?" Constable sought to confirm. "It seems to me, Mr. Torrance, that there isn't anybody round here who isn't."

"And you'd be right there, inspector," said Walter. "We all seem to be at it, one way or another. Except Ewan, of course – if you're talking about the actual hard graft, he never needs to get his hands dirty, but that's because he's rolling in it. But then, you'll have guessed that already, if you've seen the 'Medea'. I'd not even like to think how much that cost him. It's like the people who have these villas built. Have you seen some of them?"

"The people or the villas?"

"Both."

"We've only seen Mr. Vere's villa close to, but thinking about it, I dare say Mr. Connor built his own place. Very smart indeed, sir, as you say. And Liza Lott has given a pretty good impression of her... international clientele, shall we say."

"Well, there you are then. You know all about it. Money no object, no expense spared. You'd be amazed at the number of people there are like Percy Vere. Sold up in the U.K., or wherever it is they've come from, moved out here with more money than they know what to do with, and desperately looking for ways to spend it. So what do they do?"

"I have a feeling you're going to tell me, Mr. Torrance."

"Aye, well, you wouldn't be much of a detective if this came as a surprise to you – they build a big house. Liza fixes everything for them, and there's a girl who knows her way around the system. It's amazing what permits she manages to get hold of. It's all in the contacts, you see – she does have a lot of friends where it counts, and the customers seem happy enough to pay to get what they want."

Constable studied Walter's face, searching for indications of an underlying meaning in his expression. "Are you trying to tell us, Mr. Torrance, that there are implications of dealings which aren't one hundred percent by the book?"

"Oh come off it, inspector," laughed Walter. "You're no fool. You know as well as I do that sometimes, things get a little shove along the way. Now I'm not saying you, but I bet you know someone in your line of work who's slipped someone the odd bottle of scotch in recognition of a bit of help. And surely you don't need me to tell you that the building business is full of people on the fiddle."

"Including yourself, Mr. Torrance?"

"Och, no!" grinned Walter. "I'm as honest as the day is long, me. You'll not find that there's much of a demand for illicit plumbing. Worse luck me, you might say, but I get to sleep at nights with a clear conscience, which suits me."

"So then, sir," joined in Copper, "who doesn't have a clear conscience?"

"I'm not going to name any names, sergeant." Walter suddenly grew serious again. "I don't want anything nasty happening to me like poor old Juan."

"So the sort of thing we would be talking about, sir, would be… ?" Copper attempted to tease out further information from the witness.

"All right, sergeant. Well, put yourself in the position of one of these clients of Liza and X-Pat's. And then ask yourself, just as a for-instance – could you tell the difference between ordinary hardwood and special mahogany imported from Malaysia at about six times the price?"

Copper shook his head. "No, don't reckon I could, sir."

Walter smacked his knee in emphasis. "Exactly – and neither could I. We're not experts, you see. Or, say you paid to have something built in solid marble? I don't know, something around your pool, or something in the bathroom. How would you know if whatever-it-was was just built out of blocks and then just clad in marble, all while you were away in the U.K. or wherever?"

"Not a clue, sir."

"And that's my point. You wouldn't know, would you, not without taking the whole thing to pieces, and who's going to do that? You'd have no need. And here's another thought – if somebody had the security people at the quarry in their pocket, who's to say they even paid for the marble in the first place?"

"It sounds to me," resumed Andy Constable, "and correct me if I'm wrong, but you may be referring to Mrs. Stone. Which seems to be straying rather from the point, when what we're seeking to do is investigate the death of Juan Manuel Laborero. So do we have some sort of a link?"

"It's not up to me to make judgements, inspector. But let's just say that that may not have been the only secret of a certain lady, I reckon. Now don't get me wrong – Roxanne's a free agent now, and she can do what she likes. You know her husband's dead, I take it?"

"Yes, we had been told that."

"Well, I was good mates with Ed Stone up until he had his nasty accident, and I don't like to think that there may have been anything between Roxy and Juan beforehand."

"You say 'nasty accident', Mr. Torrance? What happened?"

"Oh, it was up at one of the quarries," explained Walter. "Ed was up there one day, checking out something or other, and he had a fall. Stupidest thing ever – you can't believe that a bloke who's been around quarries all his life is going to go climbing a rock-face without so much as a hard hat on, but by all accounts, that's what he did. Killed instantly, Juan said. He told the police all about it."

"Juan was there?"

"Aye. It was a weekend, and Ed had taken him along. Just as well, really, because he told the police he saw the whole thing when he reported it. And of course he had the terrible business of telling Roxanne. I think that may be what brought them closer together."

"Yes," said Constable, "I imagine it must have been a dreadful shock for her. You could see how that could happen."

"Well, inspector, I'm not one for gossip, but maybe Roxanne wasn't so cut up about Ed's death as some people might be. Oh,

I don't know that there was anything wrong between them or anything like that, but for a start, it meant that she inherited the whole building supplies company, which was worth shedloads of money, so I dare say that helped her to get over it. And as I say, Juan was around to give her a hand."

"So, Mr. Torrance, we're back to Juan again, and as I say, I'm rather more interested in his movements at Friday's party than any other time. So if we can focus on that…"

Walter gave a wry smile. "The party. Hmmm. More like a game of hide-and-seek, I'd say."

"Now that, sir, is a very odd remark. From what everyone else has told us so far, it was just a pleasant social occasion."

"Might have started out as such, guv," put in Dave Copper. "Didn't end up that way though, did it? Maybe Mr. Torrance can give us some pointers as to when things changed."

"True. Mr. Torrance, so far we're woefully short on specifics. Times and such. Can you help us out on that?"

"I'll give it my best shot, inspector." Walter thought for a moment. "Right. I didn't stir too much out of the big room, because I was talking to Percy when I first arrived, and he's got a very generous hand with the whisky bottle, so you can imagine I didn't want to stray too far. And then Eve came up, and I was with her after that. In fact, inspector, if you're looking for a suspect, you'll not find one in me, because I was in plain view of everyone the whole time."

"Yes, but the point is, was everyone in plain view of you? I take it they weren't. From your remark about hide-and-seek."

"Let me see… I did see Juan early on, but I couldn't tell you exactly when." Copper sighed in the background. "Hold your horses, laddie. I'm still thinking. Now Juan had gone off somewhere at one point, because Tim Berman was looking for him, which must have been about a quarter past ten. Aye, because Roxanne and Ewan had come back in about five minutes before… "

"Do you mean back in from the garden, sir?" interrupted Copper.

"That's right. So then Tim went out to look for him, but he came back in a few minutes later to say he couldn't find him. Mind you, it's no wonder – it was as black as your hat out there."

"So did you see Mr. Laborero after that?" asked Constable.

"No, inspector, I did not, but then, I wouldn't have had much chance. I left a few minutes after that, because I didn't want to be too late. I had some thoughts of getting an early start."

"Really, sir? What, with the fiesta weekend and everything?"

"Well, inspector, I'm not much of a man for fiestas and such. We lose enough work-time round here as it is with all that malarkey. I'd rather put in an honest day's work, so I planned to pop in here and see if I could get a few things sorted out ahead of Tuesday. Fat chance – when I turned up here, one of Alfredo's lads was on the gate, and he turned me away. No wonder – you can't get much in the way of drains laid with a dead Spaniard in your trench, can you?"

Chapter 10

"Breakfast, boys," announced Eve brightly as she arrived with a heavily-laden tray. "Sorry about the hold-up, but I'd run out of sausages, so I had to get some more out of the freezer, and I had to make sure they were defrosted properly, because I don't want to go killing off my customers, do I?"

"Preferably not," replied Constable drily. "We've got enough to do as it is."

Eve's hand flew to her mouth. "Oh, what am I saying? Oh, that's dreadful. Andy, I hope you don't think that I... I mean I wouldn't... "

"Don't worry, Eve," Constable soothed her. "Anybody can do a foot-in-mouth. You should hear some of the things my sergeant here come out with."

"I'll just let you have your food then, shall I?" Eve hurried away.

"That, guv, was one of the best breakfasts I've had in a long time," stated Dave Copper as he wiped up the remaining smears of baked bean sauce from around his plate.

"She does a good breakfast, does Eve," agreed Walter Torrance. "Girl in a million. I'm surprised someone doesn't snap her up."

"There you are, David," smiled Andy Constable. "What finer recommendation could you have than that? Somebody who can do you a breakfast just the way you like it."

Copper was spared any further teasing by the timely arrival of Eve herself. "Everything all right, boys?"

"Just what the doctor ordered," said Constable. "We are fortified for the rest of the day. And I haven't forgotten that you said you had things to tell us." He cast a sideways glance at Walter.

"That's fine, inspector," responded the Scot. "A nod's as good as a wink to a blind horse. I dare say this is all about Juan, and you'll be wanting to know whether I've told you the truth or not, so I'll leave you in peace to have your wee chat." He rose to his feet. "Be seeing you, Eve." He winked at her. "Be gentle with them."

As Walter left, Constable looked around the terrace, which had emptied of customers save for a solitary elderly man immersed in a Spanish newspaper on the far side of the terrace. "If you're free, Eve, no time like the present." He indicated a seat at the table.

As Eve sat and drew breath to begin, Dave Copper's mobile leapt into life.

"Hello… oh, yes, Alfredo… okay… what, now? Hang on – guv, it's Alfredo. He wants to go and make that little visit he was talking about. You remember."

"Oh, to Mr…. yes, of course. Right now?"

"He says so. He wants us to meet him at the house."

"Look, Eve, sorry, but duty calls. We're going to have to postpone this. Come on, Copper. We're off."

"It's a conspiracy, isn't it, guv?"

"Shut up and get the car keys."

At X-Pat Connor's villa, Alfredo's police car had just pulled on to the empty drive as Constable and Copper arrived. As the Spaniard climbed out, he greeted his British colleagues with a smile. "Thank you for coming, Andy and Dave. I do not know, but I think maybe we will be quicker if we have three people, and also it could be that you see something that I do not."

Dave Copper surveyed the vacant parking space in front of the house. "Looks as if Mr. Connor's gone off somewhere." And in response to Alfredo's slow smile, "You knew, didn't you? You knew he wasn't around, so you chose now. You reckon there's something to find, don't you? Do you think Connor's mixed up in all this?"

Alfredo remained calm in the face of Copper's growing excitement. "I do not know anything for sure, David. I do not know a reason why Mr. Connor should kill Juan Manuel. This is not to say that there is not such a reason. But I am a policeman like you – I am a suspicious person. And we have the opportunity to see if there are some things, not only about Mr. Connor, but about many of the other people in the case, which are not as they should be."

"He's right, Copper," pointed out Constable. "This is probably the perfect place. Everybody involved has got a link here. Connor lives here, so does Philippa Glass, Juan worked from here, so does Tim Berman and Walter Torrance…"

"I thought we were ruling him out, guv. From what he told us about being with somebody all evening."

"Well, maybe," admitted Constable dubiously. "I'll have a bit more confirmation before I finally cross him off the list. But even so, you can bet that all the others – Liza Lott, Ewan Husami, and Roxanne Stone – have got business links with Connor, so who knows what there is to find." He turned to Alfredo. "You're in charge – over to you."

A weary-looking Philippa Glass answered the door. Apprehension leapt into her eyes. "X-Pat's not here," she blurted, "if that's who you're looking for. He's gone out… to see someone."

"This is not a problem, Philippa," replied Alfredo smoothly.

"It is not Mr. Connor we wanted to see. But I have spoken to my superiors about this murder of Mr. Laborero, and they have agreed that it may help if I can examine his office to look if there is any helpful clue there. With your permission, of course."

"You want to do a search? What, all of you? I don't know…" Philippa hesitated. "Have you got a warrant?"

"No," said Alfredo calmly. "That I do not have. I will not have a document from the judge until Tuesday. Of course, I can wait until Tuesday if you refuse to let me into the house. But I'm sure you would not wish to do that." He smiled.

"So… you want to see Juan's office?"

"And maybe the other offices as well, if that is all right? I hope you do not object?"

"Oh. I suppose not. You'd better come in," said Philippa grudgingly, and held back the door. "It's down those stairs in the basement," she continued. "The light is on the left. I think I'd better come with you."

"No, no, Philippa, you do not need to do that. My two friends here will give me all the help I need."

"Watch and learn, Copper," murmured Constable in an undertone as the three policemen descended the stairs. "That is as smooth an unauthorised entry as I have ever seen. Well done, Alfredo."

"It is not illegal," protested Alfredo laughingly. "But sometimes, we have to be a little faster than the paperwork. Now… " A short corridor faced them, with doors left and right. "Do we work together, or do we have one office for each person?"

"Split up," suggested Constable. "We can cover more ground."

"Then I will look in here," said Alfredo, indicating a cubby-hole whose notice-board was covered with notes and signs in Spanish. "I think this will be Juan's room." He disappeared through the door.

The office Andy Constable entered was evidently the one occupied by Tim Berman. Rifling briskly through the papers on the desk and in its drawers, nothing sprang instantly to his attention. A small two-drawer filing cabinet alongside the desk seemed crammed with architectural plans, design drawings for furnishings, and commercial catalogues from a plethora of companies from all over the world detailing the bewildering and unending selection of woods on offer. On the notice-board was a large-scale map of the area dotted with variously coloured pins, presumably indicating the location of various work projects. Posted beneath it, and seeming to lack relevance, was a large-scale nautical chart of a section of coastline, with a prominent 'X' written on it in marker pen and the figures 12.30 alongside. The place indicated was distant from any marked town or village – only a single narrow road seemed to lead there. *'Cala de los Pescadores'* was the legend. Constable trawled his memory banks to dredge up a translation – 'Fishermen's Cove'. As he mused over what, if any, meaning the chart had, he was interrupted by Dave Copper's excited voice.

"Here, guv, come and have a look what I've found." Constable followed the sound to the room next door, which was noticeably more spacious and better furnished – evidently X-Pat Connor's own office. A desk in pale Scandinavian wood, whose top was inlaid with a sheet of exquisitely-veined marble, matched ledger-laden bookshelves and a side table where a computer with a large flat-screen monitor slumbered, its single eye dormant. An aggressively modern floor lamp arched its metallic neck in an extended curve to finish in a bulbous cream acrylic shade over the chrome and white leather deep swivel chair in which Sergeant Copper was seated, swinging gently back and forth as he studied the documents in his hands.

"What have we got?"

"These, sir." The papers appeared to be invoices from a

company called 'Costamatcon S.A.', made out to Connor Construction at the address of the villa, and listing a variety of what Constable assumed must be building supplies.

"So? They're a couple of bills for some sort of materials, I suppose. You can't tell what, because everything's referred to by a product code, and I for one don't intend to burrow through all the suppliers' literature to find out what's what."

"You don't need to, guv." Copper's tone was triumphant. "Take a closer look. It's not two bills – it's one. Well, it is and it isn't. Look – same invoice number on each, same date. Same materials – twenty-five cubic metres of whatever it is, a hundred and fifty cubic metres of something else, and eighty metres of some other thing. But on this one you've got a charge of x-amount for each thing, and a total of six thousand, six hundred and fifty Euros – on the other one, the price for everything is doubled, and the total comes to thirteen thousand, three hundred! Now there's a nice little earner for someone!" Copper leaned back and grinned at his superior in satisfaction.

Constable nodded slowly in agreement. "Very good, sergeant, as far as it goes. But don't leave the job half-done. Continue with your excellent deductions to the logical conclusion."

"Okay, guv. I see it like this. We can't be sure who this supply company is or what they're supplying, because we haven't got any names. But let's just guess, as a reasonable supposition, that it might be Roxanne Stone. We know she does building materials. She supplies stuff to X-Pat Connor at a certain price for the building works, together with two versions of the invoice – he then pays the proper bill, and puts the dodgy one into his customer's file. Then when, say, Percy Vere comes to pay for his villa, out comes the dodgy bill in justification of the charges, and Percy ends up paying over the odds, and he's got no clue that he's been diddled."

"A very cunning little scam," mused Constable, "and

probably exactly the sort of thing that Walter Torrance was alluding to with his not-so-subtle hints. But now we've got actual evidence of what he meant. And it's reasonable to suppose that Juan Manuel Laborero was smack in the middle of it. Well done, Copper."

"Thanks, guv. Any luck your end?"

"Not so's you'd notice. I've had a brief browse through Tim Berman's stuff, but nothing jumped out at me. Except... Ah, Alfredo!" he said, as the captain appeared in the office doorway. "Have you managed to find anything useful?"

"I do not know," replied the Spaniard. "I have looked at the papers, but there is much there and I do not have time to... do you say 'examine'... everything. I can send my boys on Tuesday to see if there is something. But I have this." He held up a desk diary. "It is Juan Manuel's. I will take it and look through it at my office. Do you have success?"

"One or two things which look a bit iffy," answered Constable, "but nothing which gives us an obvious reason for murder at the moment. We're still chewing things over. But we've just got to take a look in Walter Torrance's office, and then we're done."

"I think I have finished," said Alfredo. "So as you do that, I will find Miss Glass and tell her we will go soon." He turned and headed towards the stairs.

Walter's cubicle was tiny and scrupulously neat. Pens were ranged in rows, papers were stacked in coloured trays in an orderly fashion, and a calendar and several notices were pinned to the noticeboard with immaculate precision.

"This," remarked Dave Copper, as the two detectives attempted to squeeze through the doorway, "is the office of a very tidy man. You know, I have trouble in imagining that he'd leave a dead body sticking out of one of his trenches in such a ramshackle manner."

"Nevertheless, Copper, stunning though your detective abilities may be, we do not conduct investigations on the basis of your imagination. Do the search."

A few brief moments' rummage revealed nothing of interest. "We did have an inkling he was out of it, guv," said Copper, climbing the basement stairs to return to the hall. "And if he's got this alibi provided by Percy Vere and his whisky bottle, then at least there's one name we can definitely cross off the list." He looked around the empty hall. "I wonder where Alfredo's got to."

"With Philippa Glass, I assume. In her previous sunny corner catching a few rays, perhaps."

The Britons emerged on to the terrace at the rear of the house, to find Philippa sitting under a sun umbrella, nursing a coffee and gazing unfocussed into space. Of Alfredo there was no sign.

"We're just leaving, Miss Glass," called Constable. "We thought Captain Alfredo might be with you."

Philippa came to herself and got to her feet. "No. I haven't seen him."

"Perhaps he left without saying anything," suggested Copper, as Philippa led the way towards the front door. As the three reached the hall, footsteps sounded on the staircase from the first floor, and Alfredo came into view.

"Ah, Philippa, there you are," he said easily. "I was looking for you. I come to tell you that we are finished, and so we go. I am sorry that we disturb you, and I thank you for your help." He flashed a broad smile. "By the way, is it not that you are working in the bar today?" Philippa started to splutter an explanation, but Alfredo turned and made his way towards the cars as Philippa closed the front door behind the police officers.

"Alfredo," said Constable in a lowered voice as the three stood on the drive. "If I didn't know better, I might think that you had been carrying out a search of the rooms upstairs of that house."

"Not at all, Andy," grinned Alfredo. "Just one room. The bedroom of Mr. Connor and Philippa Glass. And I think you will be interested to see what I have found hidden in the drawer of Philippa's... cabinet of drawers, is this the word?"

"Chest of drawers? Dressing table?"

"Yes. Dressing table." He held out a hand in which nestled three coloured and laminated cards the size of a credit card.

"What are those?" asked Copper.

"Identity cards. Spanish identity cards for foreigners. And they are good. Very good." Alfredo's voice was heavy with irony, causing Dave Copper to look more closely at the photographs and details on the items.

"Well, well, guv," he said. "Look – same trick again. These have all got the same layout, same numbers, same nationality, same... well, I assume that's the address... same signature – but three different faces."

"Yes," confirmed Alfredo. "And you see the original nationality? It is Morocco."

"This is beginning to develop quite nicely, Copper," said Constable as the two climbed back into the car. "I think we're starting to get a few interesting items to chew over."

"Where do you want to chew them over, guv?" asked Copper, starting the engine. "Back to the Runcorn?"

"Not likely," riposted Constable. "We'll only get Eve'd again, and I'm not sure I'm ready for that yet. And I don't fancy that other place up by the cop-shop – we'd probably run into Liza Lott or Roxanne Stone again. I'll tell you what – let's go for something completely out of character. Let's just go back to our own villa and put our feet up round the pool with a beer in our hands."

"Brilliant idea, guv," responded Copper. "I always think better when I've got a beer in my hand."

"Debatable," said Constable with a note of humorous reserve. "But we'll test the theory."

At the '*Casa del Torero*', the pool was giving off sparkling reflections from the sun, an invitation which Dave Copper felt unable to resist. A swift sprint to his room, and he was back in his swim-shorts and heading for the water while his superior adopted a more leisurely approach, opening two bottles of beer and placing them at the ready as Copper plunged into the deep end. A few minutes later the younger man emerged from the pool, shook himself like a spaniel, and plonked himself down on a sun bed alongside the one already occupied by Andy Constable.

"That feels good, guv," he grinned. "You know, I could almost feel I'm on holiday." He took a swig of beer. "If only we didn't have things like dead bodies and suspicious characters and suggestive clues to take into account, I reckon we might actually be able to enjoy ourselves."

"Yes, well, I think we ought to pretend we *are* actually on holiday for a moment, and forget about everything else for just five minutes. I am going to close my eyes and think about nothing in particular. If I start to snore, nudge me." As if on cue, the sound of the doorbell echoed through the villa. "Bloody hell! Can't a man get any peace around here, even on a Sunday?"

"Like I said, guv, it's a conspiracy."

"Well, don't just lie there dripping, man. Go and find out who it is, and tell them we don't want any."

As Dave Copper picked his barefoot way through the arch leading to the front of the building, the murmur of conversation could be heard. Constable thought he could recognise the tone of voice, and his suspicions were confirmed as Copper reappeared leading their visitor.

"Look guv… it's Eve come to see you." A bright smile lit his features, and only the momentarily upturned eyes gave him away.

"Well, I've really come to see both of you," said Eve, casting an admiring glance up and down Dave Copper. He unconsciously stood a little straighter and pulled his stomach in.

"I know you wanted to talk, Eve," said Constable, heaving himself from the comfort of his lounger and leading the way to a patio table and chairs in the shade of an awning. "I'm sorry we had to put you off earlier, but I'm afraid Alfredo was quite insistent. But I thought you were tied up at the restaurant."

"Phil turned up at last," explained Eve. "She said something about not feeling well, but then she said you two and Alfredo had been snooping up at their villa, and he'd made some remark to her about work, so she'd decided she couldn't get away with it, I suppose. So I thought, as she's there, and Alfredo's sister is in the kitchen as well helping the chef, I could actually get away and have a word. You know, away from everyone else."

"In that case, David," suggested Constable, "it would probably be a good idea if you go and get your little book so that you can make some notes." And as Copper hurried up the steps towards the first floor, "And you'd probably better put some clothes on while you're about it."

"Oh, don't worry on my account, darling," simpered Eve, as the still-damp sergeant rolled his eyes and vanished indoors.

"We'll just hold on until he's back," said Constable, and a few moments uneasy silence ensued until Copper, now in T-shirt and fresh shorts, rejoined them, pad and pen at the ready.

"So then, I suppose we ought to be a little more formal, Miss… sergeant, have you had a chance to make a note of Eve's full name?"

"Stropper, love. Eve Stropper. But everyone who comes into the bar calls me just Eve." She sighed. "Oh, I spend so much time behind that bar – sometimes it's a relief to escape. But that's really why I wanted to talk to you. You wouldn't believe some of the things I hear – well, when people have had a drop to drink, they talk, don't they? Some of the things Philippa and I have found out, they'd make your hair curl. If I wanted to take up blackmail, I could pack that job in straight away."

"That's interesting, guv," put in Dave Copper. "That's the second time somebody's mentioned blackmail."

"Yes, well," preened Eve, "fortunately I'm not that kind of girl."

"You say you have things to tell us, Eve." Constable sat back and folded his arms. "And as we stand a fair chance of not being interrupted, now that Miss Glass has stepped into your shoes at the bar, why don't you go ahead and do just that? Now, is this about the things that happened the other night at the party, or the people involved?"

"Well, both really, Andy… inspector. Now I wasn't going to say anything about Philippa, being as she's my best mate, but I suppose it's all out now anyway."

"Excuse me… exactly what is all out?"

"About her and Juan. They've had this thing going for a while now, and she swore nobody knew, and she made me promise not to say a thing, but obviously somebody blabbed, the way they always do. And that's what the argy-bargy was about."

"Argy-bargy? That's the first we've heard of anything like that, isn't it, guv?" said Copper. "Argy-bargy between her and…?"

"X-Pat, of course. I don't know who tipped him off that there was something going on, but he had this huge row with Phil on Friday night. Well, I say huge row, but it wasn't voices raised or anything like that, but for all that, you could see that X-Pat was getting worked up – you know, his neck going red and his eyes bulging. What happened was, it was getting a bit dark, and I think Juan had been outside seeing off the last of the Spanish boys who were going, and Phil followed Juan outside when she thought nobody was looking, but I think X-Pat must have noticed her, and not long afterwards, he went out into the garden after her. Then about five minutes later, she came back in."

"Did you speak to her at that point?" asked Constable.

"I couldn't really not," said Eve. "She was in a terrible state, crying and everything, although of course she was trying to hold everything in so as not to make a fuss, so she was sniffing a lot and she had to borrow my handkerchief, and she told me X-Pat had said 'If I find he's laid a finger on you, he's a dead man'. Horribly jealous, he is."

"You say he said 'if'. So it sounds as if he was still in some doubt as to what had gone on?"

"Yes, I still don't think he knew for sure. I don't know who had told him or what they'd said. It might have just been some sort of a hint for all I know. But that's sometimes enough for him. He's got a shocking temper on him sometimes."

"Did Miss Glass say anything else?"

"No, not then, because just then Wally Torrance came up and joined in, and I thought, thank the lord, because I didn't want to get caught up in anything, because I'm all for a quiet life, me. So then we were carrying on pretending nothing was wrong, and then about five minutes after that, Liza came up and asked Phil where Juan was, and Phil said 'How should I know?', as if she didn't care a bit, and she said X-Pat might know, because he wanted Juan too. I thought to myself, 'You're treading on thin ice there, love', but I didn't want to butt in, and then Liza said 'Oh my God! I'd better go and find him before X-Pat does', and then she said something which I didn't quite catch because Percy came over to top up the glasses, but it was something about 'needing to be certified, or else none of us is safe', and off she went into the garden, leaving me and Phil with Wally and Percy. And it's a good job Percy had those bottles of wine, because normally he can't keep his hands to himself when he's had a drop or two. I don't mind really, I suppose, because he's a nice enough old buffer, but a girl likes to be asked, doesn't she?" Eve favoured Dave Copper with what was obviously intended to be an inviting smile.

Constable thought for a moment. "This is the first hint that we've had of any tensions involving Mr. Laborero. I think we'll need to speak to your friend Philippa again, because she wasn't exactly forthcoming on the subject before."

"You don't just want to talk to Phil," said Eve quickly. "I mean, she may be no saint where Juan was concerned, but she's not the only one." Constable's raised eyebrows invited her to continue. "I know Roxanne was messing about with him, and that was when Ed Stone was still alive. Mind you, now I come to think of it, it might not have been that long before he died in that horrible accident at the quarry, so for all I know he may have died before he found out. I hope so. Ed was a lovely man – I liked him, and it's dreadful when you know something about someone's other half but you feel you daren't say anything. I don't go poking about in other people's relationships. That's probably why I'm still single."

"So you reckon that Roxanne Stone was involved in an affair with Juan Manuel Laborero before her husband's death?" said Copper. "Sounds as if he had a bit of a taste for the married ladies, eh, guv?"

"Well, sergeant, at least there's one option we can rule out – we can be certain that the late Mr. Stone didn't kill him." Constable allowed an incongruous touch of black humour to creep into his response. "But going back to Mrs. Stone… "

"Oh, actually she was very upset by Ed's death, by all accounts. That's what everybody told me. Gossip in the bar again, I'm afraid – well, you can't switch your ears off, can you? But it just goes to show, you never can tell how people are going to react to these things. Anyway, one way or another, I reckon Juan managed to console her, or take her mind off it, or whatever way you want to put it. I suppose talking things through helps, and Juan was the only one around, so he was the man to do it. At any rate, what with the business and everything, it looks as if

Roxanne came to rely on Juan quite a lot, and she bought him a new car as a thank-you just afterwards."

"What, that blue jobbie?" asked Copper. "Nice thank-you!"

"Yes," agreed Eve. "I know one or two people probably put two and two together and thought Rox and Juan might have been a bit more than work partners. I think that they might have wondered what she was thanking him for. But that was then, and this is now, and you know what it's like with relationships – sometimes they just move on. Like Juan did. And you probably don't know, but these days, Rox seems very close to Tim, but I've no idea how he felt about it."

"So that would mean... hang on... " Dave Copper thought it through. "No, that wouldn't make sense. Tim Berman wouldn't have anything against Juan if Juan's relationship with Roxanne Stone was over."

"Don't ask me, darling," replied Eve. "I've long ago stopped trying to work out how men's minds work. You'd have to ask him."

"Whereas X-Pat Connor... " continued Copper thoughtfully.

"Ooh, now that reminds me," butted in Eve. "Rox was another of the ones who went off looking for X-Pat on Friday night. I never knew he was so popular. Not that he's really my type. I don't know, there's just something about him... "

"Do you have any idea what time that would have been?" asked Constable, determined to stop Eve going off down a sidetrack of irrelevance, and taking pity on Dave Copper who was attempting to make sense of his increasingly jumbled notes.

"About ten o'clock, I think," said Eve. "She said there was something she needed to have out with him. Something about protecting herself. So I said the last I'd seen of X-Pat was when he'd gone outside, so off she went out into the garden, but then a few seconds later, X-Pat and Liza came in through the door from the kitchen. They must have come round through that way from the garden, so I don't suppose Rox ever found him."

"So did she come back?"

"Oh yes. A few minutes later I noticed Ewan was over the other side of the room, so I popped over and told him that Rox was going on about protection, and I thought he'd probably want to be in on it, because he's the one who organises all the security guards for all the building sites… "

"Through one of his cousins." Dave Copper couldn't resist the remark.

"That's the one," said Eve blithely. "Anyway, he went out to find her, and they came back in together at about ten past, I suppose." Suddenly, Eve seemed to run out of steam. "That's about all I remember." She smiled apologetically. "You'll think it funny, but for all that I work in the bar, I don't actually drink all that much, so what with having had quite a long day at work, and Percy and his top-ups with his famous fizz, I just sat down in one of his great big chairs and I think I must have drifted off. I didn't really come to until somebody nudged me because people were starting to go home. Good job I didn't have far to go."

"So then," summarised Constable, "you never saw any more of Juan Manuel."

"No, I didn't," confirmed Eve. "Oh, there was one thing I forgot. I don't think I would have seen him much, even if I hadn't dozed off. I bet he was going to leave early anyway, because he'd told me early on that he wanted to get away and check something, because he had something big happening on Tuesday. He said it was worth a lot to him, whether he did it or not."

"Did he explain?"

"No, darling, he didn't. He was very mysterious. I don't have any idea what he meant." Eve shook her head sadly. "I don't expect I ever will."

Chapter 11

"Well, well, well," said Dave Copper as he returned from seeing Eve off the premises.

"And well exactly what?" returned Andy Constable, who had resumed his place on the sun lounger, lain back, and closed his eyes.

"It's all starting to shape up quite nicely, isn't it, guv?" Copper threw himself down on the next-door lounger, which groaned in protest at the sudden load, and leant up on one elbow. "The first story we hear from everybody, this guy Juan is the finest thing since sliced bread and everybody's best buddy. But talk to a few people, and all this extra stuff comes out of the woodwork. What do you make of it, now that Eve's spilt a few beans?"

"What I make of it, David," replied Constable, eyes still closed, "is that Eve's beans, as you put it, aren't the only things which require something of a rethink. We have all manner of seeds which, if we nurture them carefully, might very well develop into fully-grown motives, given a drop of extra daylight."

"Nice metaphor, guv," murmured Copper. "Not even remotely mixed."

"Mock not, sergeant," growled Constable. "We higher ranks are supposed to have an intellectual advantage over you more menial oiks." He opened one eye and laughed. "So instead of lying there cluttering the place up, why don't you go and have a root through the fridge? There must be something in there out of which you can construct a couple of sandwiches. We will fortify ourselves with something to eat, plus perhaps a second beer if you have left any, after which we shall recharge our brains with a siesta, and then I suggest we go on a little gardening expedition and do a little more digging. Agreed?"

"Agreed, guv. Just one question, though."

"Which is…?"

"How come you can get away with the digging comments, and I can't?"

"Privilege of rank," sighed Constable, settling back and smiling. "Your reward will come in heaven."

"Can't wait," muttered Copper, as he climbed the spiral stairs in the direction of the kitchen.

"Who do you want to start with, guv?" asked Copper as, a restful couple of hours later, he ran his fingers through his tousled hair and then began to fasten his trainers.

Constable turned back from the window where he had been watching the sun which, already starting to decline towards evening, was losing its fierce whiteness and beginning to take on hints of yellow and orange. "It seems to me," he replied, "that this whole business revolves around the building of these villas. And since Mr. X-Pat Connor is at the centre of that particular web, I think we ought to go and have a chat with him."

"Plus," pointed out Copper, "we know where he lives. We might stand a chance of actually finding him."

"True," said Constable, "although he wasn't there this morning, was he? Let's see if he's re-appeared – we can surprise him."

"It might not be easy tracking down the others, sir. Not on a Sunday. Fiesta, too."

"We shall improvise, sergeant," said Constable airily. "Enlist your famous power of positive thinking – that should do the trick."

At X-Pat Connor's house, the black car was in its previous position on the drive, and X-Pat himself answered the door in response to the detectives' ring.

"Oh. It's you again," he said ungraciously. "Now what?"

"I do apologise for disturbing you again, Mr. Connor." Andy Constable declined to be put off. "But I would appreciate it if you could spare us a couple of minutes."

"I suppose you're nowhere near sorting out this Juan thing?"

"I don't know that I'd say that, Mr. Connor. I think we're making some progress. But as I think I mentioned before, we have got some things to clear up, so we do need to have a further word with everybody who was present on Friday night."

"You can't talk to Phil – she isn't here."

"No, we are aware of that, sir. I think she's working at the restaurant at the moment, isn't she? I'm glad she's feeling better than she was this morning."

"What?"

"This morning, Mr. Connor. We did manage to have a few words with her when we called this morning." X-Pat looked nonplussed. "When you were out, sir. We called in for a few moments with Captain Alfredo. Why, didn't she mention it?"

"No, she did not," said X-Pat shortly.

"Ah well, maybe she didn't have the opportunity," smiled Constable blandly. "So anyway, may we…?"

"I suppose you'd better come in." X-Pat held back the door and indicated the direction of the living room. "Take a seat. Well, Mr. Constable," he said, with an effort to resume his previous bonhomie, "what is it I can do for you?"

"Here's the thing, Mr. Connor," began the inspector. "When we first started to talk to people – oh, not just yourself, but pretty much everyone we spoke to – the universal impression we got was that Juan Manuel Laborero was liked by all, and to a great extend the lynch-pin of your operation. In fact, we learn, of several people's operations. But, alas – as with so many first impressions, it turns out that this one wasn't quite accurate. We've had conversations with various people since then, and it appears that there were those who had – or thought they had – reasons not to be quite so favourably disposed towards him."

"Like who?"

"Well... like you, Mr. Connor. Just to take a random example."

"Now who, I wonder, could have told you such a thing?"

"You won't mind if I keep my cards close to my chest for the moment, I'm sure, Mr. Connor. But, going back to the first point, how am I to resolve this apparent contradiction between what we were first told about the dead man and the second version we heard?"

"I would imagine, inspector," said X-Pat, "that it would be the same in any situation. Nobody likes to speak ill of the dead."

Constable leaned forward to give his words more emphasis. "Yes, but the point is, Mr. Connor, that Mr. Laborero *is* dead." A harder note crept into his tone. "And therefore, sir, I would be very grateful if we could avoid the pussy-footing about, and try to get to a few facts and some names. Any chance of a bit of co-operation on that front, do you suppose?" He held X-Pat's eyes in a challenging gaze.

"Okay." The builder sighed. "So, maybe you're right. Juan might have had a lot of friends, and he was a very useful guy in lots of ways, but there were a few people who weren't that fond of him. I know he'd certainly had one or two rows with Tim Berman, but I don't know how serious they were."

"Any idea as to the subject of these rows? Do you happen to know whether they were of a personal nature, or were they tied up with business in some way?"

"Couldn't tell you, inspector. I don't make a habit of going around listening at keyholes."

"Always assuming that the doors with the keyholes in them have actually been fitted, sir," commented Dave Copper. "Could there have been disagreements about the scheduling of the works? Was somebody messing somebody's plans up?"

"Come on, sergeant," replied X-Pat. "You've said it yourselves. You're here investigating a murder. Who gets excited about a few bits of wood?"

"That, sir, would be related to how exciting the wood is, I expect. We've been told there are some quite exotic timbers involved. Maybe somebody might get rather cross, or worse, if they thought their time or their money was being wasted."

"I suppose it all depends on the price, doesn't it, sergeant." X-Pat's tone grew momentarily grim. "Everyone has their price, don't they? I couldn't answer that one – that's one of the many things I delegate. If you want to know, you'd better ask Tim."

"We shall, Mr. Connor," said Constable, "just as soon as we can. You wouldn't by any chance know where we might find him at the moment, would you? Of course, I dare say he'll be here in his office downstairs on Tuesday, but I'm afraid our time is rather short, and we have a flight to catch on Tuesday, so if you can point us in the right direction… "

"I'll do better than that, inspector." X-Pat leaned over the back of the sofa, picked up a telephone, and dialled. "Tim… yes. Look, I have two charming British policemen sitting here in my house asking all sorts of questions about Juan. And now they want to talk to you… yes, again. So if you're not too tied up, how would you like to pop over to the house, and we can both get them off our backs… Fine. See you in ten." X-Pat beamed as he replaced the phone. "Happy, gentlemen?"

"Very kind of you, sir," responded Constable, echoing the smile. "But not quite finished, I'm afraid. You see, we skirted round the matter of personal motivation earlier on, but I'm afraid I can't ignore it. Which brings me to the rather delicate subject of Miss Philippa Glass." X-Pat grew very still. He looked at the inspector fixedly and waited. "How can I put this?" continued Constable. "It appears that there was a suspicion in your mind that the friendship between Miss Glass and Mr. Laborero might have gone further than simple friendship. And you were reported, on the strength of this suspicion, to have made threats against Mr. Laborero."

"Gossip!" snorted X-Pat. "I can guess who told you that. I wouldn't believe everything you hear, inspector. There's nothing wrong between Phil and me, but even if there were, I don't think she'd be too happy to pay the price if I caught her playing around, which I don't for a minute believe she was."

"Everyone has their price, sir? Isn't that what you said?"

"Phil is far too comfortable where she is," retorted X-Pat firmly. "I don't think she'd want to risk everything, do you? So, if you've no more insulting questions to ask, I suggest that you might be happier waiting for Tim Berman outside in the street." He stood. "Okay?"

Dave Copper and Andy Constable stood at the foot of the steps to X-Pat Connor's house.

"Angry? Jumpy? Guilty? What do you reckon, guv?" asked Copper.

"Could be any of them," surmised Constable, "or even a mixture of all three. I'm not leaping to any instant conclusions, but you have to admit, the mask has cracked, hasn't it? I suggest you move the car out into the road – we don't want to give any further excuse for a display of the alleged shocking temper."

As Copper complied, Tim Berman drove up in a rather dilapidated white pick-up truck.

"What's all this, then?" he said as he climbed out. "X-Pat thrown you out already?"

"We'd finished our conversation, Mr. Berman," explained Constable smoothly, "so we didn't see the need to take up any more of Mr. Connor's time."

"So now you're going to take up some of my time," said Tim, casually leaning on the truck's bonnet. "I suppose you've thought of some more of those questions you were going to ask me."

"Do you know, Mr. Berman, as it happens, we have. We've been able to learn quite a lot from our various interviews with those involved… "

"Interviews? This is beginning to sound very formal, inspector. Are you going to start cautioning me next?" Tim's flippant tone was contradicted by a dawning look of apprehension in his eyes.

"Nothing of the sort, sir," Constable reassured him. "We're nowhere near that stage. As yet. But we've been given some information that… shall we say, the financial dealings surrounding the building operations of Mr. Connor's business weren't entirely transparent. Any comment on that?"

"I've been grassed up, haven't I?" said Tim. "Look, why don't you tell me straight what it is I'm supposed to need to defend myself over."

"Very well, Mr. Berman. Plain talk. We have been told by a source who should know what they're talking about, and whose accuracy I see no reason to doubt, that sometimes the customers don't quite get what they pay for. Now one might easily conclude that Mr. Laborero might have had a problem with such an arrangement. That could give you a motive, sir."

"What, a motive to kill Juan? Don't be ridiculous! All right, I'm not going to deny it – I've cut a few corners here and there, and we've all got to earn a living, haven't we? But there's a world of difference between a few little fiddles, and stuff that's going to land you in prison or worse."

Andy Constable refused to be deflected. "Ah, but it's not just you, Mr. Berman, is it? You have quite a close working relationship with Mrs. Stone over the supply of building materials, don't you? I've also heard it mentioned that perhaps that relationship goes further than the professional."

"And what has that got to do with anything, inspector?" Tim sounded furious. "Okay, Roxanne and I have a nice little earner going with the materials, and you don't mind paying a bit of – how shall we say – commission to anyone who helps you out along the way. As long as nobody gets too greedy. Has it not crossed your mind, inspector, that that might be how Juan fitted into the picture?"

"Many things have crossed my mind, Mr. Berman," replied Constable calmly. "The fact that you went looking for Mr. Laborero on the fatal night, for instance. I ask myself why. And the fact that you said you couldn't find him in the darkened garden. I ask myself why not."

"Yes, well, before you start chucking accusations in my direction, you can also ask yourself this. Who is going to get into bigger trouble – me, or someone who is capable of blowing the whistle on some very powerful people? If you want a motive, try looking there for one. And now, if you will excuse me, I think I need a drink." He climbed back into his truck, slammed the door violently, and drove off in a spray of gravel.

"You know what, guv?" remarked Dave Copper. "I think we're starting to get under a few people's skins."

"Excellent," responded Andy Constable. "That's just the way I like my suspects. And I think our Mr. Berman has given us the perfect hint as to the next one on our list."

"Ewan Husami, by any chance?" hazarded Copper. "He'd fit into the 'powerful people' category a treat, wouldn't he?"

"My thoughts exactly, David. Shall we go and find out if Mr. Husami is taking a fiesta sundowner on – what did Walter Torrance call it – 'that great big boat of his'? Let's see if his hospitality extends to offering a drink to a pair of thirsty detectives."

The road into San Pablo was heavy with traffic.

"Bit busy, guv," said Copper. "Something going on, do you reckon?"

"Of course!" Constable snapped his fingers. "I know exactly what's going on. It's the main fiesta parade on the Sunday, isn't it? That's where they're all going. Let's hope we can park."

As Constable and Copper walked up the pontoon of the marina towards the 'Medea', Ewan Husami could be seen lounging casually on the after-deck, speaking unhurriedly into his mobile. Completing the call, he replaced the phone on the table, a self-satisfied smile touching his lips, and as he picked up a cut-glass tumbler, ice chinking in its amber contents, his eyes met those of Andy Constable waiting at the foot of the gangplank.

"Well, well, inspector," said Ewan. "This is an unexpected pleasure." He did not sound remotely surprised. "Two visits from the forces of law and order in two days. I wonder what I've done to deserve such an honour."

"Well, Mr. Husami," replied Constable, "unfortunately, it seems that the more we talk to people, the more questions arise and the fewer answers materialise. So we hoped to catch you to have a further word, if we may."

"And again, not a social call, I assume. This will be about the unfortunate Juan, no doubt."

"Exactly so, sir."

"'Sir' again," smiled Ewan. "I have no idea why, but I always get nervous when a policeman calls me 'sir'."

"Gets to talk a lot to policemen, does he, guv?" muttered Dave Copper out of the side of his mouth. "Wonder why that would be."

Ewan either ignored or failed to notice the aside. "I suppose you had better come aboard." He waved the two detectives up the gangplank, and gestured to seats alongside his own chair. "Now, as we've already established that you're not on duty, I expect you'll take a drink. I have a very good single malt here," he indicated his own glass, "which my Scottish relatives would probably ostracise me for adulterating with ice, but as they're far away in the cold and I'm here in the warmth of a Mediterranean evening, I'll do as I please. Will you have the same?" In response to his guests' positive response, he rose and busied himself at the bar with bottle and glasses.

"You're very kind, Mr. Husami," said Constable. "And yes, you're right. We may not be on duty, but I'm afraid Mr. Laborero's death won't just go away, and that means that neither will the investigation into it." He sipped.

"Justice never sleeps, inspector?"

"I'd try not to put it too pompously, sir, but in essence, you're right. And so, despite this extremely agreeable whisky, I'm afraid I need to talk to you about the case."

Ewan leaned back in his chair, reached into a nearby locker, opened a box, and drew out a cigar, which he proceeded to light in a leisurely fashion as the inspector looked on in silence. He did not offer the box to the others. "Do you know what talks loudest around here, inspector?" he asked after several long moments, releasing a stream of smoke. "Money." He waved a hand to indicate the boat, the marina, the town bathed in the glow of an early Mediterranean evening. "This is a good place to be. And if it wasn't for the building trade on the Costa, there would be a lot of people a great deal worse off. Oh, I don't just mean in the building business itself, although I dare say you've heard enough stories about the hard times. Well, I can assure you, the times are not hard for everyone. One way and another, we provide a lot of money to the government – local government too, if you know what I mean."

"I believe I do, Mr. Husami. We've already gathered that much of the business depends heavily on… personal contacts? Would that be a good way of putting it?"

"I see you understand me, inspector. So I think you'll agree that the last thing I needed was for Juan to be taken out of the picture. I needed him for the contacts, because, let's be brutally honest, not everyone wants to do business with someone like me."

"Why would that be, sir?" enquired Copper. "From what you told us before, you've got businesses coming out of your ears."

"Some of our clients have rather fixed ideas," smiled Ewan. "Perhaps some of the Spanish – maybe a few of the East Europeans. I mean, I may sound Scottish, but I don't exactly look it."

"I still don't get it."

Ewan laughed. "I admire your innocence, sergeant. Let's just say that I'm a wee bit…" He searched for the right word. "… tanned for the liking of some clients."

"Oh." Dave Copper blushed as he caught on.

"So you see," continued Ewan, "Juan was very valuable. He looked after me, and I looked after him."

"Financially." Constable's statement was blunt.

"Yes, financially. And in other ways."

"But you weren't the only person he handled matters for."

"Indeed not, inspector. But just how well he looked after some other people, I really wouldn't care to say. But you might like to speak to Liza Lott – she has dealings with far more people than I ever do, being in contact with the public, so she may be able to help you out there."

Nice swerve, thought Constable. "That reminds me, sir," he said, as he emptied his tumbler and replaced it on the table. "Just one thing before we go. We've been told that on the evening of Mr. Laborero's death, Miss Lott was looking for him, and apparently she was concerned over the question of certification, and there was some mention of safety or security. It seems she was quite agitated, and I gather she went looking for you. Can you throw any light on what this may be all about?"

"If it's a question of certification, then perhaps she was worried about the signing-off of one of the building projects. It doesn't seem a likely topic of conversation for a house-warming party, does it? And as for security, inspector, then no doubt that would be something related to the site guards."

"How cynical would it be to ask if these would be yet more of your Moroccan cousins, Mr. Husami?" Constable raised an eyebrow.

"Ah, inspector, I do appreciate your sense of humour," responded Ewan. "But when the money is talking, who cares where the labour comes from, as long as it's cheap?"

Chapter 12

"That guy," remarked Dave Copper, "has got evasion off to a fine art." He leant against one of the ornamental cast-iron lamp standards adorning the promenade along San Pablo's sea front.

"Impressive, wasn't it?" agreed Andy Constable wryly. "I can never quite make up my mind whether people like that are evasive for the sheer hell of it, or because they've actually got something to hide."

"Both, I bet, guv. He's let enough things drop there to give one, as you might say, furiously to think."

"Been reading more 1930s detective fiction late at night, sergeant?"

"It's where I learnt all my best detective skills, sir," grinned Copper. "Anyway, do you propose to take Mr. Husami's hint and have further words with Liza Lott?"

"Why not? She's on the list. The only question is… " Constable stopped short. "Hell's teeth, Copper! How in the name of all that's holy did you do that?"

"What, guv?" asked the bewildered Copper.

"That!" Constable turned Copper through 180 degrees and pointed along the promenade. There, approaching a mere fifty yards away, a model of purposeful sophistication from her dark hair drawn back into a smooth chignon to the vivid scarlet patent shoes which matched her neat clutch bag, in a short clinging dress in a bold geometric black-and-white pattern and wearing white-rimmed mirrored sunglasses, came Liza Lott herself. "If you tell me that this is the product of your infamous power of positive thinking, I shall personally strangle you!"

"Nothing to do with me, guv," protested a smiling Copper. "But who says an honest policeman never gets an even break?"

As Liza Lott drew nearer, her pace seemed to falter for a moment as she recognised the two officers, but Constable was too quick to allow her to take avoiding action. "Miss Lott!" cried the inspector. "This is a happy coincidence. My colleague and I were just talking about you."

"Were you?" Liza sounded disconcerted.

"Oh, just in the way of normal chat," Constable reassured her. "I hope you don't mind me saying so, but you're looking extremely glamorous this evening. On your way somewhere nice, are you?"

"As it happens, yes, I am."

"Oh, that's a shame. I needed to have a further word with you, and this would have been the perfect opportunity. I don't suppose… you couldn't spare us a few minutes, could you? If I offer to buy you a coffee…?"

"Um… well, I suppose so."

"I hope whoever it is you're meeting won't mind if you're a couple of minutes late. Shall we…?" Constable indicated the glassed-in terrace of a smart ice-cream parlour on the opposite pavement. He stood back and invited Liza to lead the way.

"Smartly done, guv," murmured Dave Copper appreciatively.

"You're not the only one who can play the idiot when the need arises," responded Constable in similarly lowered tones. "Lull them into a false sense of security. Works nearly every time."

The coffee order executed, Constable leaned forward confidentially. "Miss Lott. You strike me as a woman with her finger very much on the pulse of things. I think you know pretty much what's going on in your little… well, perhaps not so little… circle of friends. Friends and business contacts, of course

– I realise that they're not necessarily the same thing. So I'm hoping you can provide me with some truths which I'm not always getting from other people."

"What do you mean, inspector? Where is this leading?"

"For a start, to the truth about Juan Manuel Laborero. When first we spoke to all the people who were present at Mr. Vere's party, everyone was singing Mr. Laborero's praises. Nobody could say enough good about him." Constable permitted himself a small dry smile. "To listen to you all, it was inconceivable that anyone should wish him harm, let alone murder him. But between you and me, the cracks are starting to show. I'm getting inconsistencies in what people are telling me. Now why would that be, do you suppose?"

Liza paused for a few seconds, then seemed to come to a conclusion. "You want the truth? Well, I hope you can handle the truth. So guess what? Juan Manuel was a scheming little rat who was only after one thing!"

Constable was taken aback at Liza's sudden vehemence. "Would it be indelicate to assume that the one thing you refer to would be…?" He let the query hang in the air.

"Actually, inspector, I lied. Two things. Apart from the obvious, which you have so cleverly worked out, if it hadn't been for the fact that he got very well paid, he wouldn't have cared a damn about whether X-Pat and I got this venture off the ground or not."

"Paid by yourself and Mr. Connor, you mean?"

"Think that if you like, inspector. But you ought to bear in mind that there are always two parties to any negotiation. Juan was a very… proficient middle-man. He had access to all the people X-Pat and I needed to start things up the way we wanted. And of course, once we started, we just kept going. Which has been fine up to now."

"And why would now be any different?" butted in Copper.

"Because of the investigation that they're talking about, sergeant."

"Of course. You remember, guv. Percy Vere told us his solicitor had mentioned something of the sort."

"So some people are running scared, is that what you're telling us?" resumed Constable.

Liza suddenly seemed to realise that she was getting into deeper water than she had intended. "I'm not admitting that there was anything illegal about our operation, inspector. There's a fine tradition around here – favours for favours, that's all." She snorted. "I dare say your friend the police captain could tell you a story or two in that line. Have you considered asking him a few questions instead of coming round bothering the rest of us? But X-Pat would have been in deep trouble if the paperwork had dried up, and Juan was the only one who knew all about it. So it wouldn't exactly have been in the best interests of either of us to go killing the man who helped us get our golden eggs, would it?"

"Personal matters aside, Miss Lott?"

"Personal matters aside," stated Liza firmly. "But as for that, Juan really didn't care what he did to get what he wanted. You try asking the sisterhood about that."

"And by the sisterhood you would mean…?"

"Mr. Constable." Liza stood. "You're not a stupid man. You work it out. And now, if you don't mind, I have somewhere to be, and I am late." Without a further word, she turned and crossed the road, and in moments was lost among the fiesta crowds still thronging the promenade and heading for the main square.

"You don't suppose she's heading off for an evening with Mr. Husami, do you, guv?" hazarded Dave Copper.

"I couldn't begin to guess," replied Constable. "But what an intriguing thought if she were. Business or pleasure, do you suppose?"

"On that subject, guv, you've still got a couple of ladies left on your list for a little light grilling. The sisterhood, as Miss Lott called them. Bit lacking in solidarity, isn't she? But if you think about it, I suppose they do fit quite neatly into the two categories."

"What are you talking about, man?"

"Business and pleasure, sir," explained Copper. "Roxanne Stone and Philippa Glass. Chalk and cheese. Hard-as-nails or kept woman. Quite a contrast. So shall we go a-hunting?"

"Copper, you sometimes have a very quaint turn of phrase." Constable heaved himself to his feet with a quiet groan. "I'm getting too old for this. And remind me never to accept any further invitations from you in future. You promised me a Spanish vacation – I didn't expect it to turn into a sort of Spanish investigation."

"No, guv." Copper struggled to keep a straight face. "But you know what they say – nobody expects the Spanish inv… "

"Don't you dare!" Constable attempted a stern glare, but couldn't quite manage to retain control of his features. He gave up the effort. "Alfredo has enough to do with one murder on his hands. You'd better not provoke me into making it two, although, given a dossier of your jokes, I don't think a jury would ever convict. Come on – let's go and check in with Alfredo and see if he's turned up anything useful."

At the branch police station at the urbanisation, all was in darkness.

"Part-timers, guv," commented Copper. "No commitment. Well, if Alfredo and his boys aren't working, I can't see that we should be beating our brains. Shall we pack it in for the evening and saunter down for a half? Or two? You can pretend you're on holiday like a normal human being."

As the detectives turned back towards their car, Constable

noticed a light in one of the offices above the shops across the road. "Somebody's working late," he remarked. "On a fiesta Sunday. That's dedication."

"Well, it's not Liza Lott, that's for sure," said Copper. "We know where she is. Maybe it's X-Pat Connor. He's got an office up there."

"Yes, but he's not likely to be schmoozing potential clients at this hour, is he? But we do know someone else who's got an office here, because Alfredo told us about it. Let's just saunter over the road and take a closer look. I have an instinct."

As the two Britons drew nearer, a figure could be indistinctly seen moving about behind the drawn blinds, and a legend in gold lettering could be discerned on the windows.

"Look, guv – 'Costamatcon S.A'," pointed out Dave Copper. "That's the company name on those invoices we found at X-Pat's office, isn't it? The company that does the building materials. Nice and snug, cheek by jowl with X-Pat's front operation. What a cosy little arrangement. Want to take a guess as to who's burning the… " He glanced at his watch. "… the mid-evening oil."

"Don't blither, Copper," said Constable. "We both know who it is. You've done it again. And when we get back to the U.K., I fully intend to have you burnt at the stake for witchcraft. If you could learn to rustle up suspects on demand like this at home, I might actually get all my scheduled days off when I'm supposed to. Now ring the damned doorbell, and we'll have that promised conversation with Mrs. Stone."

In response to the bell, swift footsteps sounded on the stairs behind the glazed door, and it opened to reveal the slightly breathless figure of Roxanne Stone. After a moment's pause, she registered the identity of her visitors.

"Oh. It's you."

"I'm afraid it is, Mrs. Stone," replied Constable in his most avuncular tones. "Sorry if we're a disappointment. Were you expecting someone else?"

"Yes... no... well, not really."

"I do apologise if we're disturbing you," continued Constable, "and it's pure chance that we're here, but we intended to call at the police station across the road to tell the Captain about some interesting information that's come into our possession, and we happened to notice that your office light was on. So on the off-chance that it might be you, we thought we might take the opportunity to have that second talk I mentioned. That's if it's not inconvenient."

Roxanne had recovered from her initial surprise. "Of course, inspector. Why not? To be frank, I'd welcome the interruption. I was just sorting out some paperwork, so a break will do me good. Come up, and I'll put the kettle on – don't they say policemen are always ready for a cup of tea? Do please go in and sit down." She led the way and disappeared into a tiny kitchenette at the head of the stairs.

"Hey, guv, what's this 'interesting information' that we're supposed to have?" hissed Dave Copper as they ascended in Roxanne's wake.

"Why don't we let her worry about that?" responded his superior in a similar undertone.

The office was furnished with two large leather sofas at right angles around a magazine-strewn coffee table in one corner, while in the other corner a desk and work station in chrome and glass were covered with files and documents apparently drawn from the open filing cabinet which stood alongside. A full shredder had been busy, to judge from the overflowing waste-bin next to it.

"Here we are, gentlemen." A smiling Roxanne deposited a tray on the coffee table and took a seat on one of the sofas, gesturing to the two policemen to seat themselves on the other.

"Here's something I don't very often get the chance to make – proper English builder's tea in mugs. All our Spanish boys bring bottles of water to work, or else they just disappear to the bar for a coffee at odd times. There's sugar there if you want it."

"Thank you, Mrs. Stone. Actually, I'm surprised to find you working. I would have thought you would be enjoying yourself with everyone else at the fiesta."

Roxanne smiled again. "Not this year, inspector. I'm afraid I've been here long enough to have grown rather blasé about the San Pablo fiesta. Very traditional, of course, but that means by definition that it's the same every year, so it's a case of 'seen one, seen 'em all'."

"So you're taking the chance to clear out some documents, by the look of it?" Copper glanced at the heaps of paperwork and the bulging refuse-bag by the shredder.

"Oh, just old files," said Roxanne. "Mostly paperwork to do with enquiries or projects that came to nothing. It was just cluttering up the place. I've been meaning to clear it all out for ages. And it gives me something to do."

"All on your own? That's a job and a half. Nobody to give you a hand?"

"Well... I thought perhaps X-Pat might pop up. After all, half of this is his. That's why you rather caught me by surprise – I half-thought you might be him. But I'm quite happy to do it by myself. Anyway, I don't suppose you want to talk about me, do you? You're still trying to find out about Juan Manuel, aren't you? So what is it you wanted to ask?"

"Actually, Mrs. Stone," resumed Constable, "it is about you – well, not specifically you, but we've had some conversations with Miss Lott and Mr Husami about various aspects of the case, and they have drawn our attention to the financial side of things. And of course, you are one of the many people whose financial dealings were intimately tied up with the activities of Mr. Laborero."

"Trust those two. Especially Ewan!" Roxanne Stone was dismissive. "That man thinks of nothing but money. He probably believes that there isn't anything that can't be bought. Or anybody!"

"And you don't agree?"

"It's not always about money, you know, inspector," said Roxanne in a calmer tone. "I was actually very fond of Juan, and I imagine the tongues have been wagging, so you'll already know that we did have a bit of a thing going at one time."

"I understand that you may have had something of a difficult time when you came to take over the business by yourself," probed Constable delicately.

"True. But that's all over now. A long time ago."

"And Mr. Laborero had… shall we say, moved on since then. And no hard feelings?"

"Look, inspector, I'm not blind, even if some people are. I don't care if he was mixed up with Philippa or not. That's their business. In fact, these days, like everyone else you meet, the only one I really care about is me."

Constable smiled gently. "So we can rule out a '*crime passionel*', then. Well, that's a step in the right direction. But it does leave us with the essential question of who might have wished Mr. Laborero harm, and for what reason. And I will happily confess that I'm a little puzzled as to why some people have praised him to the skies in one breath, and then damned him in the next. Would you have any thoughts on that?"

"More than you could possibly imagine, inspector," scoffed Roxanne. "In fact, if you were to come asking who would want Juan out of the way because they've got some nasty little secret, I could tell you plenty of stories."

"I'm here, Mrs. Stone," said Constable quietly. "Try me."

Roxanne seemed to make up her mind. "Right, inspector. For a start, I wonder how Ewan would fancy spending a lot more time with his father's side of the family. Some things can quite easily get you deported. Or worse. And I wonder what the sentence is these days for bribery of public officials. Fortunately, in my business, I don't come into contact with the authorities much, but I can think of one or two people who do. And would you like to find out what the inside of a Spanish prison looks like? I don't expect you would, and I'm sure I wouldn't. So you can see, there's a lot more for you to think about than the possibility of a non-existent crime of passion."

"Another crack in the facade of unity, guv," commented Copper as the two officers climbed back into their car. "When did all these lovely people start turning into ferrets in a sack?"

"About the time we started asking awkward questions, would be my guess," returned Constable. "Which makes things interesting. And now, if my calculations are correct, there's just one person outstanding on our talk-to list, and I shall pre-empt your fabled mystical powers by declaring positively that it is Miss Philippa Glass, whom I confidently expect to find behind the bar at the Runcorn."

"Does that make me superfluous to requirements, guv?"

"Never that, sergeant. You can have the pleasure of chauffeuring me back to the villa. We shall then stroll across to the bar, purchase a couple of drinks just as if we were innocent holiday-makers, and engage Miss Glass in casual conversation. We may glean all sorts of information without her even realising it."

"And you think she'll buy that, guv?" Dave Copper sounded highly dubious.

"Not a chance," laughed Constable. "But I thought I'd give your power of positive thinking a go. I could do with dusting off my acting skills."

At the Runcorn, two or three of the terrace tables were

occupied by young couples in the final stages of a meal or lingering over a bottle of wine, while the interior was silent save for the murmur of a television perched high in one corner of the bar, broadcasting a game show to an audience of empty chairs and tables. Philippa Glass, neat in jeans and a shirt knotted at the waist and with her hair caught back in a practical ponytail, was briskly straightening bottles behind the bar, replacing glasses in their racks, and seemingly engaged in the routine operations of tidying up at the end of the day.

"Good evening," she called as the two officers entered, accompanying the greeting with a bright professional smile. "Oh, hello," she added as she recognised her new customers. The smile faded slightly.

"Good evening, Miss Glass," replied Constable.

"It's Philippa. That is unless you're going to tell me that you're on duty and you've come to ask me more questions." Philippa's manner was confident and assured, a far cry from the nervousness she had displayed earlier in the day.

"By no means, Miss Glass… Philippa," returned Constable. "We've just come in for a quiet drink to relax. It's been quite a full day."

"Yes, I guess it has." Philippa's tone held reservations. "Anyway, what are you having?"

"You seem very quiet in here this evening," remarked Constable as Philippa poured their drinks. "Is it normally like this on a Sunday?"

"No, normally we're very busy," replied Philippa. "But most people have gone into town for the fiesta procession and the fireworks, so there's not much going on. We won't get much more in the way of customers tonight, so the cook's just gone as well."

"And you're here on your own."

"Yes."

"Not quite the image of the Spanish bar that everyone thinks of at home, though, is it?" commented Copper. "I mean, crowds of happy tourists, all the local Brits in here talking about football and the winter fuel allowance, landlady perched on a bar-stool doing her Peggy Mitchell impersonation – it's not quite the social whirl of the T.V. programmes, is it. I bet it can get quite lonely at times."

"I suppose so," admitted Philippa.

"Still, if you've got friends… "

Philippa broke off from unloading a glass-washing machine and rounded on Copper. "You're fishing, aren't you?" she said suspiciously. "I might have known. Never trust a policeman. You come in here all innocent, but you're still sniffing around to see what dirt you can find out." A thought struck her. "You've been talking to Eve, haven't you? Well, if you want to know something, why don't you come straight out and ask me?"

"We've been talking to a number of people, Miss Glass." Constable declined to reveal the sources of any of his information. "But yes, it has been mentioned that there were tensions between certain people over the nature of your friendship with Mr. Laborero."

Philippa flushed. "I wish people would mind their own damned business instead of gossiping about things that don't concern them," she said hotly. "And I don't see what good it does for you to start stirring up trouble for me where none exists."

"You know, Miss Glass, I think you're deceiving yourself if you think no trouble exists," countered Constable patiently. "We've heard from more than one source that you and Mr. Laborero were involved with one another, so I think it's pointless for you to deny it. On top of that, we know perfectly well that Mr. Connor had got wind of the relationship, and that there was some sort of confrontation between you and him at Mr. Vere's house. And, in addition, I can't so far find anyone who will tell me that they saw Mr. Laborero after you followed him out into the darkened garden on the night of the party. Now, in my book, that all adds up to quite a lot of trouble."

"It's all lies," blustered Philippa, with a quaver in her voice. "I told X-Pat, Juan and I were just friends, nothing more, and if he believes me, I don't see why you shouldn't. It's mad for anyone to think I had anything to do with his death. And as for Friday night, you can say what you like, but nobody can prove that I was the last one to see him alive, because there were loads of people looking for him that night. I was with Eve a lot of the time – you just ask her if you don't believe me."

"We already have done," said Constable shortly. "And what she tells us, I'm afraid, goes nowhere near clearing you of suspicion. And I have to tell you that the Spanish police also have items in their possession that have nothing to do with your personal relationships – items that they may well want you to explain."

"But it's not as if Juan knew anything about me." Philippa was sounding increasingly desperate. "Well, not that I'd want to kill him for, anyway. You want to look at some other people if you want that sort of motive."

"And where might I want to look, Miss Glass?"

"Tim," blurted Philippa. "Juan got bashed with a piece of wood, didn't he? Well, Tim's the wood expert around here. I wouldn't want to be in his shoes. The police are going to want to check up on his actions, I bet, and there are a few others who've got some explaining to do." She seemed to recover a little of her self-possession.

"Including your Mr. Connor?" suggested Constable gently.

"Look," said Philippa. "X-Pat's got nothing to do with this. I'm very happy with him, and we've got a very good life together, so why would I put that at risk?"

As the two detectives left the now deserted Runcorn, the sky over the hill, beyond which the old town of San Pablo nestled around the harbour, was suddenly lit up by extravagant showers of red and silver sparkling light, as the sound of distant explosions drifted through the night air.

"Fireworks tonight, guv," said Copper. "Looks as if the Spanish like to celebrate their fiestas with a bang."

"Fireworks tomorrow, with a bit of luck, if I can get my thinking straight," replied Constable. "I am damned if I'm going home without this case sorted out. I'm sure we're nearly there. I need a good night's sleep." He turned and headed for the '*Casa del Torero*'.

Chapter 13

"Tea up!" carolled Dave Copper as he pushed open the door of Andy Constable's bedroom with a bare foot. "Eight o'clock! Can't moulder in bed on our last day!" He stopped short. The bed was certainly not being mouldered in. The shutters stood fully open with the sun streaming in, the bedclothes were thrown back, but of the inspector there was no sign. Viewed from the balcony, the pool below lay silent and ripple-free. "Fine," muttered Copper as he placed both steaming mugs on the balcony table and slumped into a chair. "I'll drink it myself, then."

The sound of the doorbell brought him swiftly to his feet again. "Daft sod's forgotten the key," he thought to himself. "Why doesn't he come round the side? And where's he been off to at this hour?" He padded to the door with a selection of quips forming in his brain.

"Good morning. I hope I am not too early to call." Captain Alfredo took in the colourful design of Copper's boxers but forbore to comment. "Have I wake you out of bed?"

"What? Oh… no," replied Copper in slight confusion. "Morning, Captain. Come on in. No, I was up. I'd just made some tea. Would you like a cup?"

"No, thank you," declined Alfredo gracefully. "I have coffee in the morning, but I have just had some. No, I am afraid I am here on business. Can I speak to Andy please? It is a little urgent."

"Oh no," returned Copper with a groan. "Don't tell me you've found another one!"

"Another one what?" frowned Alfredo.

"Another dead body. This place is starting to look like Cabot Cove!"

"Cabot…? I do not understand."

"Never mind. But is it?"

"Is it what?"

"A body!" Dave Copper felt as if he was hanging on to his sanity by his fingernails.

"No, no, not at all. Sorry." Alfredo was apologetic. "I did not mean to make you think that. No, it is just that I have some information, and I think it will be useful if you know it as soon as possible because I am sure it will be important for the investigation. So I have come to tell you and Andy."

"You can't, I'm afraid. He's disappeared."

"What?" Now it was Alfredo's turn to look disconcerted. "When did this happen? Why have you not told me this at once?"

Dave Copper laughed. "No, I don't mean disappeared as in… 'disappeared'. I just mean he's not here. I just took him some tea, but he's nowhere to be seen. He's obviously gone off somewhere for one of his thinking sessions. He does that. Do you want to come in and wait?" He stood back from the door to allow Alfredo to enter. "Mind you, I've no idea where he's gone or how long he'll be, but I could make you a coffee if you like. We've only got instant, I'm afraid." And as Alfredo smilingly shook his head, "Well… have a seat anyway. I'll… er… I'll get some kit on, then."

The white sand beach stretched north from the San Pablo headland for several miles in a gentle curve, with the city of Alicante rising out of the morning haze in the distance. At seven-thirty, the sun had not yet had the chance to dispel the fresh chill left over from a night of clear skies, but there was already a promise of warmth as the day grew older. Apart from a very distant solitary figure walking a large dog, Andy Constable was alone as he strolled along at the water's edge, shoes in his hand, stepping over the edges of the gently-lapping wavelets with a faint smile on his face. Just like every case we ever get, he thought. The facts come at you in a constant procession, and at the start of things, you've no idea which is going to be important and which you can ignore. And just as crucial, which facts are not what they seem to be, and which ones are going to point you in completely the wrong direction. He gazed up at the blue sky with just a few ribbons of tinted clouds low towards the horizon. Last day in Spain. Time for marshalling the facts into some sort of order, and where better than a lonely beach with no distractions and a clear brain? Right – what have we got?

Juan Manuel Laborero, obviously. You don't get a murder case without a victim, and how many times had it been said that the victim is so often the most important clue when starting any investigation. Constable had always insisted on drilling that vital rule into every junior officer who had ever worked with him – know the man, and you know his murderer. Well, not invariably, but it was a very good place to begin. And nothing was ever as simple as it first appeared. At the start, it had seemed that Juan was the darling of all and sundry, charming, helpful, blessed with a string of excellent contacts which oiled the works for everyone. Constable smiled to himself. First impressions, eh? It was quite a journey from Percy Vere's description of Juan as 'keeping the wheels turning' to Liza Lott's characterisation of him as 'a scheming little rat'. The question was, how to disentangle the various strands of information. 'Know the man' is a very fine maxim, he thought, but how often do you actually know the victim other than from what others say about them? Once in an extremely blue moon, was the rueful reply. So everything's hearsay, and everything is slanted according to the relationship between the victim and the informant. So what was Juan Manuel Laborero to each of the people in the case?

It was clear that there were two sorts of relationships, the personal and the professional, and sometimes a convoluted mix of the two. Take Philippa Glass, for instance. It was pretty clear from what Eve Stropper had told the detectives that there was a continuing affair between Juan and Philippa which was nowhere near as secret as the latter appeared to believe. Was she fooling herself, or were the increasingly desperate denials a way to divert attention from herself and towards her notoriously short-tempered and violent lover, Xavier Patrick Connor? But Philippa was not the only woman to have been involved with Juan. Although it had not been spelt out in so many words, it seemed obvious that Liza Lott and Juan had also had an affair in the past. How serious it had been was impossible to tell, but it was evident that it had left some sort of scars on Liza's psyche. 'Only after one thing', Liza had said of Juan. No woman likes to think she is being used, so could it be that Liza's groomed and glossy exterior hid a seething resentment over Juan's treatment of her, a resentment which had tipped over at some as-yet-undisclosed trigger? And there again, there seemed to be no attempt to conceal Roxanne Stone's emotional involvement with Juan, at least not after the death of her husband. Beforehand, it looked as if the participants in the affair had at least preserved some half-decent discretion in preventing the relationship coming to the attention of the late Ed Stone, again according to Eve, but afterwards was a different matter. But on Roxanne's evidence, her affair with Juan was long over, and apparently with no hard feelings on her part. She professed a total lack of interest as to whether Juan was involved with Philippa Glass or not. But on the other hand, Roxanne was described by Eve as being 'very close' to Tim Berman at present. Constable laughed quietly. If it weren't for people in the business of supplying alcohol, he thought to himself, I wouldn't get half the information that comes my way. Maybe it's something in the personality of pub landlords and barmaids that encourages confidences and draws out facts which sometimes people would prefer remain concealed. And coupled with Eve's snippet, and Walter Torrance's evidence that Tim went looking for Juan on the night of the party, was it possible to construct a scenario whereby Tim was holding some sort of lingering grudge, however unjustified, over Roxanne's previous involvement with Juan, which might cause him to wish the Spaniard harm? In Eve's view, somebody had tipped X-Pat off about Juan and Philippa. Could that have been Tim, in an attempt to get someone else to do his dirty work for him and keep his own hands clean? Far-fetched, but not impossible.

Constable restrained himself. Let's not get too far ahead of ourselves, he thought. Constructing over-elaborate accusations on flimsy evidence was never going to be productive, when there were much more obvious explanations. Of course Roxanne was very close to Tim, but that needn't necessarily mean emotionally. They worked in very close association, supplying and handling materials all through the business of villa construction which lay at the heart of the narrow circle of people caught up in the case. The two diverging invoices were the only piece of concrete evidence of Walter's assertion that the building business was full of people on the fiddle, but they did not stand alone. Running all through the conversations which Constable had had with suspects and witnesses alike was a constant stream of references to bureaucracy, permits, contacts, and cash flow. Liza and X-Pat were in perpetual negotiation with the authorities for the permissions without which their businesses simply could not function. Ewan Husami was the spider at the centre of a web of enterprises supplying design services, work personnel, and travel arrangements for builders and their clients alike. Was it possible to imagine more fruitful soil for the propagation of a culture of corruption where, according to Ewan, everybody had their price? And a brown envelope full of unmarked notes had been found in Juan's own car. Where had they come from, and what was the meaning of 'the next three'? Three what? Projects? Permits? People? And how much did twelve thousand Euros buy in whatever context? Who was the buyer? And could even Walter himself be ruled out, or was his pointing the finger at Roxanne and Tim, subtle though it was, a classic diversionary tactic to draw attention away from his own wrong-doings? After all, it was in Walter's own trench that the body of the dead man had been found. And everywhere you looked, in the whole convoluted network of contacts, there was Juan Manuel Laborero. He was the man who knew everyone, he was the man who knew everything about everybody. The cliche from all those dreadful old gangster movies, thought Constable – 'you know too much!'.

Constable grunted. In my case, he mused, there's too much I don't know. There was the question of the two anonymous communications, for instance. At least it was plain who was the recipient in each case. The note to Ewan clearly contained some kind of threat, but why had it been found on Juan's person? Was it from him to Ewan, but had he not yet had the chance to pass it on? Or was it from a third person, in which case, had Juan intercepted it before it got to Ewan, or had Ewan received it but then afterwards passed it on to Juan? What could the reason be for doing so? What a blessing it would be, thought Constable, if this blasted fiesta hadn't closed down all the avenues of forensic investigation. I might not feel as if I were thrashing around in treacle, and I might know who'd had their mitts on some of these things instead of having to guess all the way through. Another threat was implicit in the message left on Juan's mobile phone. The text spoke of dangerous business, and private arrangements, but were the business and the arrangements of a personal or commercial nature? And was the threat an actual physical one such as a violent man might use, or was it the more impotent threat of a woman who felt her position to be insecure? Yet another matter where a little technical assistance would answer a myriad of questions.

What about that coastal map on Tim Berman's office wall? Did that have any significance, other than the obvious one of showing a good place to fish? According to Walter, Tim enjoyed fishing, but he was not the only one. So did the many cousins of Ewan Husami, some of whose identity cards had been found hidden, not so efficiently, among Philippa Glass's property. But what did the 12.30 written on the map mean? Mid-day, or midnight? The latter time might be a very convenient cover for something which someone did not wish to be observed. Constable had his own very clear views as to what the likely explanation for this might be. But as to why the cards would be in Philippa's possession was not at all clear to him. Was she in some way mixed up with the activities concerned, or had someone else taken the opportunity to conceal, not very expertly, a piece of damning evidence when the police came calling? Except, of course, that nobody had expected the police to come calling at that particular time, and Philippa was the only person in the house when they did. So was she, for all her professions of innocence, somehow involved with Ewan Husami in some manner which had not yet been revealed?

This is ridiculous, thought Constable. So far, all I'm getting is more and more questions and precious few answers, with suspects coming out of our ears. There must be some positive factors. Well, for a start, we can narrow the field. Wipe out that gaggle of building workers who were there at the start of the party. They were long gone by the time Juan met his fate – indeed, he saw them off the premises himself. And at least Percy Vere seemed to be in the clear. For all that he would have very obvious reasons to dislike Juan Manuel if ever the latter's presumed underhand dealings in connection with Percy's villa should come to light, there was no hint that they had done so, and indeed, Percy had been among the foremost in lauding Juan's talents. Of course, that might have been all pretence – a few unguarded words overheard would have been sufficient, and Percy was not an unintelligent man. Indeed, Percy had overheard certain things at his party which might admit of an other-than-innocent explanation, but as far as could be ascertained, Percy was in plain view during the entire evening, throwing himself into his pleasurable duties as host with gusto. No, after Juan had disappeared into the dusk of the garden, Percy had never had the opportunity to seek him out. And even if he had, Constable could not quite visualise the elderly dapper gentleman creeping around a darkened garden with a baulk of timber in his hand, intent on wreaking vengeance on his betrayer.

Eve too could be eliminated. If there were one thing Eve could be accused of, it was her ready willingness to reveal information, a far cry from her self-professed discretion. By all accounts, she had never left the interior of the villa between her arrival and her departure, and indeed, a great deal of her time had been spent in Percy's company, or else directing the long list of people who were at one time or another looking for Juan out into the darkened garden where he had last been seen. At one time or another, mused Constable. Timings could very well be at the heart of the mystery. A re-visit of Dave Copper's notes might prove productive, but there was still something elusive as to which, out of all the motives under consideration, was the one which held the key. The killer motive, he thought with a smile.

The inspector looked at his watch. Half past eight. Time to get back to the villa, before Copper started to put two and two together over Constable's absence and called out the local force on a missing person search. He trudged up the yielding sands towards the grass-dotted dunes and, reaching the road, sat and dusted off his feet, replaced his trainers, and began the walk up the long curving hill in the direction of the '*Casa del Torero*'.

"Morning, guv." Dave Copper opened the apartment door to his slightly-puffing superior. "What happened to you, then? I thought you'd done a runner because it had all got too much for you."

"Nothing of the kind, young David, as you should be very well aware. When did you ever know me allow a case to get the better of me? No, I just wanted a bit of quiet time to chew over all the facts and the people, so I've been for a walk along the beach. And very agreeable it was."

"Get anywhere?"

"Only to the end of the beach." Constable gave a grin. "No, I've had a few thoughts, some of which I hope I can hit on the head… "

"Ouch! Not very tasteful, under the circumstances, guv."

"Hmm, no, perhaps you're right." The inspector cast his eyes briefly upwards. "Sorry, Juan. But no, in answer to your question, I'm still thinking."

"That's what I reckoned, guv. That's what I told Alfredo."

"Alfredo? He's been here?"

"He's still here. He turned up a while ago. For a minute, from what he said, I had the ghastly feeling that they'd turned up another body, but fortunately not. One's enough, I reckon. But apparently there's some information come his way which he thinks is important, so he popped in here to pass it on. He's sat down by the pool waiting. I offered him a coffee, but he said no."

"I'm not at all surprised," said Constable. "I've tasted your coffee. But I could murder a cup of tea." He lifted his eyes once more. "Sorry again, Juan. Right, let's find out what is so urgent that it brings the police chief calling before breakfast."

"Good morning, Andy." Alfredo stood and offered his hand. "I would apologise for calling on you so early, but I see that you are up even before me today."

"Absolutely," confirmed Constable. "I've been down at the beach to have a bit of a think. You know, fresh day, fresh air, fresh thoughts. You never know what's going to occur to you when you've got no other distractions."

"I know what you mean," agreed Alfredo ruefully. "Some days, I am so busy that I do not actually have time to do my job."

"David says you've got something for us. Oh, thanks," he added, as Dave Copper placed two mugs of tea on the table, and the three sat. "Sure you won't have something?"

"No." Alfredo shook his head. "But I thought you should know this thing. My Commander has been in contact with me, and he has news which I think may be important. He has been told that Juan Manuel Laborero had made an arrangement for seeing a senior officer at the regional police headquarters in the city at half past twelve o'clock tomorrow. I have looked in his office diary that we found, and it is so. There is the time noted, but it does not say for what."

Dave Copper was taken aback. "That's a bit of a turn-up, isn't it, guv? Have they got any idea what it was all about, Alfredo?"

"Yes and no. He informed them that he had information for them concerning a serious crime, which he would be willing to reveal to them in exchange for personal immunity."

"And did he give any inkling as to what this crime was?" asked Constable. "Because it seems to me that there's no great shortage of crimes and misdemeanours going on around here, from everything I've heard so far."

"No, that was all," replied Alfredo. "He refused to say anything more before the meeting."

"And you knew nothing of this?"

"No. It was all done with very great secrecy. I think he must have been afraid of what would happen if the fact should be known."

"And he was right," said Constable heavily. "And I would be prepared to bet a very large amount that, if we knew what he was intending to reveal, we'd have this business wrapped up in five seconds flat. Oh well," he continued, getting to his feet, "we'll just have to rely on good old brain-power."

"You know, guv, in a way, it's almost a pity that Alfredo didn't have another body to chuck into the mix this morning. It might have made things easier."

"What?" Alfredo sounded incredulous. "You say you want another murder?"

"Well, no, not actually another murder as such," explained Copper hastily. "But the guv here's got a theory – one murder can be a pig to sort out, but if you've got two, sometimes you can make a link which points you in the right direction. Remember that business at Dammett Hall, guv? The only trouble here is, I can't see how on earth we're going to be able to make a connection, no pun intended, between Mr. Rookham and his electrics and Juan Manuel and his building works."

"Yes, well, you keep thinking, sergeant," said Constable condescendingly. "I'm sure you'll come up with something if you towse your brain hard enough. In the meantime, if you'll excuse me, Alfredo, I'm going to go and have my shower. I missed it this morning because I didn't want to wake Sleeping Beauty here too early." He nodded to indicate Copper. "He needs all the beauty sleep he can get. And brain rest," he added, as he started up the stairs to the upper floor. "We'll talk things over between ourselves – that's if I can get Copper here to think sensibly for a change – and come up and see you later, if that's okay." He vanished into his room, and moments later the sound of a running shower could be heard.

"Is he angry with you?" enquired Alfredo delicately.

"No, no, don't worry about that," smiled Copper. "That's just his way. He gets a bit snappy sometimes when he's frustrated. I reckon he's probably suffering from information overload, but he'll sort himself out."

Suddenly, a loud cry echoed from above.

"What the hell…?" Copper sprang in the direction of the spiral stairs, as Andy Constable, dripping and wrapped in a hastily-flung towel around his waist, appeared in the doorway of his room.

"David – you're a bloody genius!"

"Dear God!" responded Copper with relief. "Hearing you yell, I thought for a minute we'd had that second murder after all."

"Stop talking rubbish," said Constable, as he clattered down the stairs to the terrace, "and get me that notebook of yours."

"Panic not, guv," replied Copper calmly, pulling it from the pocket of his shorts. "Here it is, always with me as instructed."

"Let's have a look." Constable grabbed the notebook and hastily leaved through the pages, flicking rapidly backwards and forwards while the others watched bemused. He finally closed the book and sighed. A slow beaming smile appeared on his face. "Gotcha!" He handed the book back. "Thank you, David."

Dave Copper laughed. "And there we have it, Alfredo. Archimedes has had his 'eureka' moment. Thank goodness you kept the towel on, guv."

"What? I am sorry, I do not understand." Alfredo looked utterly baffled.

"By George, he's got it!" chuckled Copper. "I take it you have got it, sir?"

"Do you know, Sergeant, I do believe I have. And when I've got myself dried off, I shall sit down with that little book of yours and go through things in rather more detail, but I think we're there."

"Do you mean...?" Alfredo caught on. "You know who killed Juan Manuel?"

"That, and a great deal besides," answered Constable. He practically skipped with delight, so far as the modestly-sized towel would permit, and saved it with a quick grab as it showed signs of slipping off. "Oh, I do love it when a plan comes together."

"And you're not going to tell us right now, are you, guv?" Copper turned to Alfredo. "That's another one of the things he does," he remarked in an undertone. "Drives me loopy."

Andy Constable ignored his junior officer. "Alfredo, if you don't mind me suggesting, here's what I reckon you ought to do. Call up all the people in the case, and tell them each that you've received some sort of new information that you'd like to discuss with them. Don't let on what it is – try and be a little mysterious if you can, but don't make it sound too serious. We don't want anyone taking fright and heading for the hills prematurely. See if you can possibly not let on that you're getting in touch with everyone, but get them together in one place today sometime if you can. Your station up at the top would probably be best – and if you'll take my advice, you might like to call in a couple of your boys as back-up and make sure you've got the keys to the cells handy. You might have one or two arrests to make."

Alfredo did not seem to object at all to Constable taking control of the case in such an incisive manner. "If this is what you wish, Andy, then of course I will trust your judgement. I will do this. You say all the people – do you really mean everyone who was at the party on Friday?"

Constable considered for a moment. "No, perhaps not absolutely everyone. I think you can leave Percy Vere out of it, and Eve Stropper's also in the clear, so you can give her a miss. After all," he smiled, "someone's got to run your bar. Oh, and don't bother with all the builder's lads – they were long gone before anything happened, so let's not clutter the place up with them. So that leaves… " He ticked them off on his fingers. "X-Pat Connor and Philippa Glass, Tim Berman and Roxanne Stone, Walter Torrance, Ewan Husami, and Liza Lott. Yes, I think that'll do."

"And then you will tell me what happened?"

"With the greatest of pleasure."

"Then I will start to call people, and I will telephone you when it is all arranged."

"Excellent. And I will now go and actually have that shower. Isn't it amazing what beneficial effects a little running water can have?" Constable took a firmer grip on the wayward towel and made his way back upstairs.

"That," commented Copper to Alfredo in reference to the retreating back, "is one very happy detective inspector. You can tell he enjoys his work."

"Sometimes there are good days," agreed Alfredo. "And now I also have my work to do. I will speak to you later." He made his way out through the terrace arch towards the road, as Dave Copper seated himself once again, leaned back, and took another sip of his by now stone-cold tea.

Chapter 14

As the captain led the way past his junior officers into the large interview room, closely followed by the inspector and the sergeant, seven faces turned towards him with varying degrees of apprehension and irritation. X-Pat Connor was first on his feet with a now customarily belligerent challenge.

"Look here, Captain, I would like to know why you've got us all up here like this. You told me you had something you wanted to talk to Phil and me about – I presume this is all to do with the business of Juan Manuel, although you weren't exactly forthcoming when you rang – and then when we arrive you put us in here with everybody else, without so much as a word of explanation, with your two dobermans lurking outside like a pair of prison guards. And here we sit round the walls, like people in a dentist's waiting room, and nobody has a clue as to what you're up to."

"Sit down, Mr. Connor," said Alfredo calmly but firmly. "It will all be explained to you."

"I hope very much that it will, captain," interposed Ewan Husami easily. "Are you proposing to put us under some kind of detention? If you are, maybe I should be giving my lawyer a ring."

"Probably another one of his bloody cousins," hissed Dave Copper into Andy Constable's ear.

"As you all will know," continued Alfredo, "I have been faced with a murder case at not a good time for me. The fiesta this weekend has caused great disruption to the police services which I can use. But by great luck, I have here Detective Inspector

Constable and Detective Sergeant Copper, who had been able to help me with another matter – the death of Mr. Rookham at the television company."

"What, the guy at CostaLot?" asked Walter Torrance. "I heard about that. But I thought that was some sort of accident. Are you telling us that these two are out here from the U.K. on some sort of investigation into... well, you tell me?"

"Not at all, Mr. Torrance," replied Alfredo. "But it was, how shall I say, convenient if you all believed that. No, my English colleagues are in fact simply here on their holiday. And when Mr. Laborero was found dead, and it seemed to me that all the people who might be involved were British, I wondered also if I could – what is the saying? – push my luck, and ask Andy and Dave here – I hope you do not mind me calling you that – to help me. Because they know much better than I do how the British mind works. They might understand how a person might not be telling the truth when the signs were not clear for me. When I first met them, I too made the mistake to think that maybe they are here working on a case. I remember saying that I hoped that they were not here on a busman's holiday. But now I am very grateful that for them it has *become* a busman's holiday."

"This is all very nice and cosy," interrupted Liza Lott, "but do you intend to cut to the chase any time soon? Is all this rigmarole a lead-up to someone telling us who killed Juan?"

"Yes," answered Alfredo simply.

"Well then, for goodness sake, drop the other shoe and get on with it," said Tim Berman.

"Then I will ask my colleague here to take over," said Alfredo, seating himself behind the interviewer's desk and gesturing Andy Constable forward. The inspector took a slow look at the circle of faces around him, smiled faintly, and perched himself on the front of the desk, as Dave Copper eased himself unobtrusively into a chair next to the door.

Constable drew a deep breath and let out a gusty sigh. "Do you know the one thing that puzzles me in this whole business," he mused, almost to himself. "How on earth did Juan Manuel Laborero manage to get away with it for so long? And why was he in a position of power over the fates of so many people?" In response to the disconcerted glances exchanged between those surrounding him, he continued. "The answer is, of course, that he was useful. How many times have I had that said to me? Since even before Juan was found dead, when Percy Vere was telling us the saga of his villa. But there is an inherent problem – there's always the possibility of a bit of grit in the oyster, and that doesn't invariably lead to a pearl. Being useful can sometimes be dangerous. If someone knows too much about you, you can feel threatened. What if a clash of interests arises? What if they decide that their interests are more important than yours?"

"But we've all got our own different interests," said Roxanne Stone. "You're not telling us anything we don't all know already. But if everyone's told you all the positives about Juan, why wouldn't you believe it? I know as far as I'm concerned, my business is going to be a great deal more difficult to run without Juan around. I'm speaking for myself, but I'm sure I'm not the only one who's going to have problems without him to help out. Now that's self-interest, if you like." She looked around the room, and was rewarded with a few murmurs and nods of agreement.

"Nice try, Mrs. Stone," responded Constable, "but I'm afraid it won't wash. The facade of universal approval didn't last very long, I'm afraid. So I've heard differing stories at different times, and I've managed to build up quite an interesting picture which, in one way or another, would give each one of you a motive, to a greater or lesser degree, to want Juan dead."

"What, all of us?" said Philippa Glass. "That's ridiculous!"

"Perhaps not all of you, Miss Glass. But enough of you to make a really complicated picture. Enough to make me consider all of you as suspects." The word fell heavily, and was greeted by a brief stunned silence.

"Yes, suspects," went on Constable. "Something of an old-fashioned word, I grant you, but then, some of my colleagues would probably describe me as something of an old-fashioned policeman." He permitted himself a dry smile and glanced at Dave Copper. "Feel free to confirm that, sergeant, if you like. Maybe that puts me out of synch with a lot of the technology we've got these days to help us out, but as Captain Alfredo here has pointed out, I haven't had access to that in this instance. And I'm working to a deadline. I'm flying back to the U.K. tomorrow, and I'm not a man who likes to leave loose ends lying around, so I've been forced to do this the old-fashioned way – good old brain-power. What my young colleague here is always advocating as the power of positive thinking. Now I'm quite fond of the old certainties, the old procedures. I don't say I always follow them, as Copper here will no doubt tell you, but it's nice to have the landmarks fixed so that you know what you're ignoring. And the landmark questions in a murder case have always been, who had the motive, the means, and the opportunity? Well, the means we're pretty certain of. I dare say the labs will confirm it quickly enough when they actually get on the case, but I don't think I'm going to quarrel with a theory which puts together a massive head wound and a blood-stained chunk of timber and comes up with the answer 'murder weapon'. So the means are pretty clear. As to the opportunity – well, I'll come on to that a bit later. But when it comes to motives, I'm practically falling over them at every turn.

"So, what did each of the suspects have to hide? There is certainly no shortage of guilty secrets, as some of you yourselves have pointed out." There was a perceptible change in the atmosphere in the room – an almost palpable sharpening of attention. Constable took great care that his gaze did not fall on any particular individual. "Yes, you may think of yourselves as a group of close friends and colleagues, but self-preservation is a powerful instinct. So, was this drip-drip of compromising facts about some others in the group an attempt by some to divert suspicion away from themselves?"

"Inspector," interrupted Liza again, "you sit there spouting generalities, but you haven't said a thing that's relevant to why we've been called here."

"Thank you for the prompt, Miss Lott. I'll come to the point if you wish. But don't disparage the power of conversation. We've learnt a great deal from our conversations with various people, and certain witnesses have given us plenty of information from which to put together our jigsaw. So I'll happily start with you. Now Mr. Vere told us all about the bureaucracy involved in the building of his new villa. I think you told us something about that yourself. And you and Mr. Connor here worked very closely together to get the right paperwork so that there shouldn't be any snags in the way of your developing schemes. But I'm thinking that some of this paperwork seems to have come at a price. One very interesting thing which our Spanish colleagues here found when they examined Mr. Laborero's car was an envelope with a significant amount of cash in it, running to several thousand Euros. Those ever-popular 'unmarked bills' so beloved in fiction. The bills might have been unmarked, but the envelope wasn't. Clearly addressed to JML – Juan Manuel Laborero – it bore the message 'For the next 3'."

"Why would you think that's got anything to do with me?" objected Liza. "It could mean anything."

"It could indeed," agreed Constable. "But Walter Torrance happened to drop into one of our conversations that it was, and I think I'm quoting him correctly from memory, 'amazing what permits she manages to get hold of'. He was referring to you, Miss Lott. And Mr. Vere himself had heard rumours about a forthcoming investigation into corruption involving fake building permits. I do wonder why such an otherwise shrewd former businessman didn't put two and two together, but then, like me, I suspect he's a bit old-fashioned, and maybe he's inclined to believe the best of everybody. I, on the other hand, being a sceptical policeman, do not. And here we had Juan Manuel, right in the middle of all the negotiations, translating where his clients could have no idea whether he was rendering the facts accurately, and generally fixing things. This may come as news to many of you, but Mr. Laborero was due to meet with the police authorities tomorrow. So we ask ourselves, with all this information in his possession and an investigation on the horizon, was he planning to turn police evidence? Did he mean to jump before he was pushed?"

Liza's eyes went from side to side, and she drew breath as if to reply, only to bite it back. Constable looked evenly at her for a moment, and then turned his attention to the other side of the room, where Philippa Glass sat, hands twisting nervously, her gaze fixed on the floor.

"Now, Miss Glass." Philippa's head came up sharply. "For no particular reason, let's turn to you and have a little chat about what guilty secrets you have to hide."

"I don't know what you're talking about," stated Philippa defiantly. "I've got nothing to hide."

Constable gave a pitying smile. "Do you know, Miss Glass, I'm inclined to agree with you. But I suspect that's because, rather like Mr. Vere, you may be disposed to believe the best of your friends. But yes, I apologise if I'm thought to be making trouble for you in your personal relationships, but I'm dealing with the truth here, and nothing should be allowed to stand in the way of that. You did have a secret. Possibly only the one – I still haven't come to a definite conclusion about some little cards which you may or may not have known about, but perhaps we'll come to those later – and even that one secret wasn't such a secret as you may have thought. Your... let's put it no stronger than 'friendship', shall we... your friendship with Juan Manuel Laborero was well known to your friend at the bar, Eve Stropper, but *baristas*, unlike barristers, are not exactly notorious for keeping secrets."

Philippa turned huge moist eyes towards her lover. "X-Pat, don't listen to him," she pleaded frantically. "There really wasn't anything in it, and we never... I mean, I wouldn't... "

X-Pat threw off the hand placed on his arm in appeal. "Don't touch me, you little... I warned you," he grated. "I told you... "

"Be quiet, Mr. Connor!" Inspector Constable's voice cut sharply through the rising tone of X-Pat's fury. "I really would advise you to say as little as possible at the moment, for your own good. If you want to consider that as an official warning, please feel free to do so." X-Pat subsided into smouldering silence, but his eyes continued to burn, and he eased himself away from his former close proximity to Philippa.

"So there, I think," continued Constable calmly, "is the illustration of your problem, Miss Glass. I mention nothing more than 'friendship', and we have a demonstration of the possible consequences. So were you afraid that your undeniably comfortable lifestyle was about to be snatched away, simply because of – forgive the bluntness – a bit on the side? Did you in fact kill Juan in a panic in order to prevent the truth emerging? Or should we consider the other side of the coin? Mr. Connor, should I entertain the possibility that your violent threats against the man who was playing around with your girlfriend, threats which I'm afraid Miss Glass herself revealed to one of our informants, were translated into reality? So there, Mr. Connor, I've got two very plausible scenarios whereby Mr. Laborero was highly prejudicial to your interests – one personal, and the one I've already referred to, in your business dealings with Miss Lott."

"This is all moonshine," riposted X-Pat. "You're grabbing facts out of the air and twisting them together to make up some wild accusations. Nobody could possibly believe all this wild fantasy."

"I think you'll find they could, Mr. Connor. But if you think that's wild fantasy, I could go much further on the evidence that I've had handed to me. For instance, consider the possibility that Philippa Glass really was in love with Juan Manuel, but that he had turned away from her. We've heard from a number of sources that Mr. Laborero was a serial ladies' man. Could it be that he had resumed a previous relationship with Roxanne Stone, and that Philippa was jealous? Or let's get even wilder in our speculations. Perhaps Roxanne killed him because he was making a nuisance of himself again and she had moved on."

"Is this why you're bringing me into all this?" Roxanne Stone sounded incredulous. "Because Philippa hasn't got the sense to stop her love-life turning into some kind of soap opera, you are seriously suggesting that that would give me a reason to kill Juan? I've never heard anything so ridiculous!"

"Oh no, Mrs. Stone," returned Constable. "I don't think any of the convolutions of Miss Glass's affairs touch you in the least. That was simply an illustration of how far the facts might stretch if we were so inclined. So let's turn to some plainer facts, which I don't think anyone will dispute. You yourself did have a relationship with the dead man – you've admitted as much yourself, but you say that it was long over. I'm quite happy to believe that – our friend Eve has confirmed as much, and told us that you are currently very much involved with Mr. Berman. Involved," he mused. "Such a useful word. A choice of meanings, both of which I'm sure are applicable in this case. There is the connotation of romance, and there's also the meaning of 'linked in business'."

"But we're all linked in business, inspector," protested Tim

Berman. "You know that perfectly well. Are you trying to make out that there's some sort of gigantic conspiracy between all of us to murder Juan Manuel and cover it up?"

"Oh, there's certainly a conspiracy, Mr. Berman," replied Constable, "but not quite of the nature you describe. No, perhaps a number of little conspiracies would describe the situation better. And I was talking about you and Mrs. Stone being in business together. Not that that makes you two special, except that we actually have some concrete evidence, if you will forgive the metaphor, in your case." He turned to Walter Torrance. "I have to thank you, Mr. Torrance, for blowing the whistle on your colleague. Not directly, I hasten to add," he said, swiftly forestalling Walter's denial. "You said yourself that you didn't want to name names. But you did drop enough hints about rackets in the building business, and there were more than enough references to fiddles involving building materials. In fact, Mr. Torrance, you've so willingly pointed us in several helpful directions that I'm inclined to conclude that you yourself haven't got a thing to hide."

"So if you're telling us Walter didn't say anything specific about us," persisted Tim, "what exactly are you saying? That this conspiracy you're talking about is based on hearsay, and not even that?"

"Lord, no, Mr. Berman. I can do a great deal better than that. We have in our possession a pair of invoices for materials from Mrs. Stone's company. A pair, but by no means identical twins. Same goods, same quantities, but some very different prices, and I suspect not in favour of the final customer. So that's what you might call a very nice little earner. Now we've been told that Mrs. Stone was searching for Juan Manuel at Friday night's party, and talking about 'protecting herself'. Would that be from the prospect of going to prison for fraud, perhaps? She told me herself that she wouldn't be keen to find out what the inside of a

Spanish prison was like. Just a hypothetical comment? Well, maybe. But Walter Torrance also told us that on Friday night, you, Mr. Berman, also went looking for the dead man, but you returned, saying that you couldn't find him. Well, it was very dark in that garden, by all accounts. So was it true that you were unable to find him, or did you find him and make sure that he didn't spill the beans when he came to have his little conference with our colleagues in the Spanish police?"

"But I had no idea about this meeting you're talking about," Tim defended himself. "And even if I had, what would be the point of killing Juan? Wouldn't that just draw more attention to whatever it was he was planning to reveal to them? I'd be better off trying to persuade him not to go ahead, or even to buy him off."

"Dear oh dear," laughed the inspector softly. "The power of money. Which, Mr. Husami, you very helpfully told us speaks with the loudest voice in these parts. Well, I imagine you would know that better than most of us, with your extensive business interests, and your extended family. Quite surprisingly extended – one might almost say implausibly so."

"And what has the extent of my family to do with your supposed investigation into the death of Juan Manuel Laborero, may I ask?" Ewan Husami seemed quite at ease as he lounged in his chair, and his voice was level and contained traces of amused contempt.

Andy Constable's hackles rose. That, he thought, is a smile which I shall enjoy wiping off this particular gentleman's face. But his tone remained calm and conversational. "Just this, Mr. Husami. Mr. Vere told us of a very interesting conversation he overheard at his house on Friday night – a conversation between you and Mr. Laborero which sounded very much like extortion amidst threats to reveal dangerous facts. There was talk of people 'getting their cards'. Mr. Vere thought this might have something to do with you divesting yourself of some business interests, but I believe that he got hold of the wrong end of the stick. I think we're talking about an entirely different set of cards. Cards which were discovered in the house of Mr. Connor, among Miss Glass's possessions."

"And quite how am I supposed to be responsible for something you have found in X-Pat's house?" Ewan refused to be perturbed. "You've got nothing, inspector. You're just fishing."

"I will tell you exactly, Mr. Husami. And it's very amusing that you should say that." Constable did not sound in the least amused. "These cards are Spanish identity cards. The sort of cards which are essential if a person is going to live and work in Spain. The sort of cards which might very well pass as genuine, were it not for one small give-away detail which would possibly never be picked up unless they were seen together. That detail being that they had different photographs, but each one bore the same number and the same name – Ali Husami. So tell me, Mr. Husami, exactly how many Moroccan cousins called Ali have you got? Exactly how many of them have you brought into San Pablo at the end of those lengthy 'fishing trips' which Mr. Torrance so helpfully told us about? And did those trips perhaps involve a rendezvous with a vessel whose home port isn't Spanish?"

The confidence drained from Ewan's expression, and he sat up and reached in his pocket, producing a mobile phone. "I think, if you don't mind, I will make that phone call to my lawyer before I say anything else."

"There will be no telephone calls," rapped Alfredo. The raised tone brought a swift reaction from the Spanish officers waiting outside, one of whom opened the door and looked enquiringly at the captain. Alfredo waved him away with a murmured word of reassurance.

"Thank you, Captain," resumed Constable. "I'm sure Mr. Husami would be well advised to seek legal advice, but perhaps not just yet. And perhaps his lawyer will be able to advise him just how many supposed 'cousins' would be enough to get him deported to Morocco once the authorities find out the facts. Once he has served any prison sentence in one of those Spanish prisons we've already mentioned, of course. Now that's all quite a problem for a man who so clearly loves the cushy life in Spain. So did the obvious and easy solution, to do away with Juan Manuel, present itself before the authorities got to hear all the damning facts?"

"And you think the Spanish authorities have nothing better to do than go looking into a few petty allegations based on nothing at all? They have much more important worries than that at the moment." Ewan's tone was mocking. "And I think you'll find I have a few friends who would have something to say about it if you try to divert them away from consideration of more serious matters."

"And I think you will find that you do not have as many friends as you think," replied Alfredo silkily. "Not everything is for sale, Mr. Husami." The two stared at each other until Ewan's eyes fell.

"Forgive me for repeating myself, inspector," said Liza Lott, her poise regained, "but all you've been doing is floating wild ideas as to why each of us in turn might have killed Juan. I'm assuming you don't think we all did it. So is there any danger of you coming to the point?"

"Of course, Miss Lott. I apologise if you think I'm being long-winded. But I believe it's important to consider all the possible reasons why the death of Juan Manuel Laborero might have occurred. But yet, for me, somehow all these various reasons don't of themselves seem to provide a strong enough motive for this murder. So is there something else? Well, yes, there is, and we've heard it mentioned by several witnesses. In fact, it was something that I was very well aware of, but it was only a chance remark by Sergeant Copper here that drew my attention back to it. He made me realise – it can take a death to explain a death."

Copper looked up in surprise. 'What did I do?' was the sentiment clearly etched on his face.

"It's a question of identity," continued Constable. He hopped off the desk and began to pace. "Who and what you are. Now, X-Pat Connor has built up his business over a period of time, as has Liza Lott. All right, perhaps those businesses may not be as flourishing now as in better times, but they have put a great deal of their personal effort into them. Ewan Husami has so many business ventures that it seems he has trouble keeping track of them all. It's a highly complex web, and surely deserves investigating, but again it's a web of his own creation. Tim Berman is a trained and skilled craftsman, whatever his business morals may be. Likewise Walter Torrance, although in his case I don't have any qualms about his morality anyway. And on the subject of morality, there's many a young lady like Philippa Glass who has done very well for herself out of a close relationship with a man with money. But Roxanne Stone? Your case is a little different, isn't it, Mrs. Stone? Because you're only where you are because of the untimely death of your late husband, Ed Stone."

Roxanne suddenly grew very still.

"And it seems strange that Ed Stone's death had never roused any suspicions before. We've heard enough hints. Walter told us about Ed's 'nasty accident', as he called it, and he couldn't believe how such an experienced quarryman could make such elementary safety errors. But, innocent that he is, and disposed to believe the best of people, he took the whole thing at face value and put it down to simple bad luck. He believed the account given by the only witness to the fall – Juan Manuel Laborero. And then Eve told us about the very generous present which Roxanne gave to Juan Manuel soon after Ed's death – the death where Juan Manuel was the only other person on the scene. That extremely smart sports car has been interpreted as a gesture of thanks for the great support which Juan provided to Roxanne immediately after she was left a widow. A widow who inherited immediate control of a very profitable venture, the building supplies company. A widow who had been involved with Juan, according to the information we've been given, even while her husband was still alive. A grieving widow who could send Juan to report the circumstances of Ed Stone's death to the police in his flawless Spanish, in such a way that no suspicion arose at the time. So here's a tale that goes back as far as you like to take it – Shakespeare told it very well in 'Hamlet' – the wife and the lover conspired to murder the husband. Not a new story at all."

"No proof," forced out Roxanne. "You haven't any proof of all this. And you won't get any. Not now that... " She stopped in sudden realisation of the import of her words.

"Perhaps no proof as yet," said Andy Constable gently. "But now the police are investigating other things. So could the facts of Ed Stone's death be concealed forever? Juan didn't seem to think so. He felt that the jeopardy in which he found himself was too great. So he devised a plan. He would confess to all his crimes – the bribery, the corruption, the involvement with illegal immigration, the fraud – and bring the whole structure crashing down in return for personal immunity. But in comparison to all the other fiddles and deceits we've heard about, Ed Stone's death stands out. All the other offences are what we might call paper crimes – the offences are largely financial, and perhaps a financial penalty, however gigantic, might deal with them. Perhaps Mr. Husami's money might talk loudest after all. Maybe... " Constable permitted himself a small dry smile. "Maybe, unlike Webster's Dictionary in the song, he's not 'Morocco bound'. But Roxanne Stone's conspiracy to murder her husband stands out. Death is one of the few things that can't be paid away with a fine. And it seems likely that, whether from Juan himself or from some other source, Roxanne got wind of what Juan intended to do. And that made her desperate."

"It was never meant to be like that, you know." Roxanne's voice sounded calm, almost dreamy. "It started out as just a silly fling. Juan was a very attractive man. He flirted outrageously – I knew very well he did it to all the women, but that didn't make any difference. It was just part of the fun. And he was very hard to resist, so… so I stopped resisting. We had our fun, and I did everything I could to keep it from Ed. I still loved my husband, you see." She raised her eyes to the inspector. "You can believe that or not as you like, Mr. Constable, but I assure you it's true. And after a while, I realised that what I was doing was stupid. It was going nowhere – it never could. So I told Juan that we had to stop – that I couldn't let Ed find out. That didn't go down well at all. He was the kind of man who wouldn't accept a brush-off. He thought that his charm meant that he would set the rules, that he would decide when something was over. So rather than cause a confrontation, I let him persuade me. We carried on. And then came that horrible day – the day Juan came back from the quarry and told me that Ed was dead, and that he had done it all for me."

"And you had never wanted Juan to do such a thing?"

"No, inspector, I swear." Roxanne grew tearful. "But I couldn't convince Juan of that. With that damned male arrogance of his, he believed that I had hinted, or encouraged, or goodness knows what – he actually thought that he and I had somehow hatched this plot between us, and nothing I could say would convince him otherwise. And he said that nobody would believe my denials." She reached for a handkerchief and dabbed her eyes.

Andy Constable let the ensuing pause grow for several seconds. "Well, well, Mrs. Stone," he said eventually. "I have to say that that was quite a performance. Your acting skills do you credit. I'm impressed. Sadly, not impressed enough, because I don't believe a word of it. You've had plenty of opportunities to give our Spanish friends and ourselves your new version of the truth, but instead you have taken every chance to propose diversionary solutions to take our attention away from you and towards the other people in this room. But one fact stares me in the face – everybody else was at risk because of what was known by a string of people, but you only had one person to worry about. With Juan gone, you could believe yourself safe. And speaking of opportunities brings me to the third leg of the tripod. Who had the chance to kill Juan during what I've had described to me as a game of hide and seek at the party? This is where I've cause to be grateful to my very assiduous colleague Sergeant Copper for his meticulous note-taking."

Dave Copper gave an abashed half-grin in response to the compliment, but it went un-noticed. All eyes remained on the inspector.

"After Juan's disappearance into the garden, everyone seems to have gone outside looking for him. Quite a procession. Philippa Glass was the first to follow him outside, and X-Pat Connor pursued her shortly afterwards. I'm guessing that there was some sort of confrontation which led to Philippa's return in a state of upset. Whether Juan was involved in that is not certain, but my guess is that he prudently kept himself away from the furious Connor. But shortly thereafter, Liza needed to speak to Juan. Instead, I think she found X-Pat Connor and succeeded in calming him down, and the two returned indoors together. Roxanne Stone was the next to head outside, at around ten o'clock – precisely at the moment at which Liza and X-Pat were re-entering the house. She had made some remark about protecting herself – something of a give-away, but Eve Stropper interpreted that as relating to the security on the building sites, and relayed it to Ewan Husami about ten minutes later. He left to find Mrs. Stone, and they re-appeared soon afterwards. But for that crucial ten minutes, Mrs. Stone was alone in the garden with Juan Manuel. Enough time for a resourceful and desperate woman to take her opportunity and, in the darkness and using a convenient item of building materials lying to hand, silence the one man who could give her away and, with swift improvisation, bury the body in the trench to delay discovery and, when Ewan Husami appeared out of the darkness just as she had finished, calmly return with him to the party inside the house. As I say, the performance of an accomplished actress. So that when Tim Berman was searching for Juan only a few moments later, he was unable to find him."

"Oh, don't all look at me like that," hissed Roxanne to the room. "You all know what that little swine was like. Not a care in the world for anyone else – all he was concerned with was screwing all the rest of us, whether it was for money or the other thing. And he deserved what he got. That bastard killed my husband, and I don't care if you think what I did was wrong. He got justice in the end, so maybe I'll get the same."

In the stunned silence which followed Roxanne's final words, Walter Torrance cleared his throat. "Inspector... does this mean that the rest of us can go?"

Despite himself, Andy Constable was amused. "Well, I'm sure you can, Mr. Torrance. I'm not so sure about the others. That's a matter for the captain now."

Alfredo got to his feet, put on his uniform cap, and assumed a considerably more formal air. "Mr. Torrance, you may go. The rest of you will wait here." He opened the door and issued swift orders to one of the officers waiting outside. "Mrs. Stone – you will come with me. I wish you to make a statement." He took an unresisting Roxanne by the arm and, followed by the other policeman, led her towards his office. The door closed behind the three.

Epilogue

"I think I've had enough of Spain for the time being," remarked Andy Constable as he whirled the dials on the combination lock of his suitcase. "I shall be glad to get back home to some ordinary British crime."

"You're not wrong, guv," agreed Dave Copper, placing his case beside the door of the apartment. "If this is a holiday, maybe I should be putting in for double late shifts to give myself a breather." He grinned. "Mind you, you have to admit – in a weird way, it's been fun."

"I admit nothing," responded Constable. "But if you're right, I think we've had quite enough fun for one holiday."

The shrilling of the doorbell greeted his remark. Constable turned his eyes heavenwards. "Oh no... not again. Please tell me... "

"I'll get it, guv." Dave Copper opened the door to be greeted by the sight of Alfredo in full police uniform leathers, a motor-cycle helmet under his arm. The smile on his face was brilliant in its intensity.

"Good morning, Andy, David. I am come to say goodbye on your last morning, and to thank you properly again for all the help you give me."

"Everything in order back at the ranch?" asked Copper.

"Oh yes," beamed Alfredo. "I have called in extra men, who are making examinations of the people in the case. I think we will be very busy for a time. And my Commander is very pleased with me – I have told him it could not have been done without you two, but I think that for the honour of Spain, he will say nothing about that."

"I've no quarrel with that," said Constable. "You take all the credit you like. I just want to get to the airport and catch that flight home."

"This is why I am here," replied Alfredo. "To make sure that you will arrive to the airport safely. Come." Ignoring the other's puzzled frown, he picked up Constable's suitcase and led the way down to the courtyard, where one of his young officers sat astride a huge gleaming police motor-cycle alongside Alfredo's own similar machine, flanking the Britons' hire car. "We will escort you to the airport."

"Good grief, you don't have to do that," laughed Constable, touched in spite of himself. "Anyway, we've got to drop the key for this place off with Liza Lott."

"I think, Andy, that Miss Lott will not be opening her office this morning," said Alfredo with a twinkle. "And perhaps not any morning soon. I believe she will have other things to do. And I will be seeing her again at my station today, so I think you can safely give the key to me to return to her. So shall we go?" He straddled his machine as Constable and Copper loaded their luggage and climbed into the car. "It will be a pleasure for me. I do not have the chance to ride one of these as often as I like." He kicked the cycle into life and, sirens wailing, led the procession into the road and away.

At the Departures level of Alicante airport, Dave Copper was struck by a sudden thought. "Here guv, we've come to the wrong place. I'm supposed to return the car downstairs. Hang on – I'll try not to be too long."

"No, that is not necessary," said Alfredo. "Give me the car keys as well – Felipe here will take your car back. It will all be in order. And he too will enjoy it, even if for only a few minutes."

He spoke briefly to his junior, who climbed into the car and, grinning broadly, roared off towards the multi-storey car park.

"Well." Andy Constable extended his hand to Alfredo. "I suppose this is where I say '*Hasta la vista*'."

"No," countered Alfredo. "We do not say that. That is just for American films with Arnold Schwarzenegger. Here we say '*Hasta luego*' – until later."

"Okay, I stand corrected," smiled Constable. "And I hope you won't feel offended if, unlike Arnie, I say 'I *won't* be back'!"

"Is it really only a week since we were last here, guv?" said Dave Copper as he looked around the departure lounge.

"It is that," replied Andy Constable, taking a seat and stretching his legs out in front of him. "This is the last chance I'll get for any decent legroom for the next few hours."

"Well, at least we won't be hanging around too long. According to the screens, the inbound flight looks to be on time. They haven't put up a departure gate for our flight yet for some reason, so I'm just going to have a stroll round, if that's okay by you."

"You go ahead. I'm fine here." Constable closed his eyes.

A few minutes later, Copper was back, seating himself alongside Constable and opening the pages of a British newspaper. "Sorry, guv, but I couldn't resist it. Somebody left it lying around. I've been starved of my usual over the past week." He headed for the football pages, spending the next few minutes uttering a series of groans, tuts, and the occasional small exclamation of delight, before turning to other news at the front of the paper. "Another health scare – apparently it's celery this time… the French are having another row with everybody else… that volcano in Iceland has blown its top again… "

Constable opened one eye. "What, the one that caused all the trouble with the flights last time? Don't say we're in for another dose of that again."

"Well, at least we should be safe today, guv. Our flight's already on its way."

"And thank goodness for that."

"Er… hang on… it says here that today should be fine, but they're worried about the cloud of ash getting into British airspace tomorrow."

"No problem, then."

"*May I have your attention, please. Will all passengers to the United Kingdom please stand by for important information concerning their flights. Thank you.*"

"What the hell's that all about? Copper, go and find out, would you – and let me have a look at that paper."

"*May I have your attention, please. DerryAir regret to announce the cancellation of their flight KY70 to London due to climatic conditions beyond their control, which have resulted in the closure of all UK airspace. Would passengers please remain in the lounge and await further information.*"

Constable seized the newspaper. "Trust the bloody Met Office to get things wrong again. What is it they're saying?" His eye fell on the paper's masthead, and he let out a snort of exasperation. "Copper, you oaf! You do realise we're stuck here for God knows how long, don't you? This is *yesterday's* paper!"

* * *

Follow Inspector Constable's first investigation...

an Inspector Constable murder mystery

fêted
to
DIE

Roger Keevil

Who killed celebrity clairvoyant Horace Cope at the annual fête at Dammett Hall? Did rival Seymour Cummings spot trouble ahead? Did magistrate Lady Lawdown take justice into her own hands? Or has her daughter Laura Biding got a guilty secret?

Detective Inspector Andy Constable and his irreverent colleague Sergeant Dave Copper must try to make sense of the whirl of gossip, rumour and secrets circling the peaceful English village of Dammett Worthy. Throw into the mix a celebrated author, a dodgy solicitor and a sponging relative, and Constable and Copper really have their work cut out!

"... an ideal book to spend a lazy afternoon with."
bookgeeks.co.uk